From

The Women's Press Ltd
124 Shoreditch High Street, London E1

D0862947

Helen L. Thompson
Susan J. Whitesides
2.7.83

Valerie Miner

Photo: Helen E Longino

Valerie Miner is the author of two previous novels, *Blood Sisters* (The Women's Press, 1981) and *Movement* (The Crossing Press, New York, 1982). She is co-author of *Tales I Tell My Mother* (Journeyman Press, 1978) and *Her Own Woman* (Macmillan, Toronto, 1975). She has contributed short stories, reviews and articles to many periodicals including the *New York Times*, *Spare Rib*, the *Economist*, *Sinister Wisdom*, *Saturday Review*, *New Society* and the *New Statesman*.

Miner teaches fiction and media in the Field Studies Programme at the University of California, Berkeley. She is working on a new novel concerning the friendship between two old women in San Francisco's Tenderloin.

VALERIE MINER

Murder in the English Department

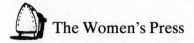 The Women's Press

First published by The Women's Press Limited 1982
A member of the Namara Group
124 Shoreditch High Street, London E1 6JE

Murder in the English Department is a work of fiction. Any
resemblance to actual persons, living or dead, is coincidental.

British Library Cataloguing in Publication Data
Miner, Valerie
    Murder in the English department
    I. Title
    813' .54[F]   PS3563. I/

    ISBN 0-7043-3890-4

Phototypeset by MC Typeset, Rochester, Kent
Printed in Great Britain

This book is dedicated with love to my family,
to Mother, Dad, John, Larry, Sherine, Kim, Dee
and Mary Anne

Acknowledgements

I believe that fiction emerges from an imaginative collectivity of writers and readers. Many people have encouraged or prodded or stimulated me in the writing of this book. I want to thank all of them and to acknowledge a few who have been especially helpful.

For their continuing inspiration and criticism over the years, I owe much to women from my writing groups: Jana Harris, Susan Griffin, Zoe Fairbairns, Mary Mackey, Kim Chernin, Eve Pell, Susan Feldman and Myrna Kostash.

For their technical advice on the manuscript, I thank Peggy Webb, Marlene Griffith, Julia Bader, Mary Dunlap, Jill Lippit, Ron Zuckerman, Ellen Reier, Joyce Lindenbaum, Deborah Johnson, Barbara Rosenblum, Helen Longino and Debbie Cogan. Any mistakes in the book are, of course, solely mine.

For their fine work in the editing and publishing stages of the novel, I am very grateful to Stephanie Dowrick of The Women's Press, London; Hope Dellon of St Martin's Press, New York, and to my agents Charlotte Sheedy and Leslie Gardner.

Finally, I thank my family for their love.

One

Christmas is always like this, Nan complained to herself as she steered through the last-minute shoppers on Mission Boulevard. Bloody Christmas morning and they're racing to Gemco or White Front for a bar of Jean Nate soap or some special ratchet screwdriver.

Nan took a deep breath and tried to exhale her irritation. She observed the local decorations. Here at the intersection of Mission and Mendez, the First Baptist Church and St Martin's Methodist Hall competed for holiday converts with garish nativity scenes. This Baptist Virgin looked as blissful as the cocaine lady Nan had met at the faculty party two nights before. Methodist Mary seemed more the valium type. Nan didn't plan to share these impressions with her sister Shirley who still believed in sacrilege. Who still attended Mass, for heaven's sake (either for heaven's sake or for Joe's sake. Polish Catholics die hard). Nan had politely declined the invitation to attend nine o'clock Mass with Shirley, Joe and the kids. She promised to get to the house by 11.30, traffic allowing.

'Jesus Christ, Jesus H Christ,' Nan yelled out the window at the broad-shouldered jackass driving the truck with a red bumper-sticker: 'Cowboys Do It Better'.

'Watch your driving, brother,' Nan called. But the cowboy had already made his left turn, and she was stuck in front of a stubborn red traffic light which just a minute ago had been green enough to take her straight to Calle d'Oro and her sister Shirley's turkey dinner.

Merry Christmas, eh? Nan glanced at herself in the rearview mirror, at her new, classy-wide spectacles which Shirley claimed made her look like a deep sea diver. Frankly, Nan thought they did a lot to liven up her face, thin Anglo features set against her black hair and brown eyes.

The ride out to Hayward always put her in a ratty mood. 'Some of

1

these strings of lights are up all year,' she spoke to Isadora, the old, red Chevrolet. 'They use the red ones for Fourth of July. And that tinsel hanging from the telephone poles there – it looks like the leaves of an electrocuted palm tree!'

Sometimes Nan worried about this habit of talking to her car. She wasn't worried about being crazy, no. She was forty-seven years old and by now she realized that a little craziness keeps you sane in this world. But what if someone looked through Isadora's windows and saw her chattering away by herself? Ah, let them look, she was more interesting than the Methodist nativity advertisement. And if a cop pulled her over? Well, she could always say she was taping a lecture on the cassette recorder. Nan had it all figured out; she had a lot of things figured out. They wouldn't arrest Dr Nan Weaver, Professor of English at University of California, Berkeley.

Ah, what the hell, she wouldn't mind being pulled over. She had heard that Robert Wendel, Class of '50 star jock, had joined the illustrious Hayward Police Force. She relished the idea of telling Robert Wendel what had happened to 'the girl brain'. He had always made her feel like some genetic mutation. 'Hello, there, Officer Wendel,' Nan would say, craning her neck at the giant basketball star. 'You still cruising the strip like you used to? Only now you've got yourself a siren and a twirly red light. Yes, sir, Robert Wendel, I always knew you would go places, your daddy being a quality supervisor at the cannery and all.'

Nan thought guiltily how she even hated the *smell* of this town – the sweet fumes of ketchup and tomato soup oozing from the cannery all day long. Berkeley wasn't Athens, but it was thirty minutes over the hills and a breath of fresh air away from Hayward. 'Damn mist.' Nan turned on the windshield wipers. A horn sounded behind her, and another huge pickup idled loudly, so close that the GMC was almost mounting Isadora. Once again, Nan found herself stranded in the Land of the Yahoos. She shifted into first and Isadora sputtered across the intersection.

Hayward, Nan reflected, was one of those city-towns forever lost in the shade of the Californian dream, over-populated by ladies in hair rollers and men in checked Bermuda shorts who never quite made it. Hayward was founded in 1848 by a failed gold miner who gave up prospecting to open a shoe shop.

Classist, she thought, I'd be called classist by my favourite communist student, Susan. And theoretically I'd accept the criticism. But Susan grew up in Beverly Hills. She didn't spend eighteen

2

years in Hayward as 'the girl brain'.

The tinny treble of 'I'm Dreaming of a White Christmas' blared through the fog from loudspeakers above the Superway Center. At the crosswalk, a Volunteer of America Santa was mindlessly clanging his bell. And the Winchell's window was stacked with green and red doughnuts.

Vulgar, is what Sister Marguerita Mary would call it. ('So very vuuuulgar', Sister had warned when she caught Nan painting her fingernails in grade school.) Nan had survived a whole childhood of Christmases in this town. She knew she was a snob. And she did have some good memories. Family things like November evenings, everyone snuggled around the radio. But she also remembered those summer days sitting at the Hayward Plunge waiting for something to happen, anything, her blood to boil over, anything.

OK, OK, Nan checked herself. Berkeley isn't much better. She was thinking about the English Department's Yule and Sherry Party.

Old Angus Murchie was leching around like there would be no new year. He was a thickly set man – looking all the more formidable in a bright red shirt.

Angus greeted her with his usual wit, 'If it isn't the shortest English professor this side of the Rockies.' He offered her a styrofoam cup of cream sherry with one hand and brushed her ass with the other.

'I have no doubt,' Nan said, discreetly moving back against the wall, 'that your perception of my mere five-foot height is accurate. No doubt, in fact, that you've tape-measured every English professor and not a few graduate students from here to Denver. However, couldn't we move on to a more appropriate conversational gambit like that new article in the *Publication of the Modern Language Association* on Milton's fear of Dianic cults. Or,' she paused, drinking the sherry too fast for tact, 'if we wanted to be informal, we might discuss where you found that fine Stewart tartan tie to match your red shirt and navy pants.'

Matt Weitz was nodding to Nan from across the room. Relax, he was mouthing silently. He would remind her later that ladies coming up for tenure could not afford to drink so much sherry nor to spill so much sarcasm.

'Ah, yes, ever the ironic lass,' Angus said, his Scottish accent surfacing briefy. 'Your sense of humour will take you a long way, my love, a long way.'

A long way, yes, thought Nan. She could see herself next year exiled to Natchez Junior College. Before she could regain professional poise, the conversation detoured. Marjorie Adams had walked up and captured Murchie's foetid attention.

Nan always felt more like Marjorie's student than her thesis adviser. Statuesque Marjorie with her long, blonde hair as elegantly coifed as any daughter of Augustus Caesar. Marjorie, who looked as if she had been born in a silk blouse and a velvet skirt. Marjorie, who always seemed to be wondering – behind her dutiful questions about course requirements and bibliographic techniques – 'Are you sure you're the real Professor Weaver? Are you sure you're in the right place, Shortie?'

'And good afternoon to you,' leered Angus Murchie, scratching the hair on his earlobe. 'How nice it is to have new faces around these dreary old faculty gatherings,' he nodded confidentially to Nan. 'I'm so glad we've broken through our stuffiness to include fresh blood – teaching assistants and so on – aren't you, Professor Weaver?'

'As you may know,' Nan said, 'Ms Adams is doing a fascinating dissertation on "Power and Love in the Novels of Irish Murdoch".'

'Quite.' Murchie stifled a yawn. 'You are the lucky devil, tending to all these fair maidens and their theses on women's literature. Ah, if I had only perceived the rewards of that vogue before I chose Milton. All I ever seem to meet are nervous young men.'

Nan realized there was no use trying to have a serious conversation with Murchie while he was soused. As he neared the end of his career he often seemed sad and desperate. After a few glasses of wine he grew irascible or predatory. Nan thought wistfully that she had never been able to have a good talk with this man who was one of the most impressive critics of his generation. What she really wanted now was to walk over and gossip with her friend Matt. But she felt reluctant to leave Marjorie in the clutches of seventeenth-century Puritanism, remembering how they also serve who only stand and wait.

Matt rescued Nan from her own virtue. Good old Matt, armed with a bottle of Calistoga Water, news about his research on E M Forster and departmental chitchat. As he steered her into a quiet corner, Nan thought how hard it was to believe that this tall, balding, distinguished professor was only forty, seven years younger than herself. Matt was one of the few faculty who sympathized with

4

what Murchie had labelled Nan's 'feminist tendencies'. And she was the only one who knew Matt was gay.

He guided her across the grey carpet to a seat by the window. Nan looked back ruefully for a moment as Murchie leaned over, pretending to smell the mistletoe on Marjorie Adams' ample bosom. She nodded to Matt.

'Listen, Nan,' he said kindly, 'this is not the place to conduct your Sexual Harassment Campaign.'

'It's not *my* campaign,' said Nan. 'Two dozen students and teachers have been active . . .'

'Yes, yes,' he nodded, 'but you're identified as the one who started it, as the ring leader. And departmental cocktail parties are not the place for discussing sexual harassment.'

'Better tell Murchie that,' she said, still glaring at him as he leaned over Marjorie.

'Listen,' Matt spoke more patiently, 'I think it's a decent political cause. But wait until you have tenure. Please. Then you can take any warpath you want.'

'We're not discussing a sport,' Nan flared back. She hated how anger showed red on her face, always advertising her feelings in meetings, in situations her mother would call 'polite company'. Oh, well, maybe in three or four years they might dismiss the blushing as menopause. And today they could assume it was the drink.

'Do you have any idea,' she continued in a lower voice, 'how many women come to me, complaining about professors making passes – touching, fondling them, writing lewd suggestions on their essays?'

'Well, you can hardly blame *me*,' smiled Matt, adjusting his tortoise-rimmed glasses as he always did when he was nervous.

'Matt, this is serious,' said Nan. 'Rapes on campus increased one hundred per cent this year.'

'Yes, pet,' Matt said with concern. His dark blue eyes held her, caressed her.

Sometimes Nan imagined that if she were younger, if Matt were straight, and if they both believed in romance, they might try a love affair. But she needed solid friends more than distracting lovers in her life right now.

Matt continued, 'Je comprends. It is a *crisis*. But let the students carry the torch for a while. If you don't get tenure, you lose this job. Colleges are so tight now you'll never get another. You'll have to go back to high school.'

'Perhaps,' she sighed, 'my ten years teaching at Pacheco High School were less prestigious, but they had a lot more to do with education.'

'Of course, sweetheart,' Matt traded her emptied sherry cup for a cup of mineral water. 'Of course you're a better teacher than all these clowns put together. But get your tenure before you do more politicking.'

'You know I've always been political,' said Nan. 'They knew that, too, when they hired me.' Often Nan wondered why they had hired her, forgetting the critical acclaim her books had received. Self-effacement came too easily. That's why she wanted this tenure. It was more than job security. It was a passport, an identity card.

'Political, yes,' said Matt. 'But affirmative action is *very* different from rampaging on about bodily assualt.'

'Matt,' Nan's voice rasped across her tight throat, 'I just cannot believe you're making fun of this.'

She stood shakily.

'Oh, friend, I'm not making fun.' Matt eased her back into her chair. 'I'm just saying that it would be ever so lonely around here without you.'

Nan bent her head back and stared at the car's beige, naugahyde ceiling. It's just when I'm alone, she thought, that all the parts of my life make sense. The English Department is embarrassed by my conscience. My friends think I work for a boring, stuffy academy. And my family sees me as some kind of hippie. Shirley hasn't pretended to understand since I gave up my precious marriage to Dr Charles Woodward. God knows what she thinks of me retrieving my maiden name or going back to college for another degree.

Nan's oblong face lengthened now as she considered the bosom of nettles to which she returned every few months for family celebrations. Her younger sister Shirley, in her early forties, was already sagging into plump middle age. Sweet, kind Shirley, brimming with good will, never knew quite how to treat her eccentric sister. Hmm, if Matt thought Nan was a den-mother, he should meet Shirley. On second thought, he shouldn't meet Shirley, considering what she and her husband Joe said about queers. Queers were the main reason they didn't want their daughter Lisa to attend Berkeley.

Nan could see the Gomez overpass now. It would be ten, twelve minutes to Shirley's house.

6

Meanwhile, Lisa, Joe and Shirley's only daughter and youngest child, was the main reason Nan was making this Christmas trip. God, she loved the child hugely – more, probably, than if Lisa were her own daughter. Sometimes Nan's only pleasure in a day of committee meetings and footnotes was a cup of coffee with Lisa at the Terrace. When Lisa had enrolled at Berkeley last year, Nan had been delighted.

She winced now, remembering Lisa's first visit to the student hospital. Nothing much, Lisa had insisted, just this funny butterfly rash on her face and sudden fatigue. Nothing they could trace. Maybe she was allergic to strawberries. Nothing much, but she had been in and out of the hospital so often last year that her parents were reluctant to allow her back to college. Briefly, Nan had played with the idea of a solitary Christmas in Mexico. She could not contain her worry for Lisa. As usual, Nan's protectiveness vied with her ambition and independence. How could she desert her niece to face a Christmas of Hayward cowboys and hospital tests?

Nan switched on Isadora's radio and swished the dial for distraction. It looked like this traffic wasn't going to unsnarl until the Desert Palms turn-off. All the stations – even FM – were clogged with carollers: 'Deck the Halls', 'Good King Wenceslaus', 'Jingle Bell Rock'. And a new disco version of 'Frosty the Snowman'. She switched back to

> *Good King Wenceslaus looked out*
> *On the feast of Stephen. . .*

Nan's mother Ruth had always preferred these religious carols. She had had a fine singing voice, something Nan definitely did not inherit, and a great memory for lyrics. Mom would be washing up in the kitchen, singing away while the rest of the family napped under bellies stuffed with turkey and mashed potatoes. Nan dearly wished Mom could be here today. She had loved these big holidays. She had such joy and faith in the family. Mom never gave up hope about Pop's promotion at the cannery. And she always said Nan would go far 'with all that will power'. At least Pop had lived long enough to see her hired at Berkeley. 'Imagine,' he said, 'Jim Weaver's kid, a big time university professor. And neither me nor your mom going past sixth grade.'

7

When the snow lay round about
Deep and crisp and even.
Brightly shone the moon that night. . .

Nan checked her watch. 11.45, Jesus god, Shirley would be steaming. Her sister probably had the entire day organized. Eggnog from 11.30–12.30. Dinner at 12.45. Presents opened at 2.30. And poor Lisa. She must be thinking Nan had deserted her.

Lisa loved her two brothers, cheered at their drag races, was bridesmaid at both their weddings. But she felt suffocated in Hayward. As she had confided to Nan one afternoon on the Terrace, 'I just don't know what to talk to them about. Do you think I'm a snob?'

'Of course not, sweetie,' Nan told her earnest niece. 'Listen, I got hooked into ten years of being a doctor's wife – before I divorced Charles and went to graduate school – because I didn't believe I had a right to feel bored.'

Lisa looked relieved. 'I'm so glad you decided not to go to Mexico. What an awful Christmas it would be with the TV, Dad and the boys whooping over the football games. I mean I love them . . .'

'Yeah, sweetie,' Nan had said, 'we marginal characters have got to stick together.'

Remembering this, Nan stepped on the accelerator.

Two

Nan pulled into the gravel driveway at precisely noon. Half-an-hour late on the nose, she noted. Since their earnest Catholic girlhoods both Nan and Shirley had scrupulously examined their own conscience and helped to calculate each other's sins. Nan had been distracted, thinking about Lisa, during the last half mile of this familiar drive past the public swimming pool, the veterans' hospital and Cordoba's Furniture Warehouse. But no matter: Isadora knew the way on her own. Isadora had been driving to Shirley's house every few months for ten years now, which was almost her entire automotive career.

Nan cut her headlights and noticed that the fog had thickened. She climbed out of the car, stretching to unknot her body from the overlong journey. Damn traffic. You'd think God could unsnarl roads on Christmas morning. Now with her arms in the air, Nan found her mouth open, gaping at the jellybean yellow ranch house. Oh, Isadora *had* made a mistake. This wasn't Shirley's place after all. And now she would be even later. Nan was climbing back into the car when she noticed someone flagging from the window. It was her nephew Bob, waving a piece of mistletoe in one hand and holding a can of beer with the other.

The surprise, Nan remembered. Shirley had promised a surprise. A big change in their life. Of course, Shirley hadn't meant that she was starting a job or having a baby (thank heaven) or getting a divorce (more's the pity). She had meant this. This jellybean yellow paint job! 'Polish yellow,' Pop would have called it. Their father was neither particularly prejudiced nor particularly aesthetic. But one of his favourite Sunday sports was driving around the tract homes in Southern Alameda County speculating on the ethnic paint jobs – 'I-ti pink,' he would say. And sure enough, to Nan's utter exasperation, the name on the mailbox would be Cellucci. Their own house had been a tedious grey and brown Anglo. But jellybean yellow! Poor Shirley lived in a jellybean yellow house. And poor Lisa.

Opening the trunk for her shopping bag of presents, Nan considered the jam of cars in the wide gravel driveway. Two broken-down Ford sedans which the boys had been repairing for the last five years, a new Mustang which Tom had bought on credit. Bob's VW with the Ferrari hood. And Joe's beat-up Buick. Nan felt a twinge of disloyalty to Isadora, as if she were leaving her in a kennel of mangy dogs. She patted the old red car on the right fender as she walked toward the house. 'I'm not going to enjoy this day any more than you,' she whispered.

Bob welcomed her with a bear hug. He was a sweet, if somewhat boring young man. Not boorish like his father, just boring. Nan reminded herself not to be snide.

'Merry Christmas,' she greeted Bob, kissing his cheek, checking again that it was, in fact, musk cologne he wore. She hoped that she had chosen as well with the silver earrings for Shirley and the silk blouse which she had splurged on for Lisa.

Joe and his older son Tom were parked in front of the Magnavox TV. A floor lamp shone on Joe's balding head.

'Hi, Nan,' Joe called, his eyes fastened to the screen. 'It's one down to go in the middle of the fourth quarter.'

Nan remembered absently how her whole childhood had been set against the radio static as Pop followed basefootbasketball year after year.

'How are ya, Joe?' She noticed once again how her diction changed when she moved from Berkeley to Hayward. Looser here, more colloquial and with a certain Country-Western twang. She was assuming her old voice, unconsciously, unavoidably.

'Just fine,' said Joe, turning from the television. She noticed that the screen was occupied by a handsome black man shaving white cream off his face.

Could they feel her irritation, her tension, Nan wondered. She thought of her friend Amy's frantic stories about Jewish family holidays, where people argued and fought from beginning to end. Matt also said his family rituals got pretty lethal. Nan didn't think that Hayward holidays were any safer; the mines were just laid deeper.

'Hi, there, Nan.' Tom waved to her. A kiss would be unthinkable to Tom, the shyer of the two young men.

'Merry Christmas to all,' said Nan. She was unpacking her presents and distributing them beneath the pink tree which shimmered with white lights and pale blue balls.

'Good game?' she asked, having promised herself to be civil, really to *try* this year.

'Naa, nothing terrific,' said Joe. 'Reruns. So how goes it, sister-in-law? You finished all your homework for Christmas?'

'Almost,' she smiled. 'How about you? How long are ya off from the shipyards?'

'Ah, the docks only closed down for two days. They gotta keep us on our toes.'

The shaving commercial flickered into a picture of a woman draped over a large, red car. Silently they all drew back to the TV. Next, a barbershop quartet quenched their mighty thirsts on Tom's favourite ale. The game would be resuming any minute now.

'So I suppose all the good women are barefoot in the kitchen,' she said to their three broad backs.

'Most of them,' Bob spoke over his shoulder. Then he was riveted by a long pass to the thirty-yard line.

'Except Lisa,' Joe said after the play was completed.

'Where's Lisa?' Nan asked.

'In her room,' continued Bob as his father's attention returned to the TV. 'She said she didn't feel so well when we got back from Mass.'

Nan frowned, remembering for some reason Mrs Ramsay's thoughts in *To the Lighthouse*, 'And Rose would grow up and Rose would suffer so.' She didn't know why Virginia Woolf was haunting her now, 'Choose me a shawl, for that would please Rose who was bound to suffer so.'

'Fucking fumble,' Joe was shouting. 'Fucking asshole fumble.'

Nan left the noisy room unnoticed.

The long ranch house was just like every other place on the block when Shirley and Joe arrived in March 1960, three months before Lisa was born. They had been so proud of this brand-new home in Desert Palms Estates, quite a step up from the old family place which they and their two small sons had shared with Pop and Mom on Kelly Hill. Here they had a big picture window and a built-in dishwasher. For the first five years Shirley and Joe almost broke their necks on mortgage payments, but since then they'd been able to afford a number of small improvements.

After Mom and Pop died, Nan let Shirley have all the family furniture.

'At least take the big oak table,' Shirley had protested.

But Nan was only too glad to witness the disassembling of the

Kelly Hill house in which she had always felt constricted.

Still, when she came out to visit her sister, it was like returning to a museum, dusty with old feelings. The stuffy furniture had absorbed all those unsaid words, had been beaten down with all the unstruck blows. Nan felt slightly uneasy here, as if she were running a low-grade fever. Snobbery. She was ashamed of her physical aversion to the plastic fuschias and the Woolworth knick-knacks and the case of unread *Readers' Digest* Condensed books. Nan knew that what really bothered her were her own ghosts. She quickened her step to Lisa's room at the end of the hall.

Nan knocked.

'Hello,' came the cheerful, high-pitched reply.

Before Nan opened the door, she speculated on the latest metamorphosis she would find inside. Last year, Lisa's room had been a foamy pink dream with the rose-petalled bedspread and cushions the colour of bubblegum. Her desk had been assembled with stuffed animals, and her walls bannered with mellow reminders that 'Friendship is the Voice of Sharing' and 'Love is a Stillness in the Heart'. It had reminded Nan of that frightening film, 'The Stepford Wives', where all the women are robotized into docile domestics. However, Lisa had maintained some marks of individuality – an atlas, the Table of Elements. And now, during the year since Lisa had started at Berkeley, it was exciting to watch the changes. First to go where the mellow posters, replaced with a huge sign protesting nuclear power. Then the desk had been cleared for a portable typewriter. The shelves were filling with new books – the Carson McCullers biography she loved, the texts on public speaking which were winning her prizes in the Rhetoric Department. Ultimately Lisa did plan a complete exit, but the family couldn't afford a dormitory this year.

Nan opened the door very, very slowly, as she used to do to tease Lisa when she was a child.

'Ohhhh, the Wicked Witch of the West,' Lisa's voice quavered now in a dramatic imitation of Judy Garland in 'The Wizard of Oz'.

'No, no, the good witch has come to save you,' said Nan, remembering the dozen Thanksgivings she and her niece had watched the old movie on TV.

The door was opened far enough for Nan to see Lisa in the heart-shaped mirror, bundled under the bed covers.

Nan hurried into the room.

'What's the matter, sweetie? How come you're in bed?'

12

'Hi Nan,' said Lisa. 'Nothing serious. Take the Grim Reaper look off your face.'

Nan noticed how the soft lamplight haloed Lisa's hair, a shade they used to call 'strawberry blonde'. She could never figure out how this golden American beauty had been produced by a union of Joe's stocky Polish genes and her own angular family.

Lisa put a feather bookmark in *Northanger Abbey*, recommended by her aunt. Nan sat on the edge of the bed, with the back of her hand to Lisa's forehead, as she had learned from mothers in the movies.

'Mighty suspicious,' Nan said, 'you coming down with Bubonic Plague on Christmas day.'

'Don't I know it,' laughed Lisa. 'Right after Mass, right before all the big cooking. Mom said, "Do you suppose it's that Feminist Disease again?"'

'Feminist Disease?' asked Nan.

'Well, you know, any time I don't want to do housework or I ask one of the boys to share chores, Mom says, "Oh, oh, you've caught the Feminist Disease".'

Nan frowned. She had promised herself not to fight with Shirley today.

'It would never occur to her to ask Dad to help,' said Lisa, with a mixture of affection and exasperation. 'If there's one reason I'll never be a housewife, it's the unfair domestic stuff. Of course there's more than one reason.'

Nan was annoyed at Lisa's tone, although she agreed with her politics. She thought about the different choices of this new generation, about the questions she and Shirley never asked. Lisa had the clarity of their hindsight, as if she stood on their shoulders, one foot on Shirley's and one foot on Nan's, seeing beyond Hayward, beyond their lives to her own. But Nan didn't resent this inheritance. If Lisa had more choices, she also had more decisions. She still had the strain of pulling away. Nan saw this tension in the taut line of her niece's mouth.

She took Lisa's hand and said, 'So if it isn't the Bubonic Plague or the Feminist Disease, what's happening, kid?'

'I don't know,' said Lisa with uncharacteristic nervousness. 'All of a sudden I felt woozy and dizzy. Nauseous. I just needed to lie down for a bit. I'm sure I'll be fine for dinner.'

'Ooooops,' gulped Nan, 'that reminds me, I ought to report for duty. Your mother will think I'm stuck in line at White Front or

13

somewhere.'

A rap sounded on the door. Nan and Lisa exchanged guilty glances.

'Come on, Mom,' said Lisa.

'Ah, I knew I'd find you two conspiring,' said Shirley. She hugged Nan and kissed Lisa on the forehead. A smile broadened Shirley's wide face. When she was a girl, the kids used to tease Shirley about her buck teeth, saying that she looked like Milton Berle. As she got older and rounder, the likeness was confirmed. Shirley was as broad and settled as Nan was wiry and 'hyper'. The only thing which marked them as sisters here was their concern for this golden child-woman in the bed. In fact, Lisa had visibly revived during the last minutes with Nan.

'Listen baby,' Nan kissed her sister. 'Sorry I'm late. The traffic was backed up between GEMCO and the Superway something awful. Season's Cheer and all that. I hope I haven't absolutely charred the turkey.'

'No, don't fret, I counted on a little leeway.'

Of course, Nan thought, Shirley wasn't going to scold her. Why was she so paranoid about her sister's criticism. They hadn't had a fight in six months. Nan knew her former therapist Annie would say that Shirley repressed her sibling rivalry. Maybe so. But Nan suspected that her sister was simply a nicer person.

'With that special warmer in the new oven,' Shirley was saying, 'it's no bother at all.'

She turned with a serious frown to Lisa. 'I wonder if we could ask the Fairy Princess to join us for some eggnog before Christmas dinner?'

Nan listened to the confused irritation in Shirley's tease and watched the guilt cross Lisa's tired face.

'Well, Mom. . .'

'I don't think the child should,' said Nan before she could remember not to interfere. Child, indeed. Protectiveness. Where did she get this protective streak? Was it because she didn't have kids of her own?

'Christmas only comes once a year,' Shirley said firmly. 'One time when you can pull yourself away from the books to be with your family.'

With that, *Northanger Abbey* was closed for the day, and the three women proceeded into the living room.

Lynda and Debbie were sitting on their husbands' laps, looking far more like sisters than Nan and Shirley. Both young women had newly permed hair. They wore complementing long dresses, one pale green and the other pale blue. It had taken Nan months to distinguish between them, to remember that Lynda was married to Tom and Debbie was married to Bob. Nan wondered how much of this was her own resistance. Debbie, with her quiet humour, was very different from earnest Lynda. She tried to be kind to the younger women, to ask about their interior decorating and their plans for children – which, from the looks of Debbie, were right on schedule. But somehow the conversation always finished with that cloying sensation, like teeth pulling on Turkish Toffee, leaving grotesque pastel strings hardening in the silence.

Joe lifted his cutglass punch cup. Nan remembered when Lisa had bought her parents the set at Penneys, a twentieth anniversary gift.

'Here's to the queen and her court,' Joe slurred, 'a Christmas toast.'

'Who won the game?' asked Nan, trying to divert the centre of attention.

'The Packers,' said Joe.

The eggnog was mollifying everyone.

'So how about a little yuletide music?' Shirley asked, in a voice Nan would have sworn was their mother's. Easy on the old nog, she reminded herself. Shirley squatted down on her thick haunches, rummaging through a collection of old Lawrence Welks for the Bing Crosby '78.

As Joe was pouring a second ample round, El Bingo joined the party.

'Now that's the way "White Christmas" was meant to be sung,' smiled Nan, pleasantly enveloped in this safe, familiar ambience. 'You should have heard the racket coming from the Superway Center.'

As always there was too much dinner on the big oak table. Too much turkey, sage dressing, chestnut dressing, cinnamon yams, turnips, parsnips, creamed onions, mashed potatoes and plenty of hot gravy. Too many sweets from Shirley's mince pie to Lynda's pumpkin pie to Debbie's black and white fudge. Far too much booze, what with all the wine Nan had brought and all the rum Joe had dumped into the eggnog. Shirley and Joe usually went broke for months after the holidays, but they would never dream of serving less. Not at a big family celebration.

Nan didn't notice the fight begin.

15

'Whaddaya mean, you want to live at Berkeley,' Joe was saying through a mouthful of mince pie.

'It's hard, Dad, the commute. I don't have any time for my college friends.'

'What's wrong with your Hayward friends, Lisa? They were good enough for the first eighteen years. Those girls from the high school are still around. You told me yourself that Darlene is working at Capwell's. And isn't what's-her-name-Annamarie at the Alameda County Hairdressers' College? What's wrong with your Hayward friends – and with your family, for that matter?'

Valiantly Lisa held back the tears.

Shirley nodded caution to her husband. She agreed with Joe about Berkeley, but she knew he wouldn't make his point this way. Nobody won when you lost your temper.

'Naw,' he waved away his wife's hint. 'don't you go giving me none of your "keep it private" looks.' He swallowed the last piece of pie as if it were Milk of Magnesia. 'Naw, I say this is family business, whether Miss Priss is going to leave home and live with all those street junkies and queers and weirdos.' He glanced at Nan, whether in accusation or apology she couldn't tell.

'He doesn't mean any offence,' whispered Bob.

Nan was staring past Joe, concentrating on a pattern in the flowered wallpaper, as if her glasses were binoculars to a freer world. She turned back to Lisa who sat silent and angry, with tears streaming down her face.

'If you ask me,' Joe said in a lower voice, 'Lisa could just as well go to the junior college like Lynda and Debbie done.' He smiled benignly at Debbie, the bearer of his imminent grandchild.

'Perhaps now isn't the best time to discuss it,' suggested Shirley. 'Being that it's Christmas and we haven't seen Nan for a month. Tell us about that trip you made, to Kansas, wasn't it, to lecture to those professors.'

'Yes,' Nan said, trying to sound interesting. 'Yes, I talked about Virginia Woolf as a forerunner in feminist criticism, showing her influence on. . .' The Berkeley idiom reflexively returned when she discussed her work. 'I mean, she was an important woman writer who. . .'

'Oh, yes,' Shirley nodded, just holding back a yawn. The others searched around the table for the last scraps of dessert. Joe was eating a creamed onion with his fingers.

'Well now,' Nan interrupted herself, 'How about opening the

presents?'

'You all go in and I'll start the coffee,' said Shirley. She looked relieved that the celebration was back in gear.

Before Shirley returned with the percolator and the tray of coffee cups, Joe had managed a grope along Nan's back to determine if she were wearing a bra. An old trick of his. This treatment occurred every holiday, but usually toward the end of the evening. No use lecturing about the finer points of sexual harassment, Nan knew, so she slid to the other end of the couch.

Shirley poured coffee and then sat down deliberately on the cushion between her husband and her sister.

Everyone's generosity was unqualified. Nylon shirts and polyester slacks and orlon sweaters – all wash 'n' wear in the latest Sears colours. They honoured Nan's strange aversion to synthetic fibres. She received a cotton tablecloth, a silk scarf, a wool muffler and a flannel nightie. Chastened, Nan thought how lucky she was to have a family tolerant of her eccentricities. Shirley regarded wash 'n' wear as unequivocal progress – one less thing to iron. But if Nan wanted to iron, well, that was her business.

Only two protests were made that afternoon, both by Shirley. Her first objection was to the big ring she received from Joe.

'Aw, it's only a zircon, hon,' he said lying with his legs across Shirley's lap. He picked up his Alka Seltzer and drank deeply. Before Shirley could protest further he added, 'Just wait 'till I make foreman; it'll be a real diamond then.'

'But Joe, we can't afford. . .' she began.

'Now don't tell me what we can't afford,' he said. 'I'm the one who brings home the money. I'm the one who'll do the affording.'

Shirley was also taken aback by the silk blouse that Nan had given Lisa. She asked if it wasn't a little too old for the girl. The girl didn't think so. In fact the present brought a smile to Lisa's face for the first time since dinner.

Throughout the evening, Nan kept stealing glances at Lisa. On the whole she looked OK. A little pale perhaps. But everyone turned grey around the gills at Christmas. Lisa would be just fine when they checked those tests at Memorial Hospital tomorrow. Nan was almost convinced that this 'mysterious illness' was a reaction to commuting between Hayward and Berkeley, a kind of cultural carsickness. Once Lisa had moved from home, Nan tried to reassure herself, she would get better. Yes, she insisted, Lisa would be all better.

17

Three

Nan always had a hangover the morning after a family gathering, no matter how little she had drunk. Today she resolved not to think about it – about the things said and not said, the covert touches, the miles of tension that hung on the walls like electrified barbed wire. She would not think about it until she had a cup of coffee.

Viennese, ground for Melita, real drip coffee. And a boiled egg in her china cup. A good breakfast wth a sunny view of the Bay from her studio flat. Bourgeois indulgence all of it, but just the remedy for family hangovers.

It would be hot today, one of those mid-winter bonuses in Northern California.

The telephone rang. Who could it be on the day after Christmas? Of course, it was Amy. Amy, whose lawyer voice was ever alert and urgent.

'So how was the Big Holiday?' she was asking.

'Fine. Fun in some ways.' Nan smiled. 'Actually it went better than I had expected. No murders.'

'Fun,' replied Amy, in that tough-kid-from-the-projects tone, that heavy Brooklyn accent. 'You're so tolerant of your family, Nan.'

'Tolerant,' Nan laughed, relieved to be talking to her old friend who also knew the treacheries of inter-class travel. 'Smug maybe, angry maybe, guilty maybe.'

'No, tolerant,' insisted Amy. 'Five minutes with my father, the Yiddish red neck, and I go bonkers.'

Nan shook her head. 'Ah, that's just your cynical, upwardly mobile act. Speaking of which, are you calling to say you've got to prepare a brief or something awful tonight?'

'Nope. I'm calling to confirm our hot movie date.'

'Fine,' said Nan. 'I'll pick you up at seven. And, say, how was your Christmas with Warren?'

'Terrific. Just the two of us, lovey dovey. Who knows why we're still happy after all these years.'

Nan laughed. 'Don't question, just enjoy.'

'Right,' said Amy, but her voice was distracted already. 'Gotta run. Bye.'

Nan returned to her sunny seat, thinking how much she loved her friend, how much she needed Amy's adrenalin and intelligence and loyalty. But sentimentality irritated Nan, so she considered the weather again. Might get as high as seventy degrees today. She thought about the Christmas holidays with Charles at Carmel-by-the-Sea. Right now she wouldn't mind a little tan to fortify her through the winter. Of course she couldn't afford it – neither the room rates nor the time. She had promised herself to finish an article. And she had promised Marjorie Adams they would discuss her dissertation this afternoon. Nan slipped her black coffee slowly, wondering if she actually *liked* Marjorie Adams. There was something about the student's old-fashioned integrity Nan admired. But sometimes that integrity became rigidity. The latter was on full display at the last departmental meeting. Nan had made a motion before her colleagues, asking them to support the Sexual Harassment Campaign in two ways. The Feminist Caucus would take a poll of all students in the English Department, asking whether they had ever been assaulted or propositioned by a teacher.

'Of either sex?' asked Angus Murchie, waiting for appreciative laughter.

'Of either sex,' Nan continued steadily. 'The second motion is that the Department formally request the Academic Senate to establish a grievance committee.'

Marjorie Adams did not approve of the Sexual Harassment Campaign. This was evident in her frown, before she spoke.

'Don't you think one could get a little, um, hysterical about these issues?' she asked hesitantly.

Nan stared at her down the huge table. Was she hearing right? Somehow she felt that if she stared, she might hear more clearly.

Murchie was nodding his grey head in considered agreement. This was the sort of 'non-academic' issue he considered inappropriate in a scholarly atmosphere. No doubt he would remind his colleagues of Nan's indiscretion during her tenure evaluation.

'I mean,' Marjorie leaned forward and spoke earnestly through her dark red lips, 'surely the complaints are justified sometimes?

But how does one know when they've been, well, provoked?'

Nan glowered at Marjorie in disbelief, remembering how hard she, herself, had fought for student representation at departmental meetings. Nan had to respect this student's courage in arguing with her thesis adviser so openly. Such a goddam stalwart character. What was her spine made from – sterling silver? Again Nan realized how little she understood this young woman.

'Doesn't that sound like "blaming the victim"?' Nan asked carefully.

'A girl learns to avoid certain situations,' Marjorie said. 'Besides, the "victim" in some cases might be the male professor unjustly accused.'

Matt interrupted with his characteristic diplomacy, 'Why don't we let the Feminist Caucus take their poll? We can consider the second motion next quarter.'

The vote was almost unanimous, with only Murchie objecting.

Nan returned to the present, checked her watch and gulped down a second cup of coffee. With this rush of medium roast caffeine, Nan was ready for all the Marjorie Adams and Joe Growskys of the world. She coasted her bicycle out of the garage. She would make it down to the office by 10.30, a good start for the day after Christmas.

Entering the university through the North Gate, Nan realized once again that the campus was never really empty. She recognized the usual holiday crowd of suntanned refugees who played an acrobatic brand of Frisbee, children on skateboards, black men summoning the ghosts of their African fathers on steel drums. For Nan herself, the campus had been a different kind of sanctuary.

Her face softened, recalling that first scary visit in the early 1950s. The campus had been different then, less 'developed', greener, more like a park. Nan Weaver had come to Berkeley for an entrance test. She remembered walking out the front door of Hayward Union High School, past the fake Grecian columns, and taking the Key System buses. Riding through the rolling hills, past Oakland's industry and into Berkeley's greenery, she had caught glimpses of San Francisco and the ocean beyond. It was like being delivered from the tense confinement of a family Sunday into a frontier where she could see past her parents' ambitions.

The high school teachers always said Nan was a bright kid. Mom hoped she might take a business course, maybe become a legal secretary. But something inside Nan insisted, even then, that she

20

wouldn't be imprisoned in Hayward. She would escape the rodeos and the embroidery exhibits. Nan had decided on that first visit, almost thirty years ago, that Berkeley would be her refuge. And indeed, she had spent the best years here – the fifties as an under-graduate, the late sixties getting her PhD, and now back again, after several years away, as a professor. An Assistant Professor.

Nan paused for a moment, astride her bicycle, to look beyond the campus to the clear view of San Francisco Bay. How the skyline had changed. Today the campus was offering up continual waves of association. She thought about the first day of classes in September 1951 and how this had seemed like the most beautiful view in the world. It still did. As a freshman (now they called it 'freshperson', a term Nan believed in, but stuttered on) during that first year, she had sat furtively in the back rows of Wheeler Hall while liberal professors professed their passions for the vernacular in Wordsworth or the mysticism in Yeats. She heard them answering questions she had been afraid to ask at Hayward Union High School. And out on Sproul Plaza, during the political rallies, she learned that some people opposed the fighting in Korea, that Americans had established internment camps for the Japanese during World War II, that Adlai Stevenson was not a dangerous Communist.

Why was she feeling so nostalgic this morning, Nan wondered. Here she was, standing in the middle of campus staring at the Bay. Maybe it was the holidays.

God, her parents had been tickled that Easter holiday she brought home Charles Woodward, dark, handsome, rich and pre-med. 'Such a nice type,' Mom had declared. Charles and Nan had fallen in love during their senior year, in 1955, early February when the tulip trees bloom over by the Ag-Econ building and the eucalyp-tus begin to glisten in their pungent sweat. He was smart, funny and kind. He would earn a good living. What else could Nan want in a husband? Charles invited her for long weekends to the Woodward family ranch in Marin County, for exciting afternoons of horses and champagne picnics, for elegant evenings of port in the parlour. Charles took her away from her small room in Kelly Hill to mas-querade parties and fancy balls on Fraternity Row.

The Bay. She got engaged because of this Bay. She recalled the night that Charles drove, with the Studebaker's top down, into the dark Berkeley hills. As they looked out over the flickering San Francisco skyline, he presented her with a huge diamond ring.

Charles offered a one-way ticket from Hayward. And love. They promised each other a life of love.

From the beginning the marriage was strained by her 'independent streak', as Mom called it. Nan insisted on teaching high school.

Why couldn't she just settle down and have children? She could afford it. God knew, none of their friends had married a doctor. No, Nan said. She wasn't satisfied. And, despite persistent feelings of unnaturalness, she didn't want to have children.

This morning, as Nan cycled past bleak Tolman Hall, she thought how the Tolman library there wasn't even built in the fifties and how it was filled with tear gas when she returned as a graduate student. Berkeley was her refuge in the late sixties, after ten years of high school teaching and marriage. After a stale and painful decade of port in the parlour which ended as port in the kitchen, dining room, bedroom and a little pocketflask which she carried for fortification on the way home from Amy, the divorce lawyer.

How had she married this unimaginative, conventional, controlling man? Nan persecuted herself with such questions until she remembered what it was like to be twenty-one years old and to believe in the immutability of love. What it was like to marry 'up' and away from Hayward. Only after this freedom, did she realize that she needed more freedom. Shirley said she was selfish. Mom said she was foolish ('Are you never satisfied, daughter, always moving on?'). Charles said she would be sorry. She heard these voices over and over. But she did not feel selfish or foolish or sorry. She felt scared and brave.

In the sixties, she was a returning student. An older woman. If she could survive Hayward and Charles, she could survive being a 'mature student'. She thought she had come back to the same campus, but the atmosphere had been changed indelibly by Civil Rights, Free Speech, Black Power, Ethnic Studies and the Anti-War Movement. Nan helped to occupy several buildings, got arrested, then acquitted. They were creating – she was helping to create – a counter-culture, a freedom of the highest order. Academic freedom. Political freedom. Sexual freedom.

Passing by the Life Sciences Building, she remembered one terrible evening filled with Professor Eastman's admonitions to her to 'hang loose, let go of inhibitions, relax'. The professor seemed so concerned about her. Personally concerned. He said he admired her willingness to change, to experiment and grow. Nan admired his mind, his intricate lectures on D H Lawrence.

22

Until once, after a moratorium meeting here in LSB, when he had kept her late, talking. Teacher and student together. Down with élitism, he murmured. Still, she wondered why he bothered about someone from the sticks. Why should he go out of his way? Suddenly, she understood.

'Just a minute', she heard herself saying as his fascination with her pendant watch turned to fascination with her breast.

She pulled away, but he was pinching her nipple through her bra.

'Professor Eastman,' she gasped, trying to knock away his hand.

'Ted,' he said, moving closer and nibbling at her ear. 'Call me Ted. We're both adults.'

'No,' she said, frightened and guilty all at once. Did he think she was loose because she was a divorcee?

'You misunderstood me,' she forced herself to speak. 'I like you as a teacher, as a friend, but. . .'

'Don't play ingenue.' His voice was seductive, his words sarcastic. 'A woman in her thirties has been around.'

She wanted to tell him that she had only slept with her husband, that she still related sex with love. And she realized how much she would sound like Shirley.

Before she could form a response, he had forced his tongue into her mouth. And Nan didn't know what to do, how to repel him. It was a perfectly spontaneous act when she bit it.

'Why you little,' he pulled away, his fingers in his mouth checking for blood. 'You little cockteaser,' he snarled, 'I've got a mind to . . .'

But Nan hadn't heard the rest. She had run from the room, down the dim corridors of the Life Sciences Building and into the clean, night air, asking herself what she had done, how she had led him on. The *Daily Cal* had just run a series of articles about 'co-ed poachers' who stole men from faculty wives. She didn't think she was a poacher. She had no designs on Professor Eastman, except as a thesis adviser. Of course she had to forget that. She dropped his class, applied for part-time status and lost her financial aid that term. The following quarter, she switched her thesis subject from D H Lawrence to Virginia Woolf.

For months she tried to dismiss the incident as trivial, as something that a 'free woman' would often endure. But friends told her not to be ashamed of her naïvete. She understood that Eastman was assaulting her integrity as well as her body. Within a year Nan was able to smile that the professor had initiated her, not into his notion

23

of sexual freedom – but into her commitment to feminism.

Now, a decade later, it was hard to believe *she* was a professor and a thesis adviser. When she lectured in Wheeler Hall about the female vernacular or matriarchal mysticism, she kept a careful eye out for bright students in the back row.

Wheeler Hall was an empty cavern this morning after Christmas. No creches or trees with winking lights and tinsel, considered Nan. Relentlessly secular. So much the better for getting work done. No student demands on her time – demands which were always so hard to refuse. After all, her conscience said, she was hired to teach. However, she needed time to write. And if she didn't write, they wouldn't let her teach. 'Paradox', according to her *Dictionary of Literary Terms*, was 'a statement or situation that seems – but need not be – self-contradictory'.

As Nan walked along the deserted corridor to her office she was disappointed to see light streaming through the frosted glass of Angus Murchie's door, which was located, unfortunately, adjacent to her own. She tiptoed so he would not hear her. Why was the old fart working over the holidays? Probably culling evidence to deny her tenure. She laughed at her own paranoia, but of all the luck, to have had Murchie reported to the Sexual Harassment Campaign during her year of tenure. Of all the luck, to have had Murchie, the most sexist professor in the department, ask to visit her class. Of course he would walk in the morning she was discussing how John Milton had exploited his daughters and his three wives. Angus Murchie, who had spent thirty years re-reading 'Comus' and 'Samson Agonistes', now knew that she 'carried her politics into the classroom'. Nan found that a peculiar allegation, as if political opinion were unsanitary, disposable material which one might check into a locker. Oh well, the tenure committee would also consider other criteria.

Could Murchie ever understand her, let alone appreciate her? When he faced tenure thirty-five years before, the procedure wasn't so precarious. He was a bright young man who had gone to the right schools where he had met the right men who cheered him on. Still, Nan doubted he was conscious of the privilege. He had an innocent aristocracy about him, as if he deserved his professorial status. He seemed surprised by and then affronted by the 'outsiders' who had broken into academia, the Jews and blacks and women. He complained most about the women. In recent years he had grown more vitriolic in putting down his female colleagues and more reckless in attempting to bed down his female students.

Nan felt relieved as she passed Murchie's office. She wondered if she would find Mr Johnson on duty. It had taken her five years to get past the stage of silent nods with the old black janitor. After a thousand evenings of Mr Johnson stopping by her door, 'just to check', they had come to a mutual liking. For a while, he tried to persuade her not to work in the sixty-year-old building at night.

'Not to scare you more than's necessary,' he had said, rubbing his grey eyebrows nervously, 'but this place isn't safe for a lady at night. Those weirdos come up from Telegraph Avenue and find ways into the building.'

How could she explain that she was working for tenure. Such an absurd system. Seven years of teaching and writing and *then* they decided if they would admit you to the club. Even her family wouldn't accept that she could get fired after all these years. As Joe said, in one of his sweeter moments, 'They'd never get rid of a good worker like you.' But Mr Johnson did understand tenure, or at least its results, because he had seen other Assistant Professors disappear.

'I guess I'm better at working than relaxing,' she explained finally.

So Mr Johnson continued to check up on her each evening, usually serving up an admonishment with his protection. Sometimes he accepted a cup of Red Rose tea in return.

Nan was thinking now that the bottle of Cutty Sark she had presented Mr Johnson, with best wishes for himself and his wife in the New Year, was probably the most successful present she had found. She was not so sure about the earrings she had given Shirley or Lisa's silk blouse. But then you could never be sure.

Nan's door was covered with maps and quotations, an amusing diversion for students while they waited to see her and an effective blind when she didn't want anyone to know she was in. Her light never spilled into the hall as did Murchie's.

On the small, square piece of corkboard by the door was an index card proclaiming:

Nan Weaver, Assistant Professor
English 20, Modern British and American Literature
English 175, Women Writers
Office Hours: Tuesday–Thursday 2–4 (and by appointment)

Underneath the white card was tacked a blue vellum envelope covered in elegant black calligraphy.

Nan knew it would be from Marjorie Adams. She unlocked her office, set down her books and walked over to the window with the letter. If Marjorie was saying that she couldn't make the appointment, Nan would explode. Last quarter one student had managed to miss four special appointments. Sometimes she felt like a self-serve filling station, open day and night. The lines outside the male professors' offices were far shorter than these refugee processions to her door. What could she do about it? She didn't want to cut herself off. This year, two students came to her after they were raped. Where else could they have gone? How could she have refused to sponsor the Feminist Caucus? Women students needed a forum to coordinate political action, a community in which to share personal problems. How different her work, her life, would have been if she had had a Feminist Caucus in which to discuss Professor Eastman's advances or the advisability of marrying Charles Woodward.

She would enjoy all this personal work with the students if the university wasn't making its own extra-curricular demands. She belonged to department committees and Academic Senate committees. They all wanted women faculty to be visible, so visible that one might imagine there were three or four times as many as there were. Sometimes she was nostalgic for that arcane, 1950s attitude that academia had something to do with books.

Remembering the letter in her hand, Nan opened the blue vellum envelope.

> Dear Professor Weaver:
>   I hope you had an enjoyable Christmas.
>   This is to confirm our appointment at 1 p.m. today.
>   Best regards,
>   Marjorie Adams

A courteous, responsible note, considered Nan, miserable at the thought of how she had become so suspicious.

Nan plugged in her electric kettle, made herself a cup of tea and sat down with Marjorie's recent chapter about the tension between power and love in *The Severed Head*. Fascinating stuff, and exquisitely written. Perhaps Marjorie revealed too much sympathy for the dour Honor Klein. How appropriate that Marjorie would select Iris Murdoch to study. What strong, determined, upper-class women they both were. How cold and detached they could appear.

Now this slander was quite uncalled for. Where was her sisterly feeling? Marjorie always tried to be respectful of Nan. She disagreed with Nan's politics, but then it was a free world. Or getting there.

As the Campanile chimed one o'clock, Marjorie rapped on the door. Nan wondered what version of Marjorie would walk in. What was featured in Vogue this month, Lolita stovepipe jeans or Dietrich slinky black velvets? When Nan had complained to Matt about Marjorie's excessive wardrobe, he had chastised Nan for being a prim, parochial schoolgirl. Matt admired Marjorie's flair. Besides, Nan thought, Matt was a much nicer person than Nan would ever be.

In walked Myrna Loy, no, maybe Joan Crawford. Marjorie's blonde hair was braided on top of her head. She wore a loose black and red forties dress, complete with shoulder pads and patent belt. Her lipstick might be called 'Crimson Passion' or 'Eve's Desire'. Her shoes were old-fashioned patent platforms, open at the toes. Nan didn't usually notice fashions, but Marjorie practically wore a sign saying, 'Annotate me.'

'Professor Weaver?' Marjorie asked politely, as if she were waking her adviser, 'I hope I'm not disturbing anything.'

'Oh, no, no,' said Nan, embarrassed at being caught in her stare. 'I was expecting you, Marjorie. Please sit down.'

The younger woman sat on the edge of a wooden chair with the tentativeness of a tanager settling on a eucalyptus branch, wary of her surroundings, unsure of proper camouflage.

Within ten minutes, both of them were submerged in the dissertation. Marjorie was sitting back more comfortably, waving her long, graceful hands as she defended her arguments. Nan enjoyed Marjorie's originality and enthusiasm. At moments like this she could see through the camp masquerades to Marjorie's complexity and tough intelligence. Perhaps, after all, she had been unfair to the young woman. Perhaps Nan was too conscious of class. She knew she was defensive about being the working-class kid from the cannery. It was something she could never change, no matter who she married or where she worked. Nan, the Buddy Holly fan, and Marjorie, the opera patron. Marjorie had once mentioned that her family owned several Corots, and Nan had not understood the

27

significance until Matt had explained that she wasn't talking about costume jewellery.

Nan sometimes worried that Marjorie and the other students could tell she wasn't smart. Oh, maybe she had a knack for common sense, but she wasn't a genuine intellectual. Nan attributed all her academic success to effort rather than intelligence. Although she was a professor at one of the best American universities, although she had published widely, she still didn't feel like a scholar. She felt like a fraud.

Marjorie, however, didn't seem to notice. In fact, she had been eager to have Nan as her thesis adviser. And right now, she was asking Nan's opinion on something as though it did matter.

A heavy knock sounded on the door.

'Come in,' called Nan, surprised.

Angus Murchie wrenched open the door, 'Well, well, I thought I heard the intense clashing of two mighty minds.' Murchie spoke with just a trace of brogue. Nan regretted this because she used to like the Scots.

Murchie was leaning against Nan's bookcase. He never stood by himself in a room. He was always leaning his portly weight on the back of a chair or against the wall. He cleared his throat to ensure their full attention. What a classic papa he would have made, if he had ever stayed married long enough to preside over a family. Nan tried to think of him as an old man, fearful of retirement, threatened by these younger women who represented a new order. But, as usual, his personality subverted her sympathy.

'Here I presumed I was all alone in these hallowed halls. Then, on the way back from my mailbox, what should I overhear but passionate argument?' He had assumed his posh Oxbridge drawl now, so much the better for hating him.

'I say, passionate argument on the day after Christmas. Before the goose is digested and the presents returned. But then Americans never did celebrate Boxing Day.' Murchie stuffed two blue aerogrammes into his pocket and fiddled with his letter opener, an overly large utensil with a moccasin-hide handle. This hunting souvenir was one of Murchie's dearest possessions. He was constantly playing with it at meetings.

Nan watched Marjorie's face lose its intensity in a demure smile. She could feel a frown cross her own forehead.

'Yes,' Nan laughed briskly, 'partners in crime.' Then she turned back to the manuscript on her desk. An awkward silence followed.

Finally, Murchie cleared his throat again. 'Yes, well, who am I but mortal man to disturb the womb of feminist criticism.' He took a long look at Marjorie, who kept her eyes on her finely trimmed nails.

'Miss Adams,' he said at last, pointing the letter opener at the young woman.

Marjorie looked up brightly.

'I should like to chat with you briefly this afternoon – after you and Professor Weaver have completed these worthy pursuits – about your readership next term. I'm considering moving you back to the sixteenth century.'

Nan could barely contain her irritation. So she exhaled it, concentrated on her yoga breathing and looked past Murchie out to the Berkeley Hills.

'Certainly, Professor Murchie,' Marjorie smiled again. 'I'll drop by within half-an-hour if that's suitable.'

'Quite suitable,' barked Murchie. 'Quite suitable.' He closed the door with a thud.

Nan took one last deep breath and smiled at Marjorie cordially, perhaps stiffly, she couldn't tell. They tried several times to resurrect Iris Murdoch. Then somehow they started arguing.

'I believe quite firmly,' said Marjorie, curling a lock of blonde hair around her Crimson Passion fingernail, 'that I read Murdoch as one mind reading another, not as a woman sympathizing with another woman. Our genitals were placed a great distance from our heads.'

'Is that why so much literature by women was ignored by critics for hundreds of years?'

'Perhaps some of it,' answered Marjorie, 'was worth ignoring.'

Stunned at Marjorie's directness, Nan wondered if the younger woman had never had to vacillate on an opinion in her privileged life? Then she wondered if she were simply jealous of Marjorie's confidence.

'Worth ignoring?' Nan repeated.

'Yes,' said Marjorie.

'Emily Dickinson?' asked Nan. 'Jane Austen? Their only recognition came as "feminine writers". Worth ignoring? Agnes Smedley? Kate Chopin?' She could barely keep her voice down. At frantic moments like this, she always felt more like a student than a teacher.

'Granted, there were mistakes,' Marjorie began.

'Mistakes?' shouted Nan. No, she mustn't shout. Angus Murchie might rush in to save Marjorie's mind from feminist assault.

'*Casualties* is more like it.' Nan's voice was quieter, if not calmer. 'Murders, exiles, rapes. Do you have any idea how few women publish serious books every year in this country and how few of those are reviewed and how few of those are bought? Just look around you. How many women are teaching literature at this university? What *writers* are they allowed to teach?'

Nan wanted Marjorie Adams to understand; at this moment she needed her, more than any other student, to understand.

'But that's changing,' said Marjorie. 'I'm here. You're here. There will be more of us.'

· Us. Nan smiled at the 'us' and at the optimism. She had always liked Marjorie's optimism.

'Actually,' said Marjorie, winding her watch, 'I should be leaving if I'm going to keep my appointment with Professor Murchie.' Even in her eagerness to go, she looked excited by their discussion.

Nan nodded, too wound up to reply.

Marjorie gathered her papers together and said, 'I do thank you for the response to my chapter.'

'Yes,' said Nan briskly, trying to recover some face.

Marjorie zipped her slim leather briefcase and exited elegantly before Nan had sunk to the full depth of her confusion.

Four

The track was almost vacant at seven a.m. However, the presence of three other joggers reassured her that indeed this running was an exercise in more than fear. Every day Nan questioned the value of jogging, especially during the first ten minutes, when she wasn't sure where she would find the steam to finish her three miles. Was this another of her endurance tests, her self-imposed penances? Her pace was slow. Even old men passed her by. But after the first four laps, she felt OK. Few runners lasted on the track as long as she did. Somewhere during the fifth lap, during the eleventh or twelfth minute, willpower gave over to internal force: she was driven along, flown above the ground. Oxygen repossessed her brain. She grew alert. She might organize her day or try to finish the sentences she had sat over for hours. Sometimes she worked through tensions from school or the family. Sometimes she fantasized. (The Distinguished Teaching Award. Tenure. A severe, but subtle put-down of Angus Murchie, Esq.) Such daydreams were the best part of jogging, like the fantasies she allowed herself before she fell asleep. But this morning the running was 'a problem-solving session', as her earnest friend Francie, who practised feminist therapy, would say. The big problem was: What could she do on New Year's Eve? Whom would she offend?

Sweat dripped down her temples. Tears streamed from her eyes. She enjoyed these signs and always felt cleansed after a run, knowing she had done something productive. Shirley regarded jogging as one of Nan's loonier activities. ('To spend all that time running around when you might be doing useful work, like housecleaning or washing your clothes or something that needed to be done, I just don't understand you, Nannie.') Both sisters were expert at cleaning, purging, always on the look out for some form of purity. Nan could feel the muscles in her back unknot and relax. It was a crisp, windy morning. She breathed in pine and cedar from the tall, swaying trees.

The New Year's dilemma felt less serious already. Would it be a smash-up evening of beer and dancing and dirty jokes with Shirley and Joe in Hayward? A quietly erotic time with Francie and her lesbian friends? A proper cocktail party at Matt's where she might make intellectual chat with her colleagues, score some career points and perhaps reward that sweet fellow Claude for his committed but discreet pursuit these past six months?

She could hear from behind her the slosh, slosh of tennis shoes in the damp earth. Damn, she thought, as a septuagenarian passed her by. She knew that running 'wasn't about competition', as Francie would say. But this guy had overtaken her twice already.

This was her tenth lap, two more to go, and all of a sudden she realized that what she wanted most on New Year's Eve was to be alone. Alone with a quiet evening, an uncluttered evening to work. Well, why not? Why not offend everybody! She could have a nice dinner and then see in the New Year as she polished off the journal article on the connections in Doris Lessing's writing between feminism and African liberation. Of course she wouldn't tell her friends; no one would believe she was spending the evening in Wheeler Hall. She would have to devise a much cleverer alibi.

Red, sweaty and limber when she got home, she had settled everything except the alibi. Shirley would take it the hardest, would regard her absence as some kind of snobbery. Nan could taste the guilt rising in her gut already. But her bones were easy from the run; she tried to remember how relaxed she was. On the front of the fridge were taped half-a-dozen snapshots. The photograph nearest the handle was of Nan, Shirley and little Lisa. Lisa must have been ten or eleven, and already she looked more like her aunt. Actually, she didn't resemble anyone in the family, with that ocean of fair hair. Both Shirley and Nan beamed at the girl, like proud mothers. Lisa stood in the middle, linking and separating them, as always.

Nan prepared her breakfast. She liked the pure colours, the white and yellow of the soft-boiled egg, steaming with its top off; the black of the coffee made richer in the dark mug.

Lisa was just one step in the tango between Nan and Shirley. Their tension seemed to crystallize long ago, just after Shirley's wedding. Once she had found her own man, Shirley was eager to help mate her sister. And when Nan finally 'landed' Charles Woodward, Shirley seemed distant, uncomfortable about their status and income. But her clearest reaction, which irritated Nan immeasurably, was sisterly relief that Nan's life was finally coming together. Nan hated the unspoken words between them. She tried to tell Shirley why she loved teaching – the ideas, the books, the life of school. She confided her frustrations with Charles, the boredom and staleness of their marriage. But Shirley said she'd get used to that. She called Nan 'restless', said, 'Even as a kid you were never settled.' At times Nan wondered if she had inherited every ounce of drive in the family. And, of course, when she finally had the courage to divorce Charles, Shirley was utterly bewildered. She saw the painful fear in Nan's eyes and couldn't understand why she was doing this to herself. During the last ten years, Shirley hadn't probed far into her sister's 'private matters'. Nan never discussed her current celibacy. As long as Nan was happy, Shirley said, that's all that mattered.

Likewise, Nan pretended to accept Shirley's family life. Sometimes she tried to imagine what Shirley did now that the kids were grown. Nan knew that she, herself, was the oddball, that Shirley had made the more commonly sensible choice for women of their class and generation. So she tried to support her sister. On Sunday mornings, before she phoned Shirley, Nan wrote a list of things to ask, things to tell, because the conversation so often sagged between them.

Nan washed out her egg cup, then the coffee mug. One of each. She would burst at the unfairness of having to do everybody else's dishes – and laundry and housekeeping.

Still, Amy had teased her last night that she was just as motherly as Shirley, just as protective of her students as Shirley was of the family. 'Too protective,' Amy had warned. 'You've got to learn to cover your own ass.'

The phone rang. It was Amy. Odd how Amy often called when she was on Nan's mind. Her friend phoned at unpredictable hours, whenever she had a moment from court or was bogged down in her research. The reasons were equally unpredictable.

'I called to apologize,' announced Amy.

'For what?' Nan asked.

'For criticizing you about the Sexual Harassment Campaign after the movie last night.'

'Yes,' said Nan quietly. She had been hurt when her old friend called her foolish. It was as though Amy were ganging up with Matt.

'And to say I'm angry with you,' Amy continued.

'Come again?' said Nan.

'Why didn't you tell me about Professor Eastman until last night?

33

Like twelve years ago?'

'You remember the quarter I dropped a class,' said Nan, 'when I had mononucleosis?'

'How could I forget, the indestructible Weaver! I couldn't believe it. But you did look awful that term.'

'I thought I had some disease,' Nan went on, 'some moral disease, to have a respected man like that come on to me.'

'Sorry,' said Amy, 'I wasn't meaning to blame you.'

'For a while,' Nan spoke quietly, 'it really shook my foundations about fairness, about safety. It showed me how tricky surviving at the Holy University could be.'

'But Nan Weaver,' exclaimed Amy, losing patience. 'It's been so many years. Why haven't you *ever* brought it up? And all this politicking you do on sexual harassment.'

'I find it hard to believe myself. I guess I thought I had told you. I thought you understood why I first got involved in this issue. At the time I thought everyone knew about me. I thought I wore it on my sleeve.'

'Yeah,' said Amy, her voice easier now. 'Francie said she felt that way after she got raped.'

Damn, Nan thought, how detached could she get, to hold this away from Amy, her best friend, for so long.

'So I just called to say,' Amy began.

Nan could imagine Amy checking her watch.

'That I understand this political campaign better,' Amy was finishing. 'But I still wish you'd wait until after tenure.'

'Thanks, Amy. We have a lot to talk about.'

'Yeah. Sometime soon. Gotta rush. Gotta be out at the jail by nine o'clock to pick up a client.'

'Right,' said Nan. 'Thanks for calling.'

Nan found herself staring out at the Bay. She couldn't go to work just yet. She made another cup of coffee. Maybe if she told Shirley about Eastman and some of her other experiences, maybe Shirley would understand her 'crazy politics'. How could she still be so ashamed? Sometimes she tried to dismiss it as insignificant. Compared to the daily violence against women – rape, mutilation, murder – what was one pass? But Eastman's assault had shaken her equilibrium profoundly. What a hypocrite she was, ranting away about women protecting themselves and not acknowledging what had happened to her. Had anything like this ever happened to Shirley? Why had she never asked?

No, she wouldn't be too hard on herself. She tried with Shirley. She tried more than Shirley did. Why was it always Nan who had to cope with her schizophrenic feelings in Hayward: Why didn't Shirley come to Berkeley for a visit? Sometimes her sister seemed too busy for her, what with supervising the bake sale at All Saints, driving what's-her-name to the prenatal clinic, organizing the fireworks stand for the Boy Scouts. Couldn't Shirley let go of the damn Boy Scouts now that Tom and Bob were married? No, she would never release the strings which bound her forever as a mummy in Southern Alameda County.

Nan thought about the last fourth of July, how she had dashed out to see the family before going backpacking in Yosemite. It was such a classic visit. She had waited an hour for Shirley outside the Boy Scout fireworks stand. An hour under the morning sun, standing in the empty lot, leaning against the dusty station wagon, one foot crunching straw, one foot fiddling in the mud rut, making notes in a new novel she had promised to review and hoping like hell that the sun wouldn't get much hotter.

There she stood, surrounded by the Big O Tire Dealer, the Quick Stop 7-11, Elizabeth's Coiffures and the A & W Rootbeer stand, which had been here on Lorenzo Boulevard since they were kids. Shirley had explained how this site was ideal for fireworks sales, right on the road to the K Mart. So many people drove by. So Nan tried to look inconspicuous, as if everyone in Hayward reviewed novels while loitering in empty lots. She glanced away when Mrs Wilson dropped off her son from their sleek yellow Coup de Ville. Mrs Wilson, who had once been Elaine Mendosa, Head Yell Leader, likewise chose not to notice Nan. Then Larry Connors arrived. Larry Connors, on whom she had the most enormous crush in the twelfth grade, but who loved Shirley instead. In his misery at Shirley's early marriage, Larry got himself hooked to a girl from Castro Valley. Nan managed to ignore the reunion by feigning fascination with the Winnebago waiting for a check-up at the Big O Tire Dealer.

When Shirley finally emerged from the fireworks stand she was apologizing for the delay and beaming about their record-breaking profits. Enough for a new tent and backpack for the kids. She spoke as if backpacking should be reserved for kids. Nan counted that she had read seventy, no seventy-five, pages during the past hour.

After the fireworks, she and Shirley went off for their favourite lunch at Burger King. The adolescent, racially integrated staff all wore brown uniforms set off with orange and white stripes. They behaved like apprentice flight attendants, smiling generously, regardless of whether you ordered a Whopper with Cheese or a small Diet Pepsi. Across the street, Nan watched teenagers piling into old Soaper's Restaurant, where she and Shirley used to stop for milkshakes when they were cruising the strip after football games. Did kids still cruise the strip?

One of the Burger King flight attendants had walked directly toward them, a sweet young woman whose little brown cap didn't look at all silly atop her cascading hair. A kid whose skirt was too short because she had grown an inch during the last month.

'Lisa honey,' said Shirley, 'can you take the bus home tonight? We need the car to pick up more fireworks at the Red Devil shack.'

'Sure Mom,' said the daughter, stewardess, niece, soon-to-be-woman. 'So what will it be for two? Lunch is my treat.'

After Nan finished drying the three breakfast dishes, she checked her watch. She would have to get moving if she were going to use this Christmas vacation to the fullest. She walked into the bathroom, took off her robe and examined herself in the long mirror. Fairly decent shape for an almost fifty-year-old woman. Her breasts were small, but firm. Nothing really sagged. But maybe that was because she wasn't wearing her glasses.

Nan remembered she was supposed to phone Lisa for the test results. By now Nan believed that the illness was psychological. Lisa's paleness was probably the same kind of anaemia she herself had suffered on leaving Kelly Hill thirty years ago. Nan had phoned a good feminist therapist, a friend of Francie's, to see if she could take Lisa. She would suggest therapy discreetly, after these test results proved inconclusive. Lisa would be willing to try it. Yes, she was much more daring than Nan's cautious self of thirty years ago.

Nan ran a comb through her hair as she dialled the Growsky's familiar number. No one answered for the first couple of rings. Probably a good sign; maybe they were off shopping in Southland Mall, near the hospital. Just as she was hanging up, she heard a low, strained 'Hello.'

'What's up, sweets?' Nan asked her sister.

'Oh, Nan,' said Shirley. That was all she said. A muffled noise, a hand over the receiver, another muffled noise. Then Shirley came on again. 'Oh, Nan, Nannie.'

'What is it?' she demanded. 'The tests, tell me how Lisa's tests went.' She was trying to sound solid, confident.

'Let me, Mom,' a small voice came from the distance. Then a more gentle tone. 'It's all right. You sit down now, Mom.'

'Nan,' she heard Lisa calling her from the other end of the phone. 'Oh. . .'

'Yes, love,' Nan said. What tone should she assume? The words came tense and stacatto-like, before she could decide. 'What was it the doctor told you?'

'Nothing conclusive,' said the younger woman with careful detachment. Nan could barely believe that this steady, brave voice was only nineteen years old. 'But it could be bad. It could be Lupus.'

'What's that?' asked Nan, afraid to hear the answer.

'A kind of arthritis that attacks the heart and connective tissues,' said Lisa, who was making As in both biology and journalism. 'It can last for a long time, completely remit or . . . kill you in a few months.'

'Oh no, no,' Nan exploded. 'I mean it couldn't be. How do they know? We'll get another opinion; try another doctor.'

'Well, we don't know anything definite,' said Lisa patiently. 'The tests were mostly negative, but that doesn't mean anything. I have the weakness, the spiking fever, the weight loss, but the freakiest thing of all,' her voice seemed to crack and then recover, 'is that funny butterfly mark on my face that I thought was from strawberries.'

Nan nodded. Then remembering she was on the phone, said, 'Yes, what about it?'

'They say it's an erythematous rash and it's symptomatic of Lupus.'

'But when will you know?'

'Well, this thing comes and goes. The tests don't always show. But they're going to take another one next month.'

'Have you considered that it might be emotional, I mean part of it. You don't have to take one opinion do you?' Nan stopped as she noticed the hysteria in her voice.

'Oh, Lisa honey, how do you feel?'

'Pretty depressed,' she said simply. 'But physically, physically I do feel better today.'

'Maybe that means some kind of remission.' Nan knew she sounded wildly optimistic.

'I doubt it,' said Lisa. 'It's supposed to be really erratic. Not much

37

I can do about it anyway. "Rest," Dr Bonelli said. But I've been resting in this damn house for a week and I'm ready to tear out my hair.'

'Listen, you do what the doctor says,' reprimanded Nan. Then, in a lighter voice, she teased, 'And if you tear out your hair, I'll buy you a wig. Remember we always wondered what you'd look like as a brunette.'

'Oh, Nan,' laughed Lisa.

Nan listened to her niece's clear, young laugh and could think of nothing to say. Tests, butterflies, arthritis, heart, kill, remit, wig, Lisa. Desperately she tried to fit it all together.

'Nan?'

Someone was calling her name.

'Yes?' she answered foggily.

'We still have New Year's Day together, don't we?' asked Lisa.

'Well, love, I don't know about that,' said Nan. 'I think we should listen to the doctor's. . .'

'The damn doctor has no idea what it's like in this house on New Year's.' Lisa lowered her voice, 'with the Rose Bowl Parade and the game and the after-game replays and the boys and Daddy hollering and Debbie and Lynda yammering on about their macramé and. . .'

'Enough said,' Nan answered, pleased at the energy in Lisa's fury. 'We'll have our day.'

Nan said goodbye. She stood up with deliberation, wiping away her selfish tears.

The friendship with Lisa had begun only a couple of years ago, when Shirley finally admitted her daughter was old enough to take the BART train out to see her aunt. Berkeley was eleven stops from South Hayward, eleven chances for murder, rape, battery. Crime was getting worse and worse in the Bay Area, despite, or perhaps because of, its utopian reputation. And Berkeley, for heaven's sake, was the end of the earth.

Lisa had prepared for that trip by reading two Willa Cather novels and buying a funky tie-dyed T-shirt like the ones everyone wore on Telegraph Avenue.

Nan searched now for her books and her ever-lost keys. It would be too simple to cast Shirley as the provincial mother. Nan and Lisa had an unspoken agreement not to scapegoat Shirley. But they would lobby for Lisa's freedom.

Nan had started the lobby years ago. Lisa was just a little girl.

38

With postcards from Holland and Morocco and the Soviet Union after she left Charles. With that birthday present atlas. With fantasies about hiking through Alaska together. Nan was conscious of being the Exotic Aunt, a strange and benevolent lady who travelled in faraway places and spoke grand ideas. She enjoyed this image, as if she were showing little Nan Weaver herself that indeed you could grow up and out of Hayward. And how she loved Lisa, more than any other person in her life.

Sometimes they would go for walks together, just the two of them. There wasn't anywhere to walk really, except the little park down by the reservoir where the Chicano boys hung out, playing their transistors and smoking thin black cigars. But Liberty Park – for all the dreams hatched there – could have been the Tuilleries or Tivoli Gardens. Perhaps they would go farther afield on New Year's, to Joaquin Miller Park or Crow Canyon. Yes, the two of them would go somewhere marvellous on New Year's Day.

Five

New Year's Eve arrived with the kind of weather that would freeze your bones – black, windy and wet, dead cold. Nan was glad she had driven to campus rather than cycled. She locked up her snug little car and walked briskly to Wheeler Hall. Would Mr Johnson be on duty this evening? For his sake, she hoped not. But if he were, perhaps they could share a toast at midnight.

No, she wasn't going to get sentimental. This was just another night. The Chinese didn't celebrate new year until February for god's sake and the Jews did it in the fall. The commercial New Year's Eve televised from Times Square was a perfect load of rubbish. Nan always had a terrible time on New Year's. First, the obligatory examination of conscience, then the list of resolutions to salve the conscience, then the drinking to swallow the resolutions. The next morning always dragged with guilt for undone deeds and hangover for done ones. Nothing could ruin a good party like New Year's.

The fourth floor was shadowy under dim corridor lights. Each wooden door was closed on a silent room. Frighteningly still. Nan remembered one night long ago when she had to stay over at the Maryknoll Retreat House, a scared child alone with the mute nuns until the next bus arrived in the morning. The convent corridor was dark and wooden like this. And she remembered walking carefully, stealthily, in search of the bathroom, willing her bladder to hold her pee so she might return to the relative anonymity of her spare cell. The convent smelled of furniture polish and stale holy water. Nan felt an inexplicable sadness for the nuns who slept alone on meticulously ironed sheets. The bathroom, she finally discovered, was at the very end of fifteen doors. The toiler paper was that cheap kind which felt more like wax paper than tissue. All the way back down the corridor, Nan prayed that she wouldn't wake any of the good sisters with the squeaking of her crepe rubber soles.

Tonight Wheeler Hall was darker than usual. Even Mr Johnson's door was shut. Just as well the old man wasn't around. He might feel embarrassed if she offered a toast for the New Year. She might feel embarrassed. As Nan turned the corner, she was startled by light streaming through the frosted glass of Angus Murchie's door.

The old coot probably didn't have anywhere to go. (No, that wasn't true. Like everyone else in the department, he had been invited to Matt's fandango. And he was quite likely to show up since Mrs Murchie was confined to the Health Spa – or upper-class detoxification centre – for the holidays. In fact, Murchie's probable presence was one of the excuses Nan had given Matt for not attending his annual party.) Nan could hear Murchie's laughter oozing from under the door sill. He wasn't alone. And Nan was almost in her office when she heard the other voice, a woman's voice. Tiptoeing back over the polished floor, Nan thought she could distinguish the dulcet tones of Marjorie Adams.

Oh Jesus, thought Nan, what had the kid got herself into? Didn't Marjorie understand that Murchie was the biggest lech west of the Rockies? Didn't she know that he had sent three of his advisees to Student Psychiatric last quarter?

But Marjorie seemed so guileless, as if her family had padded her against all misfortune. And her trust in Murchie was not so different from Nan's own respect for Professor Eastman years ago. What kind of woman works with a male professor at night? A serious woman, a scholarly woman, a woman who, perhaps naively, has come to regard herself as a student rather than a prey. Perhaps Angus did have a legitimate reason to work tonight? Nan couldn't believe he was completely evil, although he was brusque, unpleasant and selfish. What did his behaviour camouflage? Fear? He was an ageing man whose private life had been unhappy and whose career was ending. Where were his tender feelings? Could Marjorie with her quiet enthusiasm move him to humanity? Did he see through her Hollywood chic?

No use speculating. 'Guesses can be dangerous when there's no way to know,' Nan's mother would say, did say, over and over. Of course Mom wasn't talking about anything as seedy as this. Mom would never imagine such dangers at The University. Seedy – of course Nan was exaggerating. How melodramatic. Probably poor Marjorie had been lured here for a drink before Matt's party, on the pretext of recovering some urgent bibliographic reference to 'Il Penseroso'. They would be off soon, Marjorie driving because

41

Murchie sounded absolutely pickled. Nan would not bother about them. She sneaked down the hall and into her own mausoleum. Going directly to her desk, she turned on the tensor lamp. She would not risk the bright overhead light spilling under the door into the hallway, as an invitation to the likes of Angus Murchie.

Tonight she would finish reading all the journal pieces and perhaps review the rest of her research. Deliberately setting aside Marjorie Adams' dissertation, Nan kicked off her shoes and began to read over the outline for her article. She was finding some fascinating stuff about Lessing's use of African landscape. Now wasn't this much more satisfying than getting drunk at Matt's? Think of all the cocktail parties you'd have to attend to find someone as interesting as Doris Lessing. Nan hadn't sat down for two minutes before she was up, fiddling with the radio to find some classical Muzak. Then she realized that Murchie and Marjorie might hear her, so she switched it off. Too much static anyway, she really had to get a better aerial. Returning to her desk, she came across a small cache of bubble gum. She unwrapped two pieces at once. This had been Lisa's package, Nan remembered. She had left it on the last visit, after they had joked about its carcinogenic, deadly additives.

God damn it, this Lupus thing wasn't possible. Not Lisa, thought Nan, crumbling the gum wrapper and flinging it into the wastecan. Not this kid with all the energy and hope in the world. Not this remarkable young woman who was going to be the orator of her generation. Just look at the way she was reacting to the diagnosis – trying to cheer up her mother. No, it couldn't happen to bright, determined Lisa. She would be a community organizer in a few years. The kid had already worked three summers in housing services and play schemes. She was remarkably socially conscious for her age, a good feminist, an altruist at heart.

An image of Lisa, withered and pale against the hospital sheets, dropped over Nan's mind. She started to cry and abruptly sniffed away the tears. Lisa would not die, Nan resolved. Guesses *were* dangerous when there was no way to know.

The Lupus had to be a false alarm. Maybe it was Lisa's hormones settling. Or maybe it was someone else's test results. As simple as that. Scandalous the way they were always mixing up other people's results. Hospitals nowadays were as unreliable as automobile factories.

Nan stared out the window at the blackness, remembering there had been a red sky tonight – sailor's delight. Warm and sunny tomorrow. Everything would be dissolved in the morning warm. She and Lisa would go somewhere extravagant tomorrow to celebrate the New Year. They would ferry to Sausalito or go counting cows up by Santa Rosa or perhaps drive to the wine tasting country.

Nan could still hear Murchie's laughter and Marjorie's softer voice. They would be leaving for Matt's party soon, she told herself and settled into work. She was contentedly absorbed in Lessing's landscapes by the time she noticed them again. (Her father used to smile ruefully and say, 'Amazing the way our Nan reads a book – like she's swimming underwater. Never hears a thing.') She tried to concentrate. But the voice of Marjorie Adams was no longer so dulcet.

'No, no,' the young woman was almost shouting. It was Marjorie Adams, wasn't it? The voice sounded strained. Hard to place.

Nan got up and walked over to her wall. She stood stiffly, as if the tension might help her hear. Their voices were quieter now. Anxiously, Nan stayed at the wall, holding her arms tight across her chest. When she did not hear anything for a minute or two, she returned, uneasily, to her desk.

'You bastard. You dirty bastard,' she heard distinctly.

Shocked at the language – so unlike Marjorie – she knew something terrible was happening. Nan imagined her being attacked. Marjorie writhing on the blue Persian rug, Murchie on top of her, like an elephant mauling a flamingo. Nan could hear Marjorie punching him and his corresponding laughter.

No more guesses tonight. Nan knew she had to intervene. Kneeling on the floor, she scrambled for her shoes. Propriety, even in disaster. What the hell was she doing? She ran out into the hall with one shoe on. By the time she reached Murchie's door, all was silent. She knocked, but heard no answer. Eerie. Nan would rather hear anything than this silence. Nervously, she rattled the door. Then she heard something. Something low. Murchie's voice. Groaning or gasping. Then the slamming open of a window. How did she know? How much was she imagining? How much had she imagined all night? Nan rattled the handle again. No sound. Bewildered, petrified, she found herself turning back around the corner. What was she doing? Oh, yes, automatic pilot. Panic always brought out the best in her. She ran back to her office and rooted around in her purse for a credit card. Joe had showed her this trick. Confidently now, she stuck the plastic card in the lock. Calmly, as if she moonlighted as a cat burglar, she released the lock. Finally Nan flung open the door to the brightly lit office.

The window was wide open. The first thing she saw was the yellow blind flapping wildly against the cold wind. Beneath the window, lying on the floor, was the enormous carcass of Angus Murchie, gushing quantities of a maroon substance that she presumed to be human blood. She saw three deep gashes in his stomach. Oh, god, she thought, tell me it isn't true. She spun around as if looking for help. Noticing his cashmere sweater on the chair, she pulled it down and tried to stop the bleeding. Oh god. Oh god. His eyes were glazed as though he were focussing on some long and winding eternity. Never had anything terrified or repulsed her so. Behind him a wave of cold night air roared through the window. She shivered and rose as if in a trance.

Nan carefully stepped over the body and looked out the window. Down below, she saw a woman with a long blonde braid down her back running toward the Northside of the campus. She must have climbed down the scaffolding being used by the masonry workers, thought Nan. What *was* she doing? This man was dying here in the room with her. She pulled down the big window and returned to Murchie.

A small, pathetic rasping came from his throat.

'It's going to be all right,' she heard herself reassure him.

More rasping.

She wiped his forehead with her hand. She wanted to call for help. Yet Murchie seemed to need her here, now, beside him. He looked more peaceful at her touch, at her reassurance. Jesus, Nan realized, if she was scared he must be terrified.

With considerable calm, Nan studied Murchie's eyes and felt his pulse, the way Dr Charles Woodward practised on her for his first-term exams. He was breathing faintly. Every second counted. No time for outside help. She would have to try to save him herself. Overcoming nausea at Murchie's alcoholic breath, she gave him mouth-to-mouth resuscitation. Eventually she recognized it was useless. Murchie was not responding. Oh god. O god, say it isn't true. Nan drew away, noticing a stain of blood on her dress. Minimal compared to the large and peculiar patterns his dark blood had made on the teal persian carpet. She sat back, telling herself that Murchie was dead. She could feel nothing for him. But she felt a great fear for Marjorie.

Marjorie. Poor, innocent Marjorie. Stupid, careless Marjorie.

44

Here was the letter opener lying next to Murchie's right hand. Underneath it was Marjorie's batik silk scarf. Nan folded the scarf, amazed to discover how profound was her instinct to protect this other woman. Nan wondered if she herself might be accused of the murder. Then she was filled with nausea from the smell of Murchie's sweat and sex. For the first time, she noticed that his pants were down around his thighs. His penis looked like a purple magic marker. She closed her eyes which were heavy and sore. Momentarily, she contemplated whether murder would be the perfect climax to every rape.

Appalled at such cool detachment, Nan forced herself to consider Marjorie Adams again. She unfolded the scarf and wiped Marjorie's fingerprints off the ugly Mocassin handle of the letter opener. Then she wiped her own prints off the window and the door knob. Again, she marvelled at her logic and dispatch. Why wasn't she shrieking? Falling apart? 'The Weavers don't behave that way,' Mom would say. 'You're holding in your feelings,' Francie would say. Amy would see it as 'working-class common sense.' Nan tuned out the voices.

She considered calling the police. But ambulances would be too late and the cops were needed for live revellers tonight. Besides, her instinctive desire was to get away, to wake from this horror. Quickly, she checked around the room for other relics of her student and, finding none, left immediately. The corridor seemed brighter now, but this was a ridiculous psychological reaction, because Nan knew there were only two lights on in the whole building – hers and Murchie's. She returned to her room, stuffed Marjorie's scarf into her purse. Calmly (where did all this calm come from?) she gathered together her books, turned off the tensor lamp and headed out toward Isadora.

But she couldn't just hop in the car and go home to a stiff glass of brandy as if the murder movie had ended. She must try to find Marjorie Adams, to *help* her. Nan turned around and rushed toward the Northside of campus. She walked past Doe Library, down by the temporary buildings, up the hill to the geography hall where she had learned about the similarity in segregation patterns between Berkeley and Kenya (blacks in the flatlands and whites in the hills). What a strange memory to fill her head now. It was such a weird, silent night, and Nan longed for the more manageable terror of the Maryknoll Retreat House. Reaching the edge of campus, Nan knew the search was useless. What had she expected? To find

45

little Miss Muffet sitting on a bench weeping? Marjorie Adams was a woman of resources; she might well have booked a flight to Kabul by now. Nan turned back and walked tensely through the dark campus, as anger mingled with her fear. Damn, god damn, she was outraged with Angus Murchie for causing this catastrophe. He was a selfish and destructive man, who, even in his death, brought trouble. Should she phone Amy and ask her to report the death? No, she did not want to be implicated. She did not want to testify against Marjorie Adams. Some things were very certain for Nan, despite this fear which knotted her stomach and buckled her knees.

So Angus Murchie was dead. The thought actually gave Nan a terrible pleasure. For auld lang syne. Such a spiteful, petty, supercilious man. She had not realized just how much she hated him. Surely, he had been a constant irritant during these last seven years here. She had imagined him as an annoying fly. But actually, he was a corrosive termite, burrowing into her dignity, a relentless threat. This death was a curious relief; she felt as if an unknown tumour had been removed. Angus Murchie is dead; long live John Milton. Deep in her conscience, Nan knew she was a dreadful person.

Suddenly she felt panicky, remembering she was a woman out alone tonight. One violence would not protect her from another. She looked around carefully, trying not to remember that eerie whistle from 'Dial M For Murder'. The campus was sparsely occupied. And the other moving shadows seemed as timid of contact as she. Odd how you had to make an exaggerated gesture of walking to the opposite side of the road to show goodwill or harmlessness. In the fifties, Nan and her girlfiend Sally used to take three a.m. walks along Strawberry Creek just for the hell of it. Ten years later, when she returned here for graduate school, people would whisper about the dangers of campus under darkness. She did not believe them. Not until a friend had been raped up by the Campanile at dusk. Now Nan was startled by the sight of two cops walking together through Dwinelle Plaza. She looked away and quickened her pace. A cold wind blew up towards the hills, and Nan held her coat around her. Of course there would be twice as many cops for New Year's Eve.

Approaching Wheeler Hall, she walked through the light pouring from Angus Murchie's window, an odd beacon in the darkness. And another light streamed toward the Campanile. Was it her own lamp? Her heart stopped. Had she been so stupid as to leave it on? No, of course not, it was Mr Johnson's. He must have arrived late .

tonight. Good enough. He would be a reliable undertaker. No doubt by morning, at least, he would check Murchie's office. Then the police would come, also the reporters.

Nan wondered about Marjorie Adams. It had been her voice? Of course it had been. She hoped that Marjorie Adams was well on the way to Kabul by now, or at least to the family estate in Maryland. She was not the kind of woman – not with that sterling silver spine – to fall apart. She was a bright one, a survivor.

Nan intended to go straight home to finish her bottle of brandy, a lease on the first night's sleep of the new year. Instead, she found herself turning up Ashby Avenue and heading for the Warren Freeway to Hayward. The Alameda County hills were peaceful at night, like so many sleeping, naked women. 'The sun to me is dark and silent as the moon,' recited Nan. This was the quote Murchie had tacked on the bulletin board outside his door, from 'Samson Agonistes'.

No, she would not be sad; she would not grieve over this terrible man. She sped through the dark. If she tried hard she could ignore the shopping centres and tract homes. All these electric lights might be stars shining against the blackness.

Six

Shirley's living room was congested with smoke and loud laughter and Barbra Streisand music. A stranger had opened the door to Nan. Probably he wasn't a stranger, this heavy-set man in the orange and black checked slacks. No, he was probably a neighbour of many years, some native son of the Golden West, proud citizen of Desert Palms Estates, whom she had met at a dozen barbecues. Nan nodded cordially to him. Remembering the dark red stain on her dress, she buttoned her sweater securely and joined the party.

'Well, if it isn't her highness, gracing us with the royal presence,' said Joe, leering from his position on the dance floor, his arms tightly around someone's wife.

Nan smiled wanly.

Shirley turned from the drinks table, smiled at her sister and nodded reproachfully to her husband.

'Hi, Nan,' called Shirley. She tried to hide the surprise behind her delight at Nan's arrival.

'What'll it be?' asked Shirley as she walked over to her, 'Red or white wine?'

Nan gave her a quick kiss.

'You haven't got anything stronger, have you?'

'Sure, Nan, wine's what you usually want, but. . .'

Noticing her sister's concern, Nan said, 'I'm just a little shook up from the drive. Crazies on the road tonight.'

Nan walked into the clean, bright kitchen, her eyes following the flowers on her sister's swishing polyester ass. Their old family kitchen on Kelly Hill had felt safe like this, a dispensary for food and other care. Until Nan was in high school she assumed everybody kept their bandaids and merthiolate in the kitchen cupboard. Tonight, for some reason, Shirley reminded her of Mom. Mom leaning across the linoleum table, listening to ten-year-old Nan confess to

48

the blood dripping between her legs. Mom's face had betrayed shock at such physical force in one so young. But she soon recovered, reassuring young Nan that this was the most natural thing in the world. The blood made Nan a woman. Now would Shirley tell her that the blood on her dress and Marjorie's scarf was the most natural thing in the world? Would she be absolved of another wound she did not inflict?

Nan glanced at her sister and realized that they had been sitting silently for some time, through several glasses of brandy.

'Look, I'm sorry,' said Nan. 'I didn't want to spoil your party.'

'Don't worry about it,' said Shirley. 'If I hear "The Way We Were" one more time, I'm going to parcel post a bomb to Barbra Streisand.'

Nan smiled at Shirley's unlikely contempt.

'So you don't want to talk about it?' asked Shirley.

What did her sister mean? Nan panicked. Blood. Rape. Wounds. Screams. Murder. Nan's mind had been spinning. Terrified, she caught herself. What had she revealed to Shirley? She must lay off the alcohol. But searching Shirley's face for the horrors of the murder story, Nan found nothing but the simple, reliable concern she had always known.

'Nothing to talk about really,' said Nan, feeling wretched because Shirley must know she was lying.

'Listen,' said Nan, reviving. 'We've gotta go back in there. This is your party. I'm fine.' she patted her sister's hand and noticed for the first time in years the similarity of their short, stubby fingers. She had always observed the differences between them.

'I'd like to have some company,' smiled Nan. 'Honestly.' Nan sat on the old brocade couch and watched the twisting and bobbing for another half-hour, or maybe it was two hours. She wasn't keeping track of the time, but she was counting the brandies. Five should do it. She watched the couples dance, saddened by their sagging bodies. Arrogant, Nan reprimanded herself. They were all younger than she. Young. Nan did still feel young, young in the sense of fresh, in working order. Young enough for tenure. Younger than these middle-aged people who were unashamedly losing form. Lisa was young in the sense of unformed. These people were. . .five brandies.

She would have to take a pile of aspirins and say her prayers if she was to avoid a hangover tomorrow. She needed to be in good shape to play with Lisa. Lisa, maybe that's why she had driven here tonight despite her intention of going home, to check on Lisa. Sweetly, Nan bade good night to Shirley. She ignored Joe who was locked in an embrace with someone whose name she couldn't remember. Looking in on Lisa, she found her sleeping peacefully. Then she curled into one of the twin beds in the boys' old room.

Something failed – either the aspirins or the prayers – because the New Year dawned on Nan with a stunning headache, a raw stomach and, ultimately, the blazing memory of what she had tried to bury. Just last week after reading a series of articles in *The Chronicle* about women alcoholics, she had realized she would have to make a resolution. The very word resolution reminded Nan of the night she had just tried to drown. Now she was weighted to the bed with a heavy fear. But hold on, maybe it had been a nightmare, one of those wish-fulfilment dreams turned technicolor by the brandy. Angus Murchie, huge in his stillness as a beached walrus, bleeding into his precious teal blue Persian carpet, his spirit already descended. Angus Murchie forever silenced. The nightmare dissolved into dawn as Nan reached over the side of the bed and pulled out a green and pink silk scarf from her purse. The dark red marks shot a hollowness through her chest. She must talk to someone before she went crazy. Matt. She would call Matt. But even as she stuck her head into the hall for the phone, she was relieved to see Lisa chattering away, barefoot in her nightgown. The child looked so well. What did the doctors know?

Lisa put her hand over the receiver and called, 'Morning, Nan. I'll be right off the phone. You ready for our big day?'

Nan nodded and returned to the bedroom. She would wait to call Matt until her head was clearer. Meanwhile, she would have to borrow some walking clothes. She rummaged through the drawers and found a T-shirt and jeans outgrown by the boys years before.

Coffee helped. And the first day of this New Year was blessed by the absence of Joe, who had an even worse hangover and was still in bed. This meant that Nan had the newspaper to herself.

Of course *The Daily Review* wouldn't carry anything about the murder. Too much news on the low riders arrested for drunk driving in Union City and the pregnant beauty queen who was refusing to forsake her title. No space for a man killed in Berkeley. Maybe he had not yet been found? Maybe it had all been a nightmare? Maybe he was killed by someone else? Could Marjorie have left the scarf on her visit last week? Perhaps on the day when Angus had interrupted their discussion of Murdochian art and passion? Were the spots ink, perhaps, or some less violent blood?

Lisa was in fine spirits, eager to go hiking somewhere off Crow Canyon road. Crow Canyon. Niles Canyon. Wildcat Canyon. Grizzly Peak. Nan loved these Western names as much as she loved the gullies and ravines and wooded hills themselves. She was never completely at ease with the landscapes in Jane Austen or George Eliot. Nor did she ever fully appreciate the pathetic fallacies in British romantic poetry. Too many lacy trees and elegant ponds. Nan was much more at home among the giant sequoias on the edge of the ocean. Maybe she should have become a forest ranger. The open spaces might have preserved her from the neuroses of Wheeler Hall. Crow Canyon had been her favourite hideout as a teenager, when she had to escape the stuffiness of the Kelly Hill house. She would hitch a ride to these wild hills, listen to the bickering scrub jays, collect pockets of bay leaves for Mom, yell at the top of her lungs and send her voice rising high above the redwoods.

This New Year's day was hot and dry. Nan imagined that she and Lisa were walking in a sauna with a window. Their conversation had an easy unevenness – tense discussion, family gossip, companionable silence. Usually Nan delighted in the meditative friendship. Today, however, she was encased in the pain of last night and the alcohol she had taken to numb the pain. She felt riddled by memories of the sudden death of Angus Murchie and the tenous life of Lisa. Silence was unbearable. She began to chatter, to move the conversation to a safe, incessant pace.

'So what do you think of this forties revival in fashion?' asked Nan, grasping for something to talk about.

'Well, I like the shoulder pads and the platform shoes,' said Lisa. 'But I can't stand that red lipstick.'

'Yes, I have a student who wears it.'

'Oh yeah?' said Lisa, 'the really smart one who looks like all the movie stars? Mildred or Mary Anne?'

'Marjorie?' said Nan as calmly as she could. 'How did you know?'

'Oh, you talk about her a lot, about how bright and disciplined she is. She sounds a little screwy to me.'

'Do I talk about her?' asked Nan, unnerved. She groped for another topic, 'Are you still planning to major in rhetoric?'

'Yes,' said Lisa, confused because they had discussed this just last week. 'And then grad school in community organizing. I don't want to give up on a family, but I want it to be a partnership. Do you know what I mean?'

Marvelling at the certainty in Lisa's voice, Nan did not answer right away.

'Of course Dad still wants me to drop school and get a job making computer chips.'

Nan laughed.

Lisa looked up quizzically.

'*My* parents,' Nan recalled, 'wanted me to get a safe job at the Telephone Company.' She paused, her voice trailing off, 'Maybe they were right. . .' Puzzled, and slightly disturbed by her aunt's behaviour, Lisa interrupted the conversation.

'Say, isn't that a marsh hawk?'

The dark bird, soaring with precision into the high, blue distance, restored them to the silent hills.

Nan watched her niece carefully, studied the resilience in her. Yes, this Lupus was a false alarm.

She hated to say goodbye to Lisa that afternoon as if, in leaving her, she was deserting all that was good and wholesome in the world. Hopefully they would see each other on campus in a few days, if Lisa were well enough for school.

For the first time in her life, Nan felt a weight descending on her, suffocating her, as she drove from Hayward to Berkeley. Always, she had felt the weight going in the *other* direction. She turned on the radio, automatically turning the dial for KCBS. KCBS reported the latest murders every hour on the hour. But, according to KCBS, the peace had been disturbed only twice this holiday weekend. An angel had been stolen from a creche outside Grace Cathedral. And an arson attempt was made at a high school in San Jose. Nan remembered Wheeler Hall in flames during some student protest years before. Now she imagined Wheeler Hall blazng to the ground with the body of Angus Murchie, world famous Milton scholar, charred beyond recognition.

'Oh, Christ!' Nan said, and hearing her own voice, she felt less crazy. 'I'll call Matt as soon as I get home.'

It was a quiet night, little traffic on the road. Hot, cold, Nan wasn't sure. She switched off KCBS, and it was quieter still.

Before she opened the third lock on the door, she could hear the phone ringing.

It was Matt.

'Oh, Matt, I was just going to call,' Nan began and then paused, registering his cool silence. He must know about Murchie. He must be phoning to tell her.

'What's the matter?' she asked hesitantly.

'Well, I give a New Year's Eve party and practically the whole department shows except my best friend,' his voice had recovered its humour now.

Nan was silent.

'Listen, pet, I'm not really angry. I'm sure you were off on some wildly important romance. Tell me, who was it – Francie or Claude?' he teased. 'Or perhaps Angus Murchie.'

'Angus Murchie?' Nan faltered.

'Of course I was relieved that he didn't show up,' said Matt. 'But strange, eh? It was just his sort of party, with all the booze and the women, and his wife out of town.'

'Yes,' said Nan quietly.

'Well,' Matt persisted, still teasing, 'I must say I was put out not to have my date there. Why do you think I give these parties except to appear acceptably heterosexual to the outside world? You and me, babe, we make terrific gossip.'

'Listen, Matt, there's something I have to tell you. . .'

When Matt was wound up, there was no stopping him. 'Now they're all talking about me and Ms Marjorie Adams.'

'Marjorie Adams,' Nan said blankly.

'What is it, love, are you playing straight woman tonight? Angus Murchie. Marjorie Adams. You know these people. They're part of the Grand Drama of Wheeler Hall.'

Nan realized that it would probably be more productive to listen, not that she had any choice.

'When did Marjorie Adams arrive on the scene?' she asked.

'Oh, lord, who knows; we all hit the drink pretty early and began whirling and dervishing about ten o'clock. Everyone dancing with everyone. And do you know, Nan baby, I believe that Armand, the new graduate student doing Chaucer, might well be a pooftah. Have you considered that enchanting possibility?'

'Did Marjorie seem OK?' asked Nan before she thought.

'Nan Weaver, what is this? Have you turned den mother again?' sniffed Matt. 'Yes, she was fine, a little Ophelia-like, all that blonde hair hanging down like a palomino. . .'

But, Nan wanted to interrupt him. How could she have been at your party? It *was* Marjorie Adams she had seen running across campus, wasn't it?

'Marjorie did seem a little skittish,' Matt continued. 'About something she lost. Manic actually. I told her to go home and sleep tight and she'd probably find it under her pillow if she were a good little girl.'

Nan was stunned at Marjorie's gall, running away from Murchie's corpse, slipping into a New Year's Eve party. It was Marjorie she had seen running across campus, wasn't it?

How obvious was her silence? She had so much to tell Matt. Still, she hesitated. Common sense? It wasn't safe to talk about life and death matters on the telephone.

'Say, what's wrong, sweet?' asked Matt, now truly concerned. 'Just what *did* you do last night?'

Besides, Nan was thinking, it might still be a nightmare. It hadn't made the news yet. Maybe she had imagined it all.

'Speak up, lady,' said Matt.

Nan chose a light tone. 'Oh, with my family. Shirl and Joe had a horrible party.'

'That explains the mood. The only cure for family is two sleeping pills and a good night's rest.'

'Three sleeping pills,' said Nan, trying to imitate his good humour. 'Will I see you at student enrolment day tomorrow?'

'Wouldn't miss it for my life,' laughed Matt. 'See you then.'

Nan pulled down the sofa bed, parted the sea green sheets and climbed in. This was all a nightmare, she repeated to herself, a nightmare. And now it was time to rest.

It took an hour of meditation, seven glasses of water and four sleeping pills before she fell asleep. She must have dreamed deeply, because she was startled awake by the plop of the morning newspaper against her screen door. Usually she had finished jogging by the time the paper arrived. The day was splendidly sunny. Nan managed to stave off the shadow of terror as she listened to Saint-Saëns, brewed some Viennese coffee, boiled her egg. She opened the window wide, to give herself the effect of sitting on a balcony.

When she unrolled *The Chronicle*, Nan was confronted with the flaccid face of Angus Murchie and the headline, MURDER IN THE ENGLISH DEPARTMENT.

Seven

The fourth floor corridor of Wheeler Hall reminded Nan of Pacheco High School where she was teaching when JFK was assassinated. Now, as on that terrible day sixteen years before, her colleagues moved like malignant shadows, their voices hushed with dark gossip.

'Terrible.'

'Shocking.'

'Tragic.'

'Incredible.'

The faculty greeted each other with single words and sober nods. Tucked discreetly in their own offices, friends speculated with friends on motive and method. Several people recalled the time when a student, raging from a bad grade, tried to stab a history professor.

Nan did not join any of these knots of people. Exchanging a few condolences, she headed straight for her office. She rang Matt, but he was not in.

Ten minutes after she had settled down to her desk, there was a quick rap on the door.

'Yes,' she said, hoping it would be Matt, 'Come in.'

And in ambled a spectacled, muscular young man carrying a load of books. His frowning face was glued to an IBM class card.

'They say this needs to be signed to get into your Mod Lit course,' he said, almost sticking the card in her eye. 'I don't have the pre-req.'

'"Mod Lit", "pre-req", are you sure it isn't shorthand you want to take?'

'Pardon me, Professor?' he said.

Professor. Honoured teacher, he reminded her. Not wise-cracking broad, she reminded herself. Nan took a deep breath. This was going to be a difficult day.

'Excuse me,' she spoke in her most professorial voice, 'but we're all rather affected by Professor Murchie's death.'

'Yes,' said the student. 'Terrible, shocking, tragic. He was my favourite professor in the department.'

Nan stared at him incredulously.

'Of course,' he hastened, 'I haven't had the pleasure of taking your class.' He fidgeted, clearing his thumbnail with the edge of his IBM card.

'No, quite,' said Nan.

A loud knock sounded on the door. Nan knew that this had to be Matt. 'Yes,' she sighed, 'come on in.'

The door was opened by a young policeman in a beige uniform. Behind him stood another cop, a full foot taller. Nan noted that they travelled in pairs, like on New Year's Eve.

'Professor Weaver?' asked the shorter man.

'Yes,' said Nan. 'May I help you?'

The tall man also stepped into the room. 'I'm Officer Ross, and this is Officer Rodriguez. We'd like to talk to you about the recent events, Professor.'

'Yes, of course,' she said. 'Please come in.'

The two dark men stood by uneasily, their eyes on the student who was still fidgeting with his IBM card.

'Shall we continue our discussion later?' she said with cool authority. This authority would belong to the policemen once the door was closed.

The student stood, stammering between fear and irritation. 'But,' he whined. 'we have to have the study list filed by the end of the week.'

Nan's face was impassive.

The two policemen shuffled nervously. Nan desperately wanted them to sit down, at eye level with her.

'And if I don't know about your class,' he persisted, 'then how can I find another one to fill the slot?'

Patiently, Nan considered his anxiety. She remembered there were more student suicides during pre-enrolment than at any other time of year. Kindness, she cautioned herself, was at a premium in the mega-university.

'Listen,' she said, 'if you need to file the list late, I'll sign the waiver. Now, I do think you should leave and allow these gentlemen to ask their questions.'

Actually, she felt grateful to the student for distracting her.

Otherwise how could she have remained so calm?

When the policemen sat down, finally at eye level, Nan noticed that they were almost as young as the student. They both assumed that detached, professional tone which Nan recognized as one of her own voices.

No, she answered, she didn't know anyone with a grudge against Professor Murchie. She hadn't seen any students hanging around his office lately. She did not know very much about his personal life. Frankly, she hadn't had a substantial conversation with him for some time. One or two exchanges over the holiday break, that was all.

Did she sound sincere and detached? Could they hear the thickness in her voice, the same thickness she felt when she used to withhold sins in confession? These young policemen were less canny than the priest. And they seemed as uncomfortable with the interview as she was.

'We understand,' began Officer Ross, who looked just as tall sitting down, 'that you and Professor Murchie had a certain amount of disagreement about the administration of the English Department.'

'Of course that's true,' said Nan, wondering which of her scrupulous colleagues had provided that information.

'Perhaps before I speak further with you,' she said, 'I should call my Amy, I mean my lawyer.'

'I doubt that will be necessary,' said Rodriguez, 'This is only routine questioning. Of course, if you like. . .'

'No,' said Nan. She didn't want to be too defensive. 'It's just that I've never known anything like this before. I want to help.'

'Then how would you characterize your disagreement?' asked Ross.

'Well, to be simple,' said Nan, 'you might say I took the more progressive view.'

'On what issues, ma'am?' asked Officer Rodriguez.

'Oh, for instance, on student representation in committees.'

'And,' Officer Ross gave his steno pad a cursory glance, 'And on sexual harassment?'

'Yes,' Nan said heavily, 'and on sexual harassment. Just what are you trying to get at?' Too defensive, she warned herself, calm down.

'We're not trying to get at anything,' answered Rodriguez, 'except, of course, the truth.'

'Yes,' said Nan. 'Of course.'

'And apparently you had some differences about scholarly criteria?' asked Ross.

'Who told you all this,' Nan asked, no longer able to hide her anger or fear.

'This morning,' said Ross. 'We talked to a Ms Ad. . .'

Rodriguez interrupted him with a critical glance. 'Afraid that we can't divulge our sources, ma'am.'

Nan was trying to convince herself that Marjorie hadn't set her up, that this 'information' about Nan was Marjorie's naive attempt to be truthful.

'Ma'am,' Rodriguez said again, 'could you just answer the question?'

'Professor Murchie and I did have our professional differences,' said Nan, 'as do a number of faculty in this department. Does that surprise you?'

'Nothing surprises us, ma'am,' said Rodriguez. 'We're just after all the pieces.'

'And the truth,' added Nan helpfully.

'Yes, ma'am.'

The interview continued for an interminable half-hour. The only thing that sustained Nan was the prospect of talking with Matt afterwards. She phoned her friend immediately.

'Matt Weitz here.' He always answered with just an edge of British inflection. When things got really bad, Matt talked about returning to Cambridge. He had done post-graduate studies in England and, in some ways, had never really left. Odd, thought Nan, to him Berkeley was like her Hayward, the backwater.

'Hi, Matt, this is Nan. How about a cup of strong coffee?'

'Sorry, friend,' he said. 'I have the honourable men of law with me, and then I must dash over to the city for an appointment. How about we ring each other tonight?'

'Sure,' said Nan, trying to sound sure. She didn't want to worry Matt, especially not in front of the boys in beige. 'Talk with you later, sweetie.' She hung up.

Would they ask him the same questions? Would they inquire about Angus Murchie's enemies? Would Matt remember all the nasty things she had said about the old bastard over late night drinks? No, of course he wouldn't. But he might worry. And an edge of doubt might creep into his voice as he talked to the police or other faculty. No. No. She was getting out of control. Paranoia had always been one of her sharpest senses.

Nan heard someone calling her name. She looked up from her badly bitten cuticles to see a grey head peeking around the door.

'Professor Weaver,' Millie, the department clerk, said. 'Sorry to disturb you, Professor Weaver.'

'Not at all,' said Nan. 'Come in.'

How different Millie was from that kid of an hour ago, roosting in her office until his academic career was settled. Millie was so much more deferential than any student. Too deferential. But Nan understood her. Millie's youngest sister had attended Hayward Union High School with Nan, a coincidence that Millie had once boldly volunteered.

'Sorry Professor,' said Millie. 'But I forgot that this urgent note was left for you earlier today.'

'Thanks so much,' said Nan, taking the blue vellum envelope, her heart pounding audibly.

She waited to open the note until she heard Millie's footsteps safely around the corner. Of course there *was* someone besides Matt with whom Nan could discuss all this. And now she wondered whether Marjorie Adams knew that she knew.

Frantically, she ripped open the letter, tearing a corner of the page with the lined envelope. As she read, Nan turned cold with angry admiration.

Dear Professor Weaver,

Just to inform you that I am still slightly indisposed today from all the holiday activities. I am so sorry I shall not be able to keep our appointment this afternoon and hope that you will forgive this very late notice.

Sincerely,

Marjorie Adams

Rather precious, thought Nan. Because of Marjorie's nervousness or her ego? And why was Marjorie sticking around here? No, on second thought, she was too smart to run off to Kabul. Perhaps the visit to Matt's party was an attempt to establish an alibi? Nan would never have had the nerve to show up so late and so visible. But then who would ever suspect Marjorie Adams? As far as anyone in the department knew, she had the most peripheral relationship with Angus Murchie, as a graduate reader. No, Marjorie was hardly a suspect. She was doing a competent job of remaining inconspicuous by staying right on the scene. There was no way for

Marjorie to know that Nan saw or heard anything that night. And perhaps it would be wisest to keep it that way.

'Nan,' a voice called. Someone knocked. 'Nan, are you there?'

'Yes, come in,' she said, wondering who. . .

'Hi, Nan,' said Lisa.

Nan stared at her niece. (The sick child. No, Nan reflected. No, Lisa was just fine.) Something was different about her. In the last couple of years there were so many changes. Lisa had became a different person. Her shyness had turned to passion in these public speaking events. She grew more active in campus politics, particularly the Feminist Caucus.

'Well, what do you think?' asked Lisa expectantly.

She stared ahead as Lisa waited for a reply. She had to pull herself together. There was something different, physically different, about her niece.

'Don't you like it?' Lisa patted her hair.

'A permanent,' exclaimed Nan stupidly. She grinned, admiring these curls which had turned Lisa from a teenager into a young woman.

'Well, we call it a friz,' laughed Lisa. 'I'm surprised your fancy student, what's-her-face, Marjorie, hasn't done it.'

'Who?' asked Nan. 'Oh. Well, it does suit you.'

'I'm glad you like it,' said Lisa, her face lighting up. 'Daddy is still crying in his beer over my long, lost locks.'

'I can imagine,' laughed Nan, realizing what pleasure it was just to smile. 'So sit yourself down and tell me what brought you to this drastic decision, honey.'

'Oh, just the classic post-adolescent need for independence from *la famille*.' said Lisa.

'They're giving you a hard time again? Listen, we have nine more months to work on them about your moving to Berkeley.'

'Afraid that's not it,' said Lisa. 'It's *this* quarter. They don't want me to come to school this quarter.'

'What?' Nan was genuinely shocked.

'They're worried about the doctor's reports. . . Even though Doctor Bonelli said the best thing was to continue my life as normal, as if. . .'

'Hold on,' Nan demanded. 'You don't believe you have Lupus, do you? You mustn't. I have a friend at John Hopkins and another at Albert Einstein School of Medicine. We'll go from one doctor to the next until we find out that you're going to be, um, until the diagnosis is clean.'

Lisa looked at her aunt kindly, reassuringly. 'I don't care about the diagnosis,' said Lisa, 'but I do care about school. I have a big debating meeting next week. Do you think we could forge a diagnosis and save the plane fare to all those eastern doctors?'

'Lisa,' said Nan, reaching across her desk and taking the young woman's hand, 'you're just wonderful, do you know that?' She squeezed the hand with as much strength, as much life, as she had. 'Would you like me to have a talk with your mother?'

'Oh, Nan, yes. Maybe you could remind her how important it was for *you* to go to college. She just doesn't understand, does she?'

'No, honey, not completely.'

Nan thought of all the old tensions this issue would raise between herself and Shirley. But Lisa was a woman now, and Shirley would have to let her make her own decisions.

'Everyone is talking about Professor Murchie,' said Lisa hurriedly, as if the death had provided a welcome distraction from her own worries. 'Even in Hayward.' She told Nan that Joe was using the murder as another argument against her going to 'that crazy school.' Nan didn't want to discuss it. And Lisa, sensing her aunt's unusual reluctance to talk, said she'd have to hurry if she were going to be back in Hayward for dinner.

Nan walked Lisa to the door. Just as she was kissing her curly forehead, Nan caught sight of two figures out of the corner of her eye.

'Good afternoon, Professor Weaver,' said Officer Rodriguez.

'Good afternoon,' Nan echoed.

Lisa regarded them steadily, betraying only an edge of fear.

Officer Ross kept his eyes on Lisa as Rodriguez continued, 'We'd like to thank you for your cooperation earlier. And we may be back to you in a few days.'

'All right,' said Nan politely.

After they passed, she hugged Lisa tightly and said, 'All right. Everything's going to be all right.'

Eight

Nan waited in the lobby of the New World Sauna and Hot Tub Emporium, hoping Amy would not be late. They gauged you by the minute here, like a roast. Half-an-hour in the small redwood sauna and half-an-hour in the resting room – a precise recipe for relaxation. Nan had looked forward to and dreaded tonight as a time to unburden herself about New Year's Eve. Somehow she would discuss it without divulging Marjorie's identity.

She would simply explain . . . her mind darted to the time again. 7.29. Amy always cut right on the edge. Nan didn't mind that Amy had changed their dinner date to a sauna. She hadn't been able to eat for a week anyway. But why didn't Amy ever leave that extra inch? The young clerk behind the polished wood counter looked serene and clean, as if she alternated her hours between meditating and sweating. Nan often felt an adolescent gawkiness when she entered the New World Emporium, one foot on the accelerator and one foot in her mouth.

'Hi, Nan,' called Amy, moving up the counter before Nan had a chance to focus. Speedy. How could Nan worry about speedy. Compared to Amy she was a regular turtle.

'Just on time,' announced Amy, perhaps implying that Nan had been slothful to arrive two minutes earlier and just wait. 'My treat,' she said before Nan could protest. Nan felt calmer already, just witnessing her friend's centrifugal force.

'Room four,' said the pacific young woman, as if bestowing on them a special mantra.

'Hope you don't mind my switching dinner to a sauna?' Amy peeled off her sweater and jeans, unplugged her earrings and popped out her contact lens. 'But I've got this case to argue next week and Warren agreed to help me with the research tonight.'

'Not at all,' Nan began to say, but Amy was already interrupting her.

'He's such a good man really.' Amy stepped through the door to the little hot room. 'I know everyone says her man is an exception, but Warren is . . .'

'An exception,' answered Nan, climbing to the top bench. 'He really is fine, Amy. Why are you so apologetic?'

'Just that, as a feminist, I know what bastards men are. I had three rape cases last month. And it sounds like a cliché to say that Warren is, well, different.'

'Perhaps it's more of a cliché to think he can't be different,' said Nan. 'I mean he is thoughtful, generous, supportive of your work.'

'There aren't too many of them around,' Amy muttered.

'That doesn't mean he's a figment of your imagination.'

Amy turned on her side, sweat dripping down her stomach. 'Warren wouldn't like being called a figment, that's for sure.'

Nan sighed and lifted her hands over her head, as if to stretch away all the tension.

'You OK?' asked Amy. Was she commanding or asking?

'Sure.' Nan waited hopelessly for the sweat to bead on her belly. Even in this she was six times slower than her friend.

'You sound sort of . . . I don't know . . . lonely, maybe.'

Nan felt tired and frightened. How much she wanted to tell Amy what had happened. And what safer place than this steamy vault? The question was, where to begin.

Amy mistook her silence for confusion. 'Lonely, you know maybe what you need is a relationship.'

'Relationship,' Nan exploded. She sat up, tentatively resting her back against the hot wood. 'I have plenty of relationships – maybe too many – with Lisa and Shirley and Matt and you. Now if you want to talk unfeminist, Amy, it's you thinking I need to be sleeping with someone to have a relationship. Lonely, I'm not. My life is very, very full – with love *and* angst.'

'Calm down,' said Amy. Then she, herself, calmed down under the shower.

Amy slumped back on to the bottom bench with uncharacteristic pensiveness. She stretched full length and stared at the ceiling. Nan thought, uneasily, of bunkbeds in a prison cell. Before the image paralyzed her, Amy spoke up, 'You're right. Projection. My therapist tells me how I'm always doing this projection number on people. I guess it was the stuff about Warren. Here I am running around worrying whether I can love a man, so I get hyped up about your not being in love right now. Pretty thick for someone with my brilliant mind, eh kid?'

Nan noticed sweat beading to the surface beneath her breasts. She began to laugh, whether out of relief or affection or hysteria, she didn't know.

'I can't believe I haven't asked you about the department, about Murchie's death, about how everyone is holding up.'

Nan lay back and breathed deeply, wondering where to begin. Should she say she had been in Wheeler that night? Should she say she was afraid that suspicion might be cast on her?

Amy, who was not very good at silences, stood under the shower again. Shiny and dripping, she emerged, looking to Nan for an answer.

'Everyone's being pretty tight-lipped,' said Nan.

'What about Matt?'

'We're planning to talk soon.'

'And that student, what's her name, the one you said Murchie was trying to seduce by sniffing her mistletoe, Mary, Maureen, what's her . . .'

'Marjorie,' slipped Nan, regretting it immediately. Had she been stupid enough to talk to Amy as well as to Lisa about Marjorie? How could she hide someone she had already introduced to the world?

'Yeah, is Marjorie broken up by this?'

'How would I know.' Nan groped for a change of topic, but her mind was full of fear.

'Sounded like you were pretty close,' said Amy, 'like she was one of your favourite students.'

'It did?' Nan recovered, answering coolly, 'No, not really.'

Above the door a light blinked, signalling five minutes for them both to shower and retire to the next stage of relaxation. Nan felt dizzy as she climbed down off the benches. She had sat in the heat constantly for half-an-hour, while her friend had been dousing in and out of the shower. Amy noticed her unnatural flush and lent an arm.

'I wondered how long you were going to bake up there, old pal.'

Nan nodded once.

'They burn witches, don't they?'

'What?' said Nan, exaggerating her bewilderment to avoid the unfinished topic of Marjorie Adams.

'And martyrs,' Amy continued good-naturedly, as she held her friend under the cool water. 'Your good Catholic girl sticks out all over the place, you know that, honey?'

Nan nodded thanks and ducked into the resting room, closing her eyes and breathing deeply while Amy finished her stint in the sauna.

By the time her friend had settled down, Nan was prepared with a new topic.

'Lisa seems to be doing better.'

'Great,' Amy responded enthusiastically. 'So you think you've finally rescued her from the torpor of Hayward?'

'She's rescuing herself.'

'So what do you feel guilty about?'

'How could you tell?' asked Nan.

'Takes one to know one. Jews and Catholics. We have an illegal monopoly on guilt.'

'I can't keep any distance about Lisa. Shirley and Joe live in a different world. I have a hell of a time accepting that.'

'Nan Weaver, you sound like one of those bourgeois jerks nattering on about the romance of the working class. You know what's better about your life-choice. And that's all you want for Lisa. You remember the narrow bigotry, the limited expectations. The same for me in Brooklyn. Don't go on like one of those working-class-is-chic kids. Do me a favour.'

'Well,' Nan frowned. 'I know my life is better for *me* now. I just wish I wasn't so critical of theirs. About potato chips and beer and TV bowling tournaments.'

'Critical of junk food and the mind corrosion of the mass media?'

'I'm serious, Amy. If I escaped, why do I get so angry at them?'

'I suppose you have papers to verify your release?'

'Sorry?'

'Nan, it's your turn to be thick. When I go home, at first I feel like an immune foreigner, then I settle right back into the old resentments. My parents' resentment that I "escaped" to a life for which they prepared me. My own resentment that they weren't Forest Hills Jews with Bach playing in the background. We're destined to be peripheral, honey. You don't belong in Hayward. And you don't belong in Berkeley.'

'That's it,' said Nan. 'Even my most basic reflexes fail me – in both places.'

'But you keep trying. I don't believe it. You keep up with Shirley and Joe in a way that would drive me to Bellevue if I visited by family more than once a year.'

'It's different,' said Nan.

'No you're different,' said Amy. 'Braver.'

'Well, I don't know.'

'Of course you don't,' answered Amy. 'That's one of the things I love about you.'

'Are you folks about finished?' asked the attendant's mellow voice over the intercom.

'Relaxed enough to rush right back to life,' said Amy.

'Thank you,' came the amiable reply.

Nine

The committee meeting had been scheduled for the first Monday of the New Year. And notwithstanding grief over the passing of Angus Murchie, the meeting would proceed.

Nan was the only person in the large room at five minutes to ten. She was always early – another survival tactic: you get there first and watch the adversary walk in. It was a pleasant room, with huge windows overlooking the campus. Millie had arrived several minutes before to draw up the long, yellow blinds and plug in the percolator. Then she had dashed out to collect the Xeroxed agendas and finish the dozen tasks which would keep Professor Nelson, the Chairperson, from looking like the lousy administrator he was. So Nan sat alone, wondering at the clarity of blue in the January sky and sipping black coffee from her styrofoam cup.

Once these meeting rooms had been as restricted as a Mormon sanctuary. When she was an undergraduate, Nan could only imagine this place. She always knew there must be large rooms here on the third floor of Wheeler, larger than those used for classes and offices. She could tell from the outside, looking up at the pattern of windows. Later, when she was in graduate school, she had a quick peek at the room when the Student Equal Rights Council had presented a petition. Never did she expect *she* might be sitting here as a token female professor.

Nan didn't know what she had expected. Her ambitions had always seemed more like dreams – so unrealistic even for 'the girl brain'. When she was in graduate school, yes, of course, she hoped to be a professor. She was doing her PhD because she loved literature and she wanted to help young people love it, too. But if you had asked her on any particular day whether she would finish her thesis, she could not say. She continued to regard herself as slow, as behind, even though, throughout her entire life, she had been early.

Hammerly and Augustine were the next to arrive. They nodded

cordially to her, filled their coffee cups, looked around irritably for cookies and then sat down, back into their conversation.

'I know this will sound a little crude to you,' Hammerly was saying to Augustine, as though Nan were as invisible as a waitress might be to them, 'but I think we should move fast to fill the job, before the university freezes any more of the budget.'

'My friend,' Augustine said, then murmured something she couldn't catch.

Nan remembered now, with some sympathy, that Augustine and Murchie were old chums, had been at Oxford together.

'I have no doubt as to your fine intentions,' recovered Augustine. 'And I know that Angus, himself, would be concerned about maintaining department positions. However, one does find it hard to bury the dead so easily, if you know what I mean.'

Nan was keeping busy with her felt pen and steno pad. Making lists. Distracting herself from the gruesomeness of Murchie's death and from these strange, implacable fears. Fear that she might be a suspect. Fear of the murder, itself, of the kind of power and morality it takes to commit such an act. Most of all fear for Marjorie Adams. How could she help Marjorie? Because she had no answers to this, she thought of Lisa. She wrote lists of doctors to consult. Of arguments to convince Shirley that Lisa should stay in school. Of plans for her first lecture and for finishing the journal article.

This week, Nan hadn't done much work on the article, or on anything else for that matter. She had barely been able to sleep at night and to stay awake during the days. She knew such events changed people at the deepest level. How was she different? Right now, she was too exhausted to tell. She felt like an actor playing herself. Nan Weaver, Professor of English, Feminist, Aunt, Murder Witness . . . All the portrayals were low key – bit parts whispered from the wings. And her friends and family, like most normal people during a catastrophe, were caught up in themselves. The few who did notice her lethargy just accepted that she was feeling a little overwhelmed and probably tired from the holidays.

Nan knew she would feel better once she had told someone. Now she felt a shell of her former self, her insides consumed by the secret. She had intended to drop by Matt's apartment with a bottle of brandy and spend an evening confessing and being comforted and plotting the rescue of Marjorie Adams. But something stopped Nan from seeing Matt that night and half-a-dozen times since then – madness perhaps – some conviction that complete silence was necessary to protect Marjorie. She was caught in a spiral, where it became more and more impossible to share her secret with anyone. Impulse had got her into this. She had cleaned up after Marjorie that night on impulse. On instinct. There was no sensible way of understanding it, no logical way out of it. Deep down she simply believed that if she didn't tell anyone – not Matt, not anyone – Marjorie would remain safe.

While everyone else wondered 'Who killed Angus Murchie?' Nan wondered, 'Who was Marjorie Adams?' For she had the answer to the first mystery, didn't she? How did she *know* Marjorie was the murderer? How could she know from a few brief words heard through the walls of Wheeler Hall? How could she know from the back view of someone running across a dark campus? These doubts would drive her mad. But what was her peace of mind compared with Marjorie's life? Yes, she would keep silent, even with Matt, a while longer.

Nan glanced up from her list as the other professors filed into the meeting. Cool, sober, formally cordial. All the places were taken except two, Matt and the student representative, Marjorie. Nan was left sitting between those two empty seats. Nelson, the Chairperson, cleared his throat, as if to summon the spirit of administration. At that moment, the big oak door creaked, admitting a visibly embarrassed Matt.

'Sorry, friends,' he smiled, 'but I had eight hundred and eighty eight class cards to dispense this morning.'

As usual, Matt managed to clear the air with the charm of a Good Humour Man. People broke out of their tense knots of conversation to greet each other and several even managed smiles.

'We have a full agenda today,' said Nelson in his broad Boston accent. 'So I'd like to begin. Discussion of the number of teaching assistants and readers for next fall. Advertisements for the junior faculty member in Victorian, the senior in seventeenth century, a replacement for Professor Murchie.'

Augustine spoke up, 'May I suggest that we acknowledge the passing of our colleague with something more respectful than plans for an advertisement.'

Augustine wasn't a bad fellow, thought Nan, a little sentimental, but decent. He had been thoroughly incapable of seeing the pain and humiliation Murchie had caused others.

'Hmmmm, yes, well, quite,' said Nelson. 'What do you suggest?'

'Perhaps a moment's silence,' offered Hammerly, clearly anxious to please Augustine and then bloody well get on with the meeting.

'Yes,' said Matt, 'that seems properly ecumenical.'

Nan frowned a little.

'No, I mean it,' said Matt, pulling off his glasses and cleaning them. 'I think it would be a fine gesture.'

'And perhaps,' added Augustine, 'a short quote, one of Angus' favourites from "Samson Agonistes",

> *With peace and consolation dismist*
> *And calm of mind. All passion spent.'*

As they sat around the table with their heads bowed, Nan wondered what moved through their minds. Augustine's thoughts were easiest to read – genuine sadness and loss. Actually, she was relieved he hadn't read four or five pages from 'Paradise Regained' to sustain them all. Hammerly was another story. Probably he was thinking about his friend Henderson at Princeton, a Milton scholar who had been itching to move out of the snow for years. Poor Nelson must be counting Murchie's committees and classes and wondering how he would ever find a replacement as expansive as their departed colleague.

And how many of them, she wondered, were silently guessing who killed Angus Murchie? There were a number of motives at this very table. Christianson, for instance: everyone knew that Murchie had had a three-year affair with Christianson's wife before she left both of them for a graduate student. And Methor – there was some old gossip about Murchie doing a reader's report on Methor's book – which was then rejected by the publisher. Perhaps not a motive for most people, but Methor bore deep grudges and was very competitive with Murchie. What about Matt? Murchie had been known to do a certain amount of queer baiting. And herself? Their personal animosity had escalated over years of his sexual passes and her political outspokenness. Everyone knew about their clash on The Sexual Harassment Campaign.

As she looked around the room, she realized with a cold rush of terror that she was the most likely suspect. As she looked around, she realized that she was the only one looking around.

Nan bowed her head thinking, surely this has been longer than a minute; surely this has been enough false grief.

The heavy door creaked again to admit Marjorie Adams. The young woman's look of surprise at the silent gathering was quickly composed into appropriate mourning.

Marjorie took her seat next to Nan with quiet dignity. But her pink lurex dress shone under the fluorescent lights. The lipstick was a new shade to match the dress. Her blonde hair was wrapped high at the back around a pink silk gardenia. Dorothy Lamour, Nan tried to remember, 'The Road to . . .' Sometimes Nan wondered if there wasn't something feminist in Marjorie's choice of attire. Compared with her own understated, academic style, Marjorie expressed a strong individuality and quite a nice sense of humour. Why *had* Marjorie come to Berkeley from her fashionable Eastern circuit? Nan thought with sympathy that this move must have been as traumatic as her own emigration from Hayward.

Nelson cleared his throat, as if everyone needed to be roused from deep despond.

'Shall we resume?' he said, then suggested that they keep the discussion of Murchie's death, the police investigation and his replacement to a minimum.

So they proceeded through the teaching assistants and the tenure questions and the faculty advertisements with vigorous dispassion. Dispassion. Nan remembered how one of her articles had been rejected for 'lack of dispassion'. It had been about suicidal themes in Anne Sexton, for god's sake, but perhaps suicide warranted an objective approach. Apparently murder did.

Nan stole a glance at Marjorie Adams. She felt chilled by her composure. Was this steadiness sustained by valium or a more expensive tranquillizer? Nan found her eyes fixed on Marjorie's fingernails, so perfectly manicured and so fastidiously matched to the silk gardenia.

The agenda was covered by 11.30, an unprecedented fifteen minutes early. No one stayed for cordialities. Those at the other end of the table left with the hasty relief of physicists escaping a nuclear testing site. Matt paused to confirm a lunch date with Nan. Then, as she turned from her friend, Nan was startled to find Marjorie Adams waiting to talk with her.

Nan appreciated the power of Marjorie's seductiveness; ingenuous politeness laced with poise.

'Yes, Marjorie,' said Nan, as though she were a grade school teaching discussing a fairytale. That was it – 'Rapunzel', with Murchie as the wicked father.

'There's something I have to say to you,' began Marjorie, saying it all with her blue, blue eyes.

'Not here,' Nan whispered. 'Perhaps we can make an appointment.' She was mesmerized by Marjorie's confidence. Yes, together the two of them could create an innocence.

'That's exactly what I mean to say,' responded Marjorie, slightly unnerved by Nan's intensity. 'I just want to apologize for missing our appointment. I know how valuable your time is, especially at this period of the year.'

'That's quite all right.' Nan was leaning heavily against a chair. She shouldn't be so stunned. She knew that a lot of rich people were impervious to danger. It was as if they never learned a whole set of survival signals.

'Well, do you think we might make another appointment,' Marjorie enquired in that patient tone that Nan, herself, used for noticeably thick students.

'Certainly,' said Nan, recovering and pulling out her diary. Tomorrow was packed with tasks that at any other point would seem crucial.

'How about tomorrow morning?' Nan suggested, having no idea how she could cancel her class.

'Oh, well, um,' Marjorie was hesitant, 'actually I'll be out of town for several days. Could we make it Friday?'

'Yes,' said Nan. Was Marjorie going to see her lawyer, or maybe she had an uncle in the Mafia who could buy her out of this nasty business?

'How about one o'clock?' asked Nan, with concerted coolness.

'Yes,' agreed Marjorie, 'that would be perfect.'

Perfect, thought Nan, as she watched this woman waft from the room. There was only one thing about Marjorie Adams that was not perfect. And perhaps Nan had even imagined that.

Ten

Numbly, Nan went about her chores the next morning. She was stunned at the dispatch with which Marjorie had arranged their 'appointment'. Not until she was eating her sandwich by the window of her office, staring blankly at the hills, did Nan admit that they *must* talk sooner, that there was really no time to waste. Was Marjorie playing it cool? Did she know what Nan knew? Did Nan know what Nan knew?

She phoned Marjorie and, finding no one home, went down to the department office to leave her a message. As Nan was checking her own mailbox, Millie called out,

'Phone for you, Professor Weaver.'

Nan had tried to get Millie to call her by her first name. But the secretary said she didn't want to appear to be showing disrespect. Or favouritism.

'Thanks,' smiled Nan.

'Hello, Nan Weaver here.' She liked Matt's British style of answering the phone and sometimes copied it.

'Nan?' Shirley's familiar voice sounded querulous, lost. She rarely phoned her sister at work.

'Hello, Shirl. How are you?'

'Just fine, honey. But Lisa isn't. I'm afraid she's in the hospital.'

'Oh, no,' said Nan, turning away from Millie's desk. She still harboured Mom's instinct for keeping bad news in the family. 'What is it, what happened?' she whispered.

'Same thing,' Shirley's voice was more anxious now. 'Who knows what it is. She's tired, feverish, sweating, vomiting. She's just awful sick, Nannie.'

'Listen, I'll be out by four o'clock, OK? And, hold on, what hospital?'

'Memorial. You know, the big new one out by Southland Shopping Mall.'

'Right,' said Nan. 'See you in a couple of hours.'

'Family troubles?' Millie inquired kindly.

Nan remembered that Millie, who was raised in nearby Castro Valley, had the same kind of family if not the same kind of troubles.

'Yes,' Nan told her. 'Better cancel that note to Marjorie Adams. It looks like I'll be running in and out of town for a couple of days.'

'Sure,' said Millie. 'I hope whoever it is gets well quickly.'

Quickly, thought Nan, as she walked back to the office. Last week she had no idea just how quickly things could happen and how slowly time could pass.

Rain follows hard on the Northern California sun in early January sheets of rain, enough to blot from your memory all warmth and wellbeing. The first part of the drive to Hayward was always against Isadora's will, especially in this rheumatic weather. Nan thought of the rains in Tanzania during the two years she taught there after graduate school. East African rains came with the sun, bathing houses and streets as if from a benign placenta. Nothing else about Tanzania had felt benign, but Nan had loved the gentle predictability of the weather. Here in this California Eden, winter promises were broken in the sky from one hour to the next.

The road was packed with trucks today. She passed two giant Macks hauling tomatoes to the canneries. She could smell the aroma of Hunts from fifteen miles away.

By the time Nan and Isadora reached Hayward, the rain had subsided. Pulling into the hospital parking lot, they almost ran over a rollerskater. Not an eight-year-old kid, but a man in his twenties. He was dancing like Fred Astaire around the parallel parking lines. Bicycles she understood. And skateboards, maybe, but now rollerskates! What next? At least he had chosen a hospital zone.

Nan noticed Joe before she saw Shirley. This sickness must be terribly serious for Joe to take a day off work. From halfway down the corridor, she could see the distress on his reddened face.

Shirley was seated behind her husband, her head in her hands. She would not be crying. Nan knew this. Shirley would not make a scene in public. She would be worrying or praying, probably both.

'Hello, Nan,' Joe said, as much to alert Shirley as to greet his sister-in-law.

Nan shook his hand and nodded. Then she put an arm around Shirley and asked, 'What's happening now, honey?'

'That's what we'd all like to know,' said Joe. 'We've been in this damn hallway for four hours straight. They won't let us see our own daughter. They won't tell us what the fuck they're doing. What do they think, we're waiting for a streetcar?'

'Joe,' Shirley said with the balance of sternness and softness she had cultivated during the twenty-five years of their marriage. 'Joe, just sit here beside me and maybe we can talk.'

Now Joe's head was bowed. He reminded Nan of a terrier mutt they once had, who would go racing after cars and then come home, his tail between his legs, having reckoned the impossibility of the race.

Shirley took her sister's hand. 'Nan, honey,' she said. 'We don't know what's going on. Lisa got sick and then fainted this morning. They've been running tests on her since we arrived. Kidneys, heart, the whole thing. Maybe you could talk to them. I mean, you know how to deal with these medical types because Charles was a doctor and all.'

Nan became the family translator, the middle-class woman asking clear, precise questions. She recalled a scene from Morogoro when a tall, skinny boy arranged for his father's amputation because he was the only one in the family with a few English words.

Not that the doctor's language was English, exactly.

'We think it may be systemic Lupus Erythematosis,' said tired old Dr Bonelli, regarding her carefully to see if she was following.

'How serious?' asked Nan.

'The type, severity, time of onset and duration may result in a highly variable pattern and prognosis. Pathologic changes are non-specific but include widespread fibroid vascular changes and disseminated arteritis.'

'So you're worried about the heart?' asked Nan.

'Among other things,' the doctor said hurriedly. 'But it really is too early to tell, much too early.'

Nan returned to Shirley and Joe with three styrofoam cups of coffee and a certain amount of news. Lisa was conscious. The diagnosis was uncertain. The family would be allowed to visit in fifteen minutes.

During that interminable quarter hour, the fight erupted.

'Stress,' muttered Joe, sipping listlessly on the cold, black liquid. 'My pal at work tells me that pressure and tension can *kill* people all right.'

'Shhh,' said Shirley. 'We don't need any talk about killing.'

Joe ignored his wife. 'What else do you expect,' he demanded breathlessly, as if he were trying to shout and whisper at once.

'Look at that guy who got killed in Nan's own department last week.'

Shirley laid her head in her palms again.

'Lisa, poor babe, has been overworked and overstressed,' said Joe conclusively. Now Nan noticed he was staring at her. 'She's in a situation she just can't handle.'

Nan nodded because she did, in fact, think he had a point. But how he was pinning it on her, she didn't understand. Well, the nurse would be here in a few minutes. Then they would all see Lisa.

'This college business is one of those stresses,' Joe persisted. 'Have they found out who killed that guy yet?'

'Joe, please,' Shirley pleaded.

'No, you listen,' Joe said. 'Lisa is just an average . . .'

Shirley reached out for his hand.

He pulled it back, shaking a finger at Nan. 'Just because some of the family's got overdeveloped heads, it don't mean we all do. She's got my blood in her, too, that kid. She's just your normal American girl.'

Nan did not know how she could keep all this madness inside her head without bursting. The murder. Marjorie's safety. Lisa's survival. Perhaps her mind could work on alternating currents, one disaster distracting her from the other.

'Joe,' said Nan, with exaggerated calm. 'If you're saying Lisa got sick because she was working too hard, then you're underestimating . . .'

'Please,' said Shirley, now standing between her husband and her sister. 'Please, both of you. This is no time to . . .'

'She's a good, simple kid,' Joe's voice was angrier now.

'Mr and Mrs Growsky,' called the nurse from several paces away, her voice loud enough to interrupt them, official enough not to crease the hospital routine.

'Mr and Mrs Growsky,' she said again as she reached a conversational distance. 'You may go in and see your daughter for about twenty minutes.' The young nurse then turned to Nan. Was she young? Nan hadn't noticed this before. She had only noticed that the nurse was someone who warranted respect because she guarded access to Lisa.

'And you,' she spoke to Nan, 'may accompany them if you wish.'

Nan nodded her thanks and caught up with Joe and Shirley as they opened the door to Lisa's ward.

Lisa's eyes, as she greeted her parents, betrayed the panic of a lost

76

child and the confused guilt of someone knowing her pain has brought trouble to other people.

Nan backed out into the hallway, surveying the four-person ward. Green curtains were drawn around the three other beds, providing at least a semblance of privacy for the sleeping, or dying, patients.

Best for Lisa to see her parents alone first, thought Nan. Who was she but some bungling fairy godmother? Maybe Joe was right about Berkeley, not all of it, but about stress at this point in Lisa's life. Look at what had happened to Marjorie Adams. Nan pulled away from the door, to allow the family some privacy.

She was pleased and embarrassed when she heard Lisa's voice, 'Nan, don't go away, Nan.'

So the three of them stood around her, like zookeepers staring helplessly at a rare bird, her flight broken by some malevolent current. (Maybe it *was* the air, Nan thought wildly, maybe they each would be struck down, the young and tender first, then the tough old crones like herself.)

Nan was surprised to see Lisa lying there with no hoses or tubes. Just Lisa, who looked so young and so pale enveloped in hospital white. Predictably, she tried to cheer up everyone.

'You know I'm just trying to play hooky from the first week of school.'

After these determined words, Lisa's voice wavered. Her fatigue was most evident in her heavy eyes.

The young nurse fluttered in and discreetly reminded the family that they could view the body for only five more minutes.

Then they were left, standing stupidly in the corridor. They returned to the bench, although the wait for the next visit would be hopelessly long. Another two hours before they might see Lisa again. Another two hours of mysterious tests.

'Look,' said Nan, breaking through the silent terror. 'This is going to be expensive . . .'

'Thanks for your wisdom, Professor,' said Joe.

'All I mean is that I've got a little bit saved,' said Nan, 'and I'd like to help out.'

'We don't need charity,' said Joe, ignoring the warning on Shirley's face. 'We've got the union insurance. Besides don't you think you've "helped" enough already.'

'Joe,' said Shirley, with more anger than Nan had seen since they were girls and Shirley found the Driscoll boy pulling their terrier's ears, 'Joe Growsky, I think Nan may have had just about enough of you today.'

Shirley noticed the old woman across from them staring. Blushing, she lowered her voice. 'We're all tired and irritable, and it's obviously not doing us any good sitting here getting at each other.'

Joe regarded his wife apologetically. Sometimes Nan forgot how much Joe relied on Shirley's good sense.

'Speaking of bills,' he said, stealing a last angry look at Nan, 'I better get back on the job before I lose it.'

'Right then,' said Shirley, still very much in command. 'I'll explain to Lisa. See you late tonight.'

'Sure, sweetheart,' said Joe with genuine tenderness. He even managed a civil nod to his sister-in-law.

The two women drove over to Southland Mall for coffee. No use sitting around the dreary hospital for hours. Shirley suggested the Gourmet Sandwich Bar next to Gorman's Ice Cream. She thought Nan would like the special Italian coffee, and maybe she would have one of those sticky Greek desserts.

Shopping. Shopping malls. Shopping centres. Shopping expeditions for birthdays and graduations and weddings. So much of their time together was spent shopping. This was a way for Nan and Shirley to be with each other without confronting each other. A re-enactment of their childhood where every Saturday morning Mom would take them to the sales. They had spent the best years of their lives shopping. Not here, of course, because Southland wasn't built until 1964, when Lisa was four. But many of these stores were transplants from the old Hayward strip on Foothill Boulevard, their owners broader and greyer and more prosperous than in the old days, yet still the kind of people you called Hattie or George. This mall was an odd conglomeration – family jewellers and small stationers next to superchain clothing stores, everything done up in primary colour neon. Such intense Americana was enough to give Nan the shakes.

Maybe this was actually a giant time capsule of late capitalism Nan wondered. Sometimes she imagined that all these people (young mothers listlessly pushing strollers until the next mealtime; old people chatting on the plastic benches; adolescent employees polishing the philodendra), all of them were tied into some bright helium balloon which would go floating up to another planet as 'Specimen Earth'. Nan was keeping a close watch on the exit signs.

Shirley, her eyes fixed on Penney's window, laughed and pointed, 'Oh, just look at that outfit.'

Nan cringed at the orange velvet jump suit. It was enough to make Marjorie Adams look inconspicuous.

'That's the outfit I was trying to describe,' said Shirley.

Nan shrugged.

'The one that Juliet Amaro wore to Crystal's wedding,' said Shirley, going on rather hectically. 'Zipped just to the decent level and tied at the waist with a black silk rope. That Juliet, you've got to admire her nerve. Her husband Mike really spoils her. She stays in bed until noon every day reading. And he says all he ever did in those Vietnam swamps was dream of someone to take care of.'

They found an empty booth in the air-conditioned recesses of the Gourmet Sandwich Bar and began a dozen conversations, none of them about Lisa. Shirley made her usual, discreet inquiries into the state of Nan's life. Any new boyfriends? What classes was she teaching this term? How was the little garden in the back of her little apartment?

Nan understood that Shirley wasn't conscious of saying 'little'. They found each other's lives confining in different ways, that's all.

As usual, Nan answered her sister's questions within three minutes. There was so much she never confided, even before the ghost of Angus Murchie. Like the tenure decision. She never told Shirley the dozen ways that it frightened her. They spent ninety-five percent of their time together talking about Shirley's life, because 'the family' was more mutual territory and also, Nan had to admit, because Shirley was more forthcoming.

'So we thought we'd take a short vacation – just Joe and me – in Reno,' Shirley was saying. 'Gladys Crosby was telling us about a casino hotel deal where they practically pay you to stay there.'

'Why don't you go somewhere on the California side of Tahoe,' suggested Nan, in what she tried to make a perfectly reasonable, friendly voice. 'You know that Nevada hasn't passed the Equal Rights Amendment, and we're trying to boycott the state.'

'How can you boycott a whole state?' asked Shirley. 'Really, that seems a bit high horse to me, just because they don't agree with your feminist politics.'

'It's more than politics,' said Nan, recognizing the pattern in this argument and noticing how they were effectively avoiding the troubled subject of Lisa. 'It's my life – and *your* life, too,' Nan could not, or would not, stop herself from arguing. 'It's just like the Civil

Rights Bill a few years back, giving equality to blacks and . . .'

'Listen,' said Shirley. 'Shall we agree to disagree? We don't want to get into an argument now.'

Agree to disagree, thought Nan wearily, remembering their mother serving tea and cordiality, suggesting they agree to disagree, reminding them that family ties were stronger than political differences. Mother admonished them that when they went out into society (such a funny phrase, as if she expected her two girls from the Hayward cannery to be invited to debutante cotillions) they must always avoid talking about religion and politics.

Nan and Shirley finished their coffee and paid the bill. As they walked out Shirley asked if Nan would be able to make it out for the Fourth of July this year.

'Sure, if I'm in town,' said Nan, not explaining her dream of going to India or Japan or somewhere very, very far away this summer. Funny how Shirley, who couldn't organize her life enough to take the secretarial courses she always talked about, was now lining up the holidays on Nan's calendar. But January to July was a big leap, even for Shirley. The holidays meant so much to her. Perhaps they were symbolic of the family closeness for which both women wished. Despite their affection, they each kept many secrets. At least Nan did, because she preferred being anonymous to being misunderstood. Someday she *would* tell Shirley about the tenure struggles, the abortion, the migraine headaches she suffered during the ten years she was married to Charles. Someday. Now they were having trouble just being straight about Lisa.

'. . . the sale at Goldman's?' Shirley was saying.

'What was that?' asked Nan, surfacing back to Southland.

'Do you want to drop round to the sale at Goldman's?' asked Shirley in a louder voice.

Nan wondered at her sister's relentless cheer.

'They've got a special on small-size summerwear,' continued Shirley. 'Didn't you say you needed a new bikini?'

Nan smiled at Shirley's long, practical memory and nodded agreeably because there was still an hour left before they could see Lisa.

Back at the hospital, the nurse informed them they would have to wait an additional thirty minutes.

When they were finally admitted to the ward, Lisa was propped up against some pillows, her hair just washed and still wet.

'You look like you've been through the laundromat,' teased Nan.

Her niece feigned the patience of Elizabeth Barrett after a bad day with father.

'More like the old-fashioned ringer,' managed Lisa. 'Don't tell me you two have been hanging around here all evening waiting for me to be liberated from medical technology.'

'We had a nice little shopping expedition,' said Shirley. 'And we bought your aunt a very sexy bathing suit. Nan is joining us on the Fourth of July, isn't that nice?'

'But it's just after New Year's,' Lisa laughed weakly.

'Don't you remember,' smiled Nan, 'how your mother made all the Christmas plans on my birthday in August?'

'Well, I hope that I'm around to celebrate with you,' said Lisa.

'Oh, sweetheart,' said Shirley. She put her hand on Lisa's cheek. 'Don't be talking like that. Don't even be thinking like that.'

Lisa pulled away, frowning and silent.

'Mrs Growsky,' said the nurse, appearing in the doorway. 'May we speak with you a moment?'

Shirley nodded nervously and then turned to Nan. 'You give her a good talking to.' She was forcing a smile. 'You pep her up, will you?'

Once Shirley was out the door, Lisa began to cry.

'I'm sorry,' she said. 'Sometimes Mom is so awful chirpy.'

Nan sat on the bed and held Lisa's hands. She was washed with fondness for her brave niece and her persevering sister. Lisa had an admirable commitment to candour, a passion for truth which would not allow her mother's compromises for survival. It was as if her honesty had blossomed from the qualities of Shirley's endurance.

'I don't want to hurt her,' said Lisa. 'It's just so confusing, so tiring, and she keeps up this happy smile while I *know* she's falling apart inside.'

Now Nan began to weep. They sat for a long time, holding each other and crying. It was a relief for both of them, the first release this terrifying day. Then they rocked silently.

Bells rang. From somewhere.

'That mean's visiting hours are over,' said Lisa. 'They told me you couldn't stay after 8.15.'

'Listen, I've got an idea,' said Nan.

'What?' Lisa smiled, in spite of herself. 'I know, you sneak under the bed and then come out in the dark. We can have a slumber party.'

'Not a bad thought,' said Nan. 'Actually, my idea was about the summer.'

'About the Fourth of July?' Lisa was forcing herself to wakefulness above the drugs.

'Yup,' nodded Nan. 'How about we skip the Fourth of July and the fourth of August and spend some time wandering around the Himalayas together? Just the two of us, kid, and thousands of sherpas.'

'Wonderful,' declared Lisa. 'Oh, I get it,' she smiled. 'It's a bargain, isn't it? I have to promise to live until the summer.'

'Much longer than that.'

'Well, Nan, I'll try. But tell me about you. How are things at school?'

'No more word on the murder,' Nan said as evenly as possible. Then she added quickly, 'My classes are good. I really like my graduate students this year. Marjorie Adams's thesis is coming along in strides.' Now why did she mention that? She shouldn't have permitted herself to think about Wheeler Hall. 'Anyway, this is all pretty boring business compared to the Himalayas. Do we have a date for the summer or do I have to go get myself another niece?'

'Oh, not that,' Lisa's voice went up in mock alarm. 'The Himalayas it is.'

The nurse walked in, followed by Shirley.

'I'm afraid,' the nurse said, 'that . . .'

'That the prison is closing for the night,' interrupted Lisa, with a grin.

Shirley, still standing behind the nurse, nodded approvingly to Nan. 'Well, Miss Lisa, you seem to be approaching your normal, sassy self.'

Shirley walked over and kissed her daughter goodbye. 'See you tomorrow then.'

Lisa waved to them and winked at Nan. 'See you in Kathmandu.'

Shirley's smile did not drop completely until they were safely in the car. And, once she began to let go, she could not stop the loud, rasping sobs.

'OK, OK, steady there, girl,' Nan comforted her sister. 'Now tell me just what the doctor said.'

'Nothing. He said that he couldn't say *anything* for another month. She could be out of the hospital in two days. He might try this drug "prednisone" or something. The sickness could disappear forever or . . .'

'Or Lisa might die,' finished Nan, losing her temper for the first time in this insane day. 'God damn. This makes no sense. It just isn't fair. She's a kid, such a good kid.'

The two women huddled together inside Isadora, Shirley silently weeping and Nan railing.

Finally, Nan calmed down, or perhaps she simply wore out. 'Look, this isn't doing us any good,' she said, stroking Shirley's hair. 'I'll have a talk with the doctor tomorrow and then call my friends in Maryland and Chicago. We're not going to sit quietly while Lisa succumbs to, to nothing.'

Shirley looked at Nan hopefully, and Nan looked back with restrained reassurance. She didn't want Shirley to expect miracles. She would just see what she could do.

Nan dropped Shirley at the door. Joe would be inside to take care of her. No, she wouldn't go in. She had had enough family for one day. Besides, she needed to get home, to try once more to sleep.

Jose Feliciano was singing 'California Dreaming' on Isadora's radio as Nan pulled on to the freeway, out of Hayward.

'Hayward is one of those anonymous California way stations that no one sings or writes or dreams about,' she said aloud, reassured by the sound of her own voice. 'A stage coach stop in the last century. Now a BART station to the plusher suburbs. Hayward has always been the kind of place where losers got waylaid on the road to their ambitions. California nightmare. California madness.'

Perhaps she was hysterical. She must be more than a little crazy to be giving herself a pop sociology lecture, especially tonight in the midst of murder and fatal disease.

She remembered once in the second grade how Sister Maria Goretti had explained that prayer was retroactive. If only Nan still believed in prayer. If only she knew to whom she could pray. Perhaps she would just try her mother's approach to crisis, making it disappear by ignoring it.

'California dreaming is vineyards,' she continued groggily, 'orange groves, quaint adobe missions surrounded by bougain-villaea, the Sierras, the Pacific Ocean. California madness is earth-quakes, the Donner Party, Zodiac murders, Altamont.'

'Holy shit,' shouted Nan, as a pickup swerved in front of her, almost amputating Isadora's right fender. She leaned on the horn. The truck driver gave her the finger. His bumper sticker said, 'I'd rather be swinging'.

More alert now, Nan watched the winding speed of Highway 580 move into the dark, forested Warren Freeway leading to Berkeley. Descending upon her was the now-familiar depression, that profound claustrophobia. And she realized why people went into madness. It was the only safe exit from the freeway.

Eleven

Marjorie arrived for her appointment spot on time, dressed as, hmmm, perhaps as Katharine Hepburn today.

A pin-striped shirt tucked into baggy linen pants held up by fashionable suspenders. If Nan tried to wear these clothes, she would look ridiculous. Was it the difference between them of six inches or twenty-five years? Neither; it was something to do with class in several connotations. Nan reckoned that Marjorie carried off the role better than Hepburn. She knew that the other side of her disdain for Marjorie's materialism was awe of her panache. Nan was not a little envious of all this classiness.

'Have a seat, Marjorie,' said Nan.

'Thank you, Professor Weaver.'

Again Nan was impressed with Marjorie's formality. The demure manner balanced the flamboyant appearance, like diplomat licence plates on a chartreuse Jaguar. Nan tried to understand: visual vs. verbal; action vs. admission; unconscious feeling vs. intellectual rationale. She imagined Marjorie was generated by great imagination and protected by deep discretion.

'How about a cup of tea, Marjorie? It's only bagged Lipton' (why was she apologizing?), 'but I suppose anything will do in this chilly weather.'

'Yes, thanks,' Marjorie accepted, 'that would be lovely.'

Her eyes, Nan noticed again, were sure and steady. She didn't look like *she* had lost any sleep during the past week, at least nothing compared with Nan's insomnia. Marjorie seemed quite composed for someone who had killed a man with his own letter opener in the room next door.

'Shocking, isn't it,' said Nan, in spite of herself.

She had intended to let Marjorie raise the issue. She must have noticed Nan's light when she climbed down the scaffolding. Marjorie must know that Nan knew.

Nan thought back to their first interview, the day Marjorie asked her to supervise the thesis. Marjorie had been terse about her life. Only child. Rich parents. Always top of her class. She was so reserved – as if Nan's asking personal questions was as inappropriate as investigating her dental history. But Nan felt more sorry for Marjorie than embarrassed for herself. Somehow the student lacked common sense and basic social skills. As Amy would say, she wasn't 'streetwise' at all.

'Shocking,' repeated Marjorie, pulling out her fountain pen and opening her pad. 'Oh, yes,' she continued almost absently, 'Professor Murchie's death, shocking.'

Death. Nan noticed she said 'death', and not 'murder'.

'Thank you,' said Marjorie, accepting the mug from Nan. She sat back in the wooden chair, bobbing the tea bag in the steaming water, waiting for Nan to speak.

'Not that he was everyone's favourite colleague,' Nan continued, thinking the young woman might need some encouragement to talk.

'Oh, Professor Weaver,' said Marjorie with alarm, 'You mustn't speak like that.'

Poor Marjorie, thought Nan, she was overcome. She noticed that her student's eyes were slightly bloodshot, that, in fact, she did seem rather tired. How *would* such an experience change you? Was she terrified? Hardened? Still in shock?

Marjorie leaned foward and dropped her tea bag into the grey waste can. 'With all the suspicion floating around us,' she said confidentially, 'comments like that could get you in trouble.'

Nan did not know how to respond to such coolness.

'Of course, I'm not meaning to imply anything,' Marjorie added quickly, almost blushing. 'It's just that everyone is so paranoid.'

How remarkable for Marjorie to identify with 'everyone'. Nan realized that she must have been staring because Marjorie asked, 'Have I upset you?'

For a frozen, horrified moment, Nan wondered if Marjorie was intentionally casting suspicion on her.

Finally, she said, 'No, you haven't upset me. No, I think I've been upset for most of the last two weeks.'

'Of course,' Marjorie said gently.

'Well, then,' said Nan, 'shall we get down to work? I do think that this last piece you submitted is very fine indeed.'

Was this her own voice? Nan wondered. Her own words? Was she actually behaving as calmly and professionally as Marjorie's deferential attention implied?

The appointment was scheduled for an hour. They became quickly engrossed. In fact, this was turning out to be one of the most satisfying sessions they had had, unscathed by petty jealousies or insecurities. Focussed by such mutual intensity, they shared a curtain against the grim violence of two weeks before. Power and love in the work of Iris Murdoch. Power and hate in the death of Angus Murchie. An appropriate wake, somehow, for the despised professor.

Marjorie's questions barely contained her excitement for their discussion. Nan thought of Lisa's idealism, how alike in tone and how different in aspiration were the two young women. While Lisa was convinced that school would give her tools to change the world Marjorie had faith that school would give her answers to understand it. And today she had a special urgency about her, as if these novels could substitute for the treacherous narrative of her own life.

The Campanile sounded two o'clock, reminding Nan that she had a class to teach in ten minutes. She was surprised when Marjorie made an appointment for the following Monday. Even now, she expected Marjorie to be called off on some emergency. But no, the young woman would stick it out, would stay around. The scene of the crime probably was the wisest sanctuary. A wiser one than Nan would seek.

As Marjorie stood, gathering her papers, Nan noticed a slight shaking in her hands. This silent self-containment was not normal, not human. Marjorie really must speak to someone, to get this gruesome business off her chest. Despite her objections to the sacrament of penance, Nan had to admit the sheer relief of confession. She wasn't sure whether it was for 'poor Marjorie Adams' or for herself that she made the next step.

Nan reached into her purse and pulled out Marjorie's pink and green scarf from which she had washed Murchie's dark blood. For a moment, Nan was lost, imagining it tied around Marjorie's hair, plaited into the braid which later hung ragged down her back as she fled across the campus.

For the first time in an hour, Marjorie lost her composure. Her blue eyes widened and her cheeks flushed brightly. She *was* human. Nan wondered if her scrutiny was sadistic. No, she needed to know that Marjorie was human. She felt a strong draw toward her now, a rush of all her bottled-up sympathy.

'Is that my scarf?' asked Marjorie, quavering on the 'is' but steady by the time she got to 'scarf'.

'I guess it must be,' said Nan. 'I found it . . .'

Marjorie interrupted her, 'Yes, I think I do recall wearing it the last time I was here.'

Remembering the black and red Joan Crawford dress Marjorie was wearing during their last appointment, Nan couldn't believe she would make up such an absurdly unstylish alibi. She must know where Nan had found the scarf. *She must know.*

'I did look around for it after that appointment,' Marjorie continued.

And so Nan learned that the younger woman's facility for analyzing fiction was well matched by her talent for creating it. Nan *did not understand* the game in which they were both irrevocably caught.

'Thank you,' said Marjorie. 'I bought it in Paris several years ago. I'm so grateful to have it back.'

Now Nan couldn't imagine Hepburn handling that line with more aplomb. 'I bought it in Paris,' Nan thought to herself. Imagine that. Imagine anything. Imagine a murder around the corner. Often during the last two weeks, especially during those early morning, insomniac walks around her small flat, Nan did wonder just how much she had imagined. No, no, she was absolutely sure Marjorie hadn't worn this green and purple scarf with her Joan Crawford dress.

Marjorie calmly finished collecting her papers. She turned to Nan as she reached the door. 'Professor Weaver, there's something I have to tell you.'

'Yes,' Nan said unsteadily.

'I want to apologize for my very rigid disapproval of your political activities.'

'My, my,' stammered Nan, 'my political activities?'

What was this woman made of, thought Nan. She surveyed Marjorie's angelic countenance and wondered if the student were crazy. Trauma made some people disassociate from reality.

Nan was sure of only one thing – Marjorie must leave. She must leave before Nan went crazy. Nan must help her to leave.

'Well, yes, I appreciate your concern, Marjorie. But I do have a class now. Perhaps we can talk about it another time?' Nan heard Marjorie's cool, assured tone coming from her own mouth. Not surprising, since Marjorie had written the entire scene, the whole unlikely plot.

Marjorie nodded cordially and was gone. Gone with the languid grace of someone who had never run across a dark campus, her hair flying, her scarf lost.

Ten minutes later, Nan found herself staring at the wall opposite, at a map of Jane Austen's Winchester. She checked her watch and realized she was going to be late for her modern literature class. She had already missed three appointments this week. She was drinking so much brandy late at night that she wasn't completely present at the appointments she did manage to keep. Maybe, after all, she should tell Matt. Otherwise, she might drink herself to death. Surely the genteel Marjorie Adams did not want two deaths on her kid gloves.

So Nan found herself knocking on Matt's door after class. (A very bad session it was, saved only by the students' blessed obsession with course requirements and grades.) When Matt did not answer, Nan felt grateful. Why, she asked herself as she walked down the corridor, why did she need to keep this terrible secret? Was she being self-destructive? Some kind of martyr? She should talk with someone. Amy? No, Amy would think she was mad, would insist on protecting her from herself. Matt was really the only person who would understand, who would talk out the questions of good and bad, of right and wrong with her, who could keep the silence. On the other hand, the more word got out, the more chance it had of leaking and drowning Marjorie Adams.

As she unlocked her office door, the phone was ringing. Marjorie Adams, maybe, asking if they might meet in some dimly lit bar to discuss the finer points of sexual harassment? Matt, maybe, who would get her to confess to what had been bothering her for two weeks. Sometimes during those sleepless early mornings, she wondered if Matt suspected her, suspected the look in her eyes to be fearful guilt rather than the cold weight of someone else's secret.

'Nan,' came an excited voice from the other end, Shirley's voice.
'Nannie, we have some news.'

'Yes,' said Nan, breathlessly switching from one drama to another. Why was she immersed in these two questions of death now? Is this what Francie called karma? If so, Nan knew why she had always distrusted those eastern religions.

'Do they know the trouble with Lisa?'

'No,' said Shirley, almost jubilant, 'but *none* of the tests are positive.'

'Oh, Shirl,' said Nan, and then she, herself, could not continue. The relief came in heavy sobs.

'Oh, now, this is no time for crying.' Shirley had done her weeping at a more appropriate time, earlier during the anxious week. 'And what's more, Lisa is feeling a little better. She'll be home tomorrow.'

'May I invite myself to supper?' asked Nan.

'I was hoping you could make it,'said Shirley. 'Say, are you OK? Your voice sounds kinda tight.'

'Fine,' said Nan, briskly. 'Just fine. And Shirl?'

'Yes?'

'Do you think you could spare time for just the two of us? I have something rather difficult to talk about. I mean, could we go off somewhere for a drink after supper?'

'Sure,' said Shirley with surprise. 'Just the two of us, honey?'

Twelve

'Suicide?' repeated Nan, not loud enough to be overheard in the corridor. Had the police planted the story as a trap? Did everyone know he had been stabbed in the stomach? Perhaps they thought it was hara-kari. She did not want to know any more than she did now.

Matt, always careful, closed the door of his office.

She waited until he sat down, his back to a seventeenth-century print of the River Cam in mid-afternoon. No maudlin dawns or sunsets for Matt, but a subtle three pm light, not unlike the colour of the Berkeley sky this grey January day.

'Shhh,' said Matt. 'I don't think it's come out in the papers or anything. I just heard one of the policemen talking to Augustine about Murchie's depressions.'

Matt stared out his window as he recalled: 'Could it be suicide' had asked the tall cop. And Augustine, who knew the old bull best, had said, 'Yes, he had been quite despondent lately.'

Matt looked back to Nan now, saying, 'Hell, I feel like I'm in a game of Clue. . . .'

'They haven't been around for two or three days,' interrupted Nan, 'the police, I mean?'

'No,' said Matt.

'So they're taking the suicide idea seriously?'

A dozen familiar possibilities collided in Nan's mind. Did Matt suspect that Nan did it, and was he going to offer aid? Did Matt overhear her conversation with Marjorie? Had Matt *himself* committed the murder and. . . So much had happened in the last two weeks that Nan had begun to doubt everything she saw or might have seen on New Year's Eve.

'This is just between us, you understand,' said Matt.

'Yes,' nodded Nan, wondering whether she should stop him.

'Murchie saw me with Enrico in the back corner of Le Croissant – I was giving Rico a little kiss – the week before the murder.'

'Oh, Matt,' said Nan. Then perhaps he *had* done it. No, that was no motive. Besides, Matt had been giving a party.

'And Murchie told Augustine,' said Matt, 'But Augustine came up to me during the New Year's party and said he appreciated my "social discretion". I think he meant my staying in the closet. He said my private life was my own bladedebladedebla.'

'Did Murchie tell anyone else?'

'No, apparently Augustine advised him to keep it quiet. But don't you see, it makes me a . . . at least in Augustine's eyes, I'm a suspect. And who knows what he'll tell the police, in the interests of a thorough investigation? Damn Murchie, he's more trouble dead than he was alive.'

'I've begun to figure that out myself,' Nan said.

They fell silent and stared out Matt's window overlooking Sather Gate. Dozens of students coursed through the ornate arches, the relentlessly healthy blood stream of middle-class America.

As she watched Matt tugging on the edge of his trim beard, she awoke to the fact that he was, after all, her old friend. Of course he hadn't committed the murder – even if he were capable of the gymnastics of leaving his own party, sneaking into Murchie's office and escaping without a trace. Besides, there had been Marjorie's voice and the blonde woman running across the campus, and the scarf.

'Well, look, if they're talking about suicide,' she said, 'then the air will clear of all these awful suspicions.'

'Yes,' nodded Matt, unconvinced.

'That would be two blessings in one,' Nan said brightly.

'Sorry?' asked Matt, cleaning his glasses of imaginary dust.

'Well,' said Nan, 'no one gets arrested and Murchie is dead all the same.'

Her friend looked very uncomfortable.

'Come on, now.' Nan leaned forward confidentially, 'You can't tell me you're not glad the bugger is gone.'

'Quite honestly, Nan,' Matt said, replacing his glasses slowly, 'I'm *not* glad he's dead.'

'I am.'

'Then this office,' he answered hotly, 'better be the only place you admit that.'

'Oh, Matt.'

'I'm serious, Nan.'

'All right,' she said. 'All right.'

'Nan,' said Matt. He looked at her as if he were a stranger. Was he thinking that if she were foolhardy enough to talk like this, she might have been overwrought enough to kill Murchie? He must remember that she hadn't shown up at his party; he must remember her alarm when he had teased her about Murchie on the phone. No, no, he couldn't suspect her. At least not for any longer than she had suspected him.

'Nan,' said this kindly, but distant man, 'you simply can't go around talking like that.'

'Of course you're right, Matt. I guess this has made me a little hysterical.' She realized she wouldn't need to confide about Marjorie now, not if everyone thought it was suicide. Not if everyone were willing to believe it was suicide.

'And something else, old friend,' said Matt, looking more like his former self, intense and affectionate, 'I do think you should drop this sexual harassment bit. . .'

'What?' she gasped.

'Now, with Murchie's death, with your mutual antagonism, well, you need to keep a low profile, Nan, at least until the tenure decision.'

'Tenure,' she snapped. 'I need you to tell me about tenure? A day doesn't go by that I don't think of the self-esteem, the financial security involved in tenure. I suppose you think I should get a good job at the Telephone Company.'

Matt looked puzzled. She ignored this.

'All the work those women put into the campaign, and you expect me to drop out?' demanded Nan, relieved by the surge of anger. She felt clear, clean for the first time all week. 'Why just yesterday *Marjorie Adams* apologized, saying she thought this was an important issue. Marjorie Adams, who has probably never used the word "issue" to refer to anything outside the New Criticism.'

'I don't see how you can be so flip, Nan,' worried Matt.

Flip, was she flip? Yes, perhaps she was feeling a little light-headed. Reckless to mention Marjorie like that.

'Seriously,' Nan went on, 'I don't know how you think we can shelve political movements until convenient times.'

'Convenient,' Matt was angry now. 'Nan, I'm the one who's talking political strategy. Can't you see that the department has had enough, well, enough emotional trauma this term. People will not be receptive . . . People will be *appalled* if you push your campaign now.'

'First of all, it's not my campaign,' said Nan.

'But you're identified as one of. . . .'

'And what does it have to do with Murchie?'

Matt spoke with more grief than exasperation, 'Nan, this issue proves your enmity with Murchie. To put it simply, if people think he committed suicide, you should leave well enough alone.'

'Well enough,' she said, damned if she were going to drop out of a protest that had taken two years to get moving. For all his sensitivity, for all his politics, Matt was still a man. God, she wished Amy were around. What a time for her and Warren to take their second honeymoon.

'Women are being assaulted every day on this campus,' she said, wondering if he understood how much she was leaving unsaid.

Nan watched her friend's knuckles harden over a paperweight, whiter than the snow inside the glass ball, the River Cam during another season.

'Listen, old pal.' Nan's voice was not quite her own, 'We'll have to agree to disagree.'

By 6 pm, she was on the way to Hayward. Usually she hated driving in the dark, but now she didn't notice it. Nothing would equal the darkness of the last week. It felt wonderful to be alone. After that fretful conversation with dear, protective Matt, this ride was feeling positively midsummer.

Suicide, thought Nan, fancy that, our poor guilt-ridden Angus Murchie so contrite about his crimes against woman that he would off himself. The sort of Miltonian morality you might pray for.

Enough of the callous act, she stepped on the accelerator. God, I *am* afraid. For me. For Marjorie. Why can't I bring myself to talk with her about it? The poor woman has probably been raped. All very well that she made a fast alibi and ran off to Matt's party. Quick thinking. But by now she must be writhing with anxiety. What *can* I do? She knows I know. Doesn't she? She knows as much of what I know as I know.

Why was there *nothing* she could do for Marjorie – or for Lisa. At least with Lisa, she was convinced of the diagnosis: Hayward Claustrophobia.

Hayward, she thought, where else can you go nowadays where people talk about neighbourhood spirit, fear of god and improved industrial parks in one conversation? OK. OK. Maybe I'm a snob. Maybe I'm effete and selfish. But I remember years and years as a girl feeling like I was drowning, trying desperately to surface. I had no idea what I'd find at the top, but I knew I couldn't breathe in that atmosphere. I understand what Lisa's going through. I remember the boredom and guilt and anxiety. I know people can suffocate, can die from that depression. Hayward is one thing for Shirley and Joe, who have all their hopes and friends there. But it's quite another for Lisa.

Of course she wouldn't mention Lisa's frustration to Shirley. She wouldn't revive the family feud. She would simply ask if Lisa might recuperate in her flat for a few days, as a change of scene.

'Absolutely not,' Joe said, as Shirley cleared the supper plates. 'You're absolutely not going back to school in that filthy town. Berkeley is probably where you caught this, this, whatever it is.'

'Oh, Dad,' pleaded Lisa. She did look much better than Nan remembered from the previous week, but not quite well enough to wrestle with her 200-pound father.

'Joe, don't you think. . .' Nan began.

Joe cut her off with a glare, proving, perhaps, that Joe did not think.

The whole evening had grown worse and worse, from tension to accusation to this terrible screaming.

'But Dad,' Lisa tried again. 'Dr Bonelli said school was a good idea. It'll keep my mind off things.'

'Your mind just needs a good rest,' said Joe.

'But what'll I do, Dad, sitting home all day?'

'You'll be with your family,' he said, 'where we can keep an eye on you. Don't you remember that a man was murdered on the same floor where your poor aunt has to work? That place is dangerous, Lisa, especially for a delicate girl.'

'Oh, Dad, you make me feel like one of those old German mantle clocks, protected in a crystal dome.'

'Not every girl is as lucky as you, miss, to have a family that really cares, that. . .'

Lisa ran from the room in an uncharacteristic display of temper, slamming the door. Nan considered how Lisa had become more and more irritable this year, dissolving her reputation as sweet young thing.

Shirley followed her daughter, nervously wringing the dish towel. She returned looking frightened. Joe had moved into the living room and turned on the TV too loudly.

'Nan,' Shirley said finally, 'I do believe you promised me a drink.' Her voice was tired, bearing none of the usual cheerfulness. 'And all night long I've been thinking about those Kalúa Coma Comas that they do down at the Pelican Bay. How about it, sister?'

Nan had forgotten her desperate invitation of yesterday afternoon. Yes, she had planned to tell her sister. Tell her what? That Marjorie Adams had committed suicide on Angus Murchie? There was no longer any need for this sisterly confidence. No need for herself. Nan remembered the betrayal she had felt when, as a teenager, she had started keeping secrets from Mom.

The Pelican Bay was considerably more swanky than seven years before when they had come here to celebrate Nan's new job at Berkeley. Sweet, sentimental Shirley. Clearly, she was prepared for a long, intimate talk.

But what could Nan tell her? Still no new lovers. Nothing definite about the job. The menopause hadn't arrived yet. A few headaches, but nothing serious.

'I hope things are OK at work,' said Shirley, as they slid into the coral naughahyde booth with a view of the San Leandro Marina.

Nan peered at the night, a quarter moon shimmering against the whitecaps, a few stars visible in the overcast sky. During the day, this was a salt water bog. But the night brought a flattering vagueness. And you could see most of the San Francisco skyline.

'Work is hectic,' said Nan, in a stalling-for-time tone, 'but the first week is always like this.'

The young waitress, bound in white satin and black net, handed them huge drink menus in the shape of pelicans.

Shirley, sensing Nan's disapproval, put her hand on her sister's arm and said, 'Now, Nan, we're here to relax.'

'Of course you're right,' agreed Nan. She read the list of rich cocktails: Chocolate Brandita, Bananacreamo, Tequila Fruitarama, and her stomach curdled. This reminded her of going to Gorman's Ice Cream Parlor with Shirley when they were kids. She hoped her sister wouldn't think her élitist for just ordering a brandy.

Shirley didn't even notice the order. Rather she was examining Nan's face. 'Now tell me, hon, what's on your mind?'

Nan took a long sniff of brandy and gazed out at the shadowy shapes of sailboats rocking in their moorings on the rough January bay. What could she tell Shirley to warrant all this secrecy and confidence? Not about Marjorie, but about Lisa.

'Lisa and I are not planning to be around for the Fourth of July,' said Nan, trying hard to avoid what she really wanted to say about Lisa.

Shirley dropped her straw in mid-slurp.

'We're thinking of going off to India and Nepal for a long trip next summer. Sounds exciting, eh?'

'India?' said Shirley.

'The Himalayas. I have a friend in the department, you've heard me talk about Matt, anyway, he went there last year. Pretty inexpensively. Once you get the plane fare out of the way, you can move around India very cheaply.'

'India,' Shirley said again.

'I want you to know that this isn't just a game to get her mind off the illness,' said Nan. 'I really mean it.'

'I'm sure you do,' laughed Shirley. She took a long drink of her Coma Coma and then asked, 'But India? Isn't it awfully crowded and hot?'

'Not in the Himalayas,' smiled Nan, 'not any more so than Southland Shopping Mall.'

'Do you really think she's going to be OK?' Shirley asked abruptly. 'Oh, please, god, she's OK.'

'I'm sure of it,' said Nan. 'As sure as I am of anything right now.'

'But what do you think it is?' asked Shirley. 'None of those tests. . .'

'Emotional, Shirley, something emotional, I'm *sure* of it.'

'In that case,' Shirley hesitated, 'this family tug-of-war is doing Lisa no good.'

Nan stared hard at her, wondering whether those were Joe's words, then feeling ashamed. Sometimes she gave Shirley no credit.

'Of course you're right,' said Nan, meaning nothing in particular, but longing to be closer to her sister.

'Then you'll stop pulling her back to school this term?' asked Shirley.

'The girl does need her own life,' said Nan.

'But she's hardly *been alive* this last month,' said Shirley. 'She's exhausted, can't sleep, eats poorly.'

Yes, Nan wanted to say, can't you see that Joe is killing your daughter with these demands. And then she thought about herself. Was she also killing Lisa? First Murchie and now Lisa. It was too much to think about. She noticed that Shirley was close to tears.

'I know she's growing away from us,' Shirley was saying.

Nan thought about Lisa's last birthday. She had asked for a

portable typewriter but Shirley had given her a reconditioned sewing machine. Of course she agreed Lisa should trade it in for a typewriter. Of course. Whatever she found more useful.

'Remember,' said Shirley, 'I've been through this one before. She's a lot like you when you was a kid, Nannie.'

Nan nodded, embarrassed and guilty, as if she had seduced Lisa with some genetic mirror.

'Nan, she'll leave us as sure as you did. I just want to make sure she's well enough to go.'

'Maybe she *should* drop school this quarter,' Nan murmured. 'But do let her come out to my apartment for a visit, to recuperate for a few days.'

Nan smiled encouragingly at Shirley.

Yes, nodded Shirley, Lisa would come for a visit. On this the sisters agreed to agree.

Thirteen

Winter Quarter always moved slowly. Everyone was depressed by the weather and still suffering from the torpor of bloated holiday bellies. Nan looked out the window of her classroom.

One of the more long-winded students (a bright woman, but verbose) intoned about incest and inspiration in Bloomsbury. 'Vanessa Bell's paintings were. . .'

Morning rain again, Nan noticed. January and now February presented impermeable grey. Streets lines with stubs of trees. And an early dark, much too early for those who would lie sleepless until after midnight. All possibilities seemed closer to Nan. Winter was a season for snuggling families or pensive solitude. But she had no heart for such satisfactions. She felt her soul was camped in a large, empty waiting room. What was she waiting for? Perhaps the official police wrap-up on Murchie's death. There had been delays on delays of the coroner's report.

The student continued, 'Few people give adequate credit to Vanessa's visual influence on Virginia's lyrical. . .'

Nan noticed that the old room with its dusty fluorescent lights and peeling ceiling seemed particularly stuffy this morning. The students looked alert, engaged, and Nan momentarily let herself feel the excitement and satisfaction of seminar teaching.

Nan gazed out the large window again. Waiting. She was also waiting for Lisa. Poor kid never did make that trip to Berkeley. She had returned to Memorial Hospital for two weeks. Anaemia. One of the things they were considering was anaemia. And when she was released, she was spent. Lisa looked paler than Nan had ever felt in Africa. She had grown so much thinner. Her skin was almost translucent, barely covering the delicate bones of her face. The doctors still did not know what was wrong, and wanted to keep her under observation like some prodigal astronaut.

'Don't you agree, Professor Weaver?' Nan focussed on a student at the back of the room, a woman with long, black hair and bright eyes who did all the readings and submitted her papers on time.

Nan looked around the class, twenty faces staring at her, waiting for her, demanding of her . . . She relished their eagerness. Usually, she flourished on it.

'Would you repeat that?' she heard herself say. She had spaced out several times lately, luckily only once in each class. Today she was fading in the middle of a seminar discussion of. . .what was it today, oh, yes, Virginia Woolf's essays on criticism. She had to 'get her act together' as Lisa would say. She had planned the class thoroughly. All the hand-outs and readings were prepared last quarter. She loved the topic. The course had an excellent reputation on campus. But, she must not keep coasting like this. She must wake up. And now she heard herself asking,

'Do you remember what Woolf says in the Hogarth Press pamphlet – that writers should consult critics, the way patients consult doctors, without the public looking on. . .'

Their faces brightened; each looked eager in her own way to jump in and argue. Nan promised herself to stay awake, to pay attention, to be a good teacher. After all, she liked teaching. She liked being a good teacher. This was her life. If she didn't get tenure, she would find somewhere else to teach. In her home, perhaps. These twenty women could squeeze into her studio if most of them sat on the floor. Sometimes she had dreams of a feminist literary institute. Dreams, she reminded herself, were for the night.

'That's about all we have time for today,' she said, over the grudging sighs of her students. 'See you Thursday.'

When Nan reached the fourth floor of Wheeler, she was relieved no one was waiting outside her door. Just a couple of notes (one from a student, another in persistent Claude's florid handwriting) tacked to her bulletin board. And a *Daily Cal*. She quickly let herself into the office, locked the door and sat down to read the student newspaper.

SEXUAL HARASSMENT CAMPAIGN
REACHES CHANCELLOR'S COMMITTEE

A campaign against sexual harassment has now garnered 5000 signatures and will be the first order of business tomorrow at the Chancellor's Advisory Committee.

The campaign, run by students and teachers from across

campus, was started two years ago by Nan Weaver, Assistant Professor of English. It. . .

Two words burned from the page: 'Assistant Professor', a term meaning 'academic without tenure'. A teacher up for losing her job. All the old fears of being penniless, jobless, a failure, welled up inside her. Of course Mom had been right about the Telephone Company. She stopped herself. Why was she so timid? Why couldn't she read victory in this article? They had all worked on the campaign for two years. Five thousand students and professors were now involved in this vital issue, and all Nan could think about was losing her job.

The phone interrupted her worries. Gratefully, she picked it up.

'Hello, pet,' came Matt's voice. 'I see you've made the headlines.'

'What do you think of it?' Nan was remembering Matt's warnings last month, wondering now if she should have listened to her prudent friend.

'I think you're a brave woman.'

'But how do you think the committee will vote?'

'Are you asking if they'll send you to the guillotine?'

'Something like that.'

'Well, I can't vote,' he answered. 'But I can take you to lunch afterwards.'

'Can't do lunch; gotta save that for my campaign sisters.'

'Dinner then?'

'How about dinner if we win and drinks if we lose,' suggested Nan. 'Lots of drinks.'

'You've got it, friend,' said Matt.

The next evening, Matt drove Nan to a celebratory dinner at the Pogo Cafe in the Castro District of San Francisco.

'So this is your idea of victory?' Nan asked ruefully. 'The Chancellor sets up a faculty committee to consider setting up a grievance procedure: some bureaucratic victory!'

'What did you expect?' laughed Matt. 'Mass castration? Of course it's victory. They took the complaint seriously for the first time. They're developing a policy.'

'You'd make the perfect English Civil Servant,' said Nan in exasperation. They were approaching the Bay Bridge. She would change her tone. She really did appreciate Matt's loyalty. 'So tell me about this restaurant we're going to.'

'Well, the Pogo is a kind of camp, punk rock cafe,' Matt explained. 'And aside from admiring their salads, I must admit to a small crush on one of the waiters, a Scandinavian guy from the Midwest who has done the *definitive* dissertation on David Hockney. Knut is determined to get a teaching job here in the Bay Area. And, well, hmmm, this is Knut's third year at the Pogo Cafe.'

This news didn't cheer up Nan at all. What would she do next year when she lost her teaching job? Certainly restaurants were no option. When she was sixteen, she had been fired from the Palace of Pancakes on Foothill Boulevard for putting too much butter on the waffles. One of the many times when Mom's lessons in generosity backfired.

From the ceiling of the Pogo Cafe hung mannequin arms and legs, painted green and purple. Over by the kitchen, a grotesque head of Sir Francis Drake was stuck on the bare branch of a potted palm. Patti Smith screamed from the loudspeaker. Nan would suggest that they go somewhere else for drinks afterward. Somewhere cosy and quiet. Somewhere outside the context of such nightmares which captured her few hours of sleep.

Knut walked over and took their order with a red sequined pen. He was a tall, handsome young man who revealed an easy sense of humour as he flirted with Matt. Nan tried to concentrate on his healthy face and on Matt's delighted gaze to distract herself from the surrounding grotesquerie. The tortured limbs reminded her of tales Sister Anna Peter used to tell about Romans persecuting Christians. Be prepared to die for the faith, Sister Anna Peter had instructed them. Sometimes lately, Nan felt she might be willing to die in exchange for faith, if god would only grant some order to the craziness of the last four weeks. Had Angus Murchie been prepared to die for his lusts? With all her imagination, Nan could never understand how they could call it suicide with his pants down like that. Was Marjorie Adams prepared to die for her self-defence? How could Nan even pretend to lead a normal life until suspicions were settled? What else could she do? As Knut left the scene, Matt turned back to her.

'Marjorie Adams seems to be getting along with you these days,' he began.

'How do you mean?' asked Nan, startled that her friend had learned to read minds. She took a long drink of ice water and stalled to catch her wits.

'Well, first she apologised for her political insults, and then you

102

told me she actually joined the SHC. Didn't I see her circulating a petition last week?'

'That did surprise me,' said Nan, but not wanting to sound intimate with Marjorie Adams, she added, 'Now all she needs to do is wash her face.'

'Nan,' smiled Matt. 'There's nothing wrong with a little make-up. What a Puritan you are! In England the punks – and I'm referring to the *men* – wear make-up. I've always fancied myself in a little green eye shadow.'

'Oh, you'd be exquisite,' said Nan. 'But you'd be wearing it for fun. Marjorie does it because she thinks she has to, to objectify herself.'

'Whoa now,' said Matt. 'Aren't you exaggerating a mite? Marjorie would have men flying after her, even if she wore a mask, just because of that gorgeous Rapunzel hair.'

That Rapunzel hair, thought Nan. How many times in the last four weeks had she dreamt about that Rapunzel hair! Gold thread through the black night. Yellow cloud floating over the dark campus. How often had she waited for Marjorie to come to the office and cry off her midnight blue mascara? How many days had she expected Marjorie to confess the murder, the self-defence, the fear? And how many nights had she lain awake, haunted by the image of Rapunzel's escape?

'Don't take it so seriously,' said Matt. 'Marjorie isn't such a tough cookie. The make-up is her covering for shyness.'

'Shyness!' exploded Nan. 'Come on now, she carries that upper-crust Eastern poise like a tiara.'

'And not very different from the shyness of someone else I know,' said Matt. 'Plenty of people would deny that you're shy. They'd say you're quite a dragon lady.'

'That's different,' Nan began.

Before she could finish, Matt was distracted by the approaching of gorgeous Knut, carrying huge California salads, overflowing with avocado, bean sprouts, tomatoes. Clearly, he had provided well for his friends. The Pogo Cafe was abundantly more generous than the Palace of Pancakes.

When Knut was out of earshot, Matt confessed, 'You know, I'm ready for a good, long romance now.'

'You?' teased Nan. 'What happened to your principles of non-monogamy? What about the "fluidness" of picking up a new man every night? What about Enrico?'

'Enrico, dear man, is only interested in passing ships,' said Matt wistfully. 'I'd like something more serious. I don't mean a husband and a white picket fence. But I wouldn't mind a little long-term infatuation.'

Nan nodded, trying to be sympathetic.

'You're not convinced,' said Matt, stabbing a tomato. 'You don't believe I can be faithful.'

'No, no, it's not that,' said Nan, sounding tired. 'But sometimes this emphasis on sex seems so, so authoritarian. If you're not in love, you're supposed to be looking. And once you find someone to desire, there's always the question of whether you're monogamous or polygamous or celibate. Do you know that one of my favourite students turned in a paper last week entitled, "Celibacy as a Political Option in Feminist Fiction".'

'Nan,' Matt spoke tentatively, 'are you sure that this sexual harassment thing isn't making you a little, well, a little cynical?'

'Oh, the old "feminist as prude" theory?' she exclaimed.

'My dear, you're the last person I'd call prudish. "Passionate" is more like it. Passionate about everything.'

'You know I've been in love since Charles,' said Nan. 'Four years with Tony. Lots of flings – some more far flung than others.'

Matt nodded.

'And, recently, I've realized that I did love Charles once upon a time. It was love. Then we grew apart.'

Matt nodded again, waiting.

'But sex is over-rated.' Nan picked up a fork, turned it over. 'Sometimes it's great fun. Sometimes it's boring. Sometimes you feel like it. Sometimes you don't. Can we leave it like that? Listen, Matt, I'm delighted that you're in love this month. But that doesn't mean I have to be.'

'Oh, you're just disappointed that there's no one in the cafe who appeals to you,' teased Matt. 'Just you wait. I'll phone you next Sunday morning and you'll answer, absolutely breathless from love-making with Claude.'

'No,' said Nan. 'I'll be *enjoying* my own company. Besides,' she grinned, 'I don't answer the phone when I'm making love.'

Matt shook his head in surrender.

Nan continued vehemently. 'And I won't be missing the struggle about whose house I'm sleeping at, whether to pack two days' worth of clothes to take with me, whether the "other person" is "into" watching TV or fucking or talking. I won't miss worrying how long the romance is going to last, whether I should be meeting new people, whether I'm leading someone on. I'll know that when the coffee grinder is gungy, it's my gunge. When the bathtub is un-washed, it's my toe jam. And I can play my records any time of the day or night.'

'OK,' said Matt. 'As you like it. You always were more practical than I. Sometimes your life seems a model of self-sufficiency.'

'I'm not saying I *won't* fall in love again,' warned Nan. 'It's just that *right now* I don't need it.'

'What do you need?' he asked.

'I need my students to learn something,' said Nan, thoughtfully. 'I want the women in my classes to gain confidence. I need my family and friends to love me.'

'Speaking of family,'' said Matt, who was almost finished with his Pacifica Celebration Salad, 'how's Lisa?'

'The same,' Nan stared disconsolately at her plate. She felt naus-eated by the profusion of green, green vegetation and full of horror that anything might grow so lush. 'But the Memorial Hospital was enough to make anyone ill.'

'She's out now?'

'Yes, for a while,' Nan shook her head. 'Until she has a relapse. She does look better. But she's been at Shirley's throat. It's as if the illness brought out a lifetime of anger about being confined in Hayward. Anyway, the family agreed that she could come visit me in Berkeley for a few days.'

Nan closed her eyes now. She wondered if having another body in the house, one used to nocturnal hibernation, might cure her of insomnia.

Matt looked concerned. 'Maybe we should skip the drink tonight. You seem ready for bed.'

'Yes,' said Nan. 'Probably so.'

After effusive goodbyes to Knut the Handsome, they left the Pogo Cafe. On the drive back over the bridge, Nan and Matt chatted randomly about Knut, the Chancellor's meeting, the mood in the English Department, Murchie's death, Nan's family. Some-times Nan thought that Matt would be the best husband she'd ever find — thoughtful, sensitive, honest. Anything was easy with him. She could say anything, ask anything she wanted. Well, almost anything. There was still one question that haunted her. How could the police believe it was suicide if Murchie was found with his pants down?

Fourteen

They all received their subpoenas on the same day, Nan later found out. Hammerly, Augustine, Matt, Millie, herself and five others from the department had been called before the Grand Jury of Alameda County.

Matt brought in a newspaper describing the investigation of Murchie's death and they sat in Nan's office pouring over the yellow columns together.

Grand Jury. Nan remembered zilch from elementary American civics. Grand Jury. She had images from an old George Raft film. Memories of Jessica Mitford refusing to cooperate with the House Unamerican Activities Committee.

The San Francisco Chronicle reported twenty-five people would be interviewed over the next couple of weeks. It was very unusual to call a Grand Jury for a routine suicide, but, as the *Chronicle* article revealed, Murchie's cousin-in-law was an Assistant District Attorney. Probably not a man to believe in suicide with the pants down.

Nan wasn't the only person alarmed. The following morning when the faculty met in the large committee room, Hammerly arrived fuming.

'Really,' he stiffened. 'This is too much. Can't they let the man die in peace and leave the rest of us to our work?'

Augustine, Murchie's friend, was silent, frowning.

'It would be one thing to have a homicidal maniac in our midst,' Hammerly continued, nervously now as everyone watched him. 'But it was a suicide, wasn't it?' He looked to Augustine who remained silent.

'Really,' said Hammerly again. 'We must be allowed to *work*. The department could disintegrate around us. We have responsibilities. . .'

'Such as filling his position,' said Augustine bitterly.

'Quite uncalled for,' said Hammerly, whose Princeton friend had

106

become one of the prime candidates.

'Gentlemen, please,' called Nelson, in his most chairpersonly tone.

'Well, it's damn annoying,' flushed Hanson, 'I don't mean any disrespect. These "investigations" might be useful if I were teaching the development of the mystery novel. However, I'm in the middle of writing a paper about Celtic myth and trying to direct three dissertations on Yeats.'

Matt smiled, almost imperceptibly, at Nan. He raised his dark eyebrows over the tortoise rims of his glasses. Nan nodded abruptly.

'The best approach,' she heard herself saying (she was staring at Hammerly because he sat on the opposite side of the room from Marjorie Adams), 'the best approach is to regard the investigation as an interesting experience. It's an inconvenience, to be sure, but little more trouble than that. No one seriously believes that anybody here committed murder.'

Murder. It was the first time the word had been uttered among them all. Shivering imperceptibly from the silence, Nan looked from Hammerly's impatient eyes to Hanson's red face to Augustine's rigid jaw. Each man was staring at her.

Finally Matt broke the tension. 'Nan's right,' he said with a trace of nervousness. 'It will be over in a few weeks. Let's try to bear with it.'

The corridors were quiet for the rest of the week. Eerie, as if they were threaded with an invisible string laid to trip criminals or ghosts. Everyone communicated from the corners of their eyes. The few greetings exchanged were subject to the closest scrutiny. Did everyone suspect everyone?

Everyone, except perhaps Marjorie Adams. Marjorie had not been called to testify. Still, Nan doubted whether this exemption would make her feel safe. Marjorie must be having the same need as Nan for the relief of talking to another person. Yet, neither woman would start the inevitable conversation.

And then one day Nan broke down, despite all her plans to let Marjorie speak first. (Best to keep quiet, she told herself. Quiet enough that Marjorie might forget. Quiet enough that Nan might learn nothing more to conceal from the Grand Jury.) But one day the silent, lonely corridors of Wheeler Hall became indistinguishable to Nan from that silent, lonely madhouse she had inhabited for the last six months of her marriage. So, when Marjorie arrived to discuss power and love in Iris Murdoch, Nan said,

'Marjorie, you were a reader in Professor Murchie's class last quarter, weren't you?'

'Yes,' said Marjorie quickly, as if to keep the admission from sticking to her crimson lipstick.

'In fact,' said Nan, 'I think I recall seeing you in his office several times during that last week.' She didn't want to push Marjorie. She just wanted to offer the opening.

'That's quite possible,' said Marjorie, with more detachment than Nan expected.

'So you must feel particularly upset about his death,' Nan tried again.

Marjorie was frowning, on the verge of tears?

That's it, thought Nan, let it out.

'Do you think it's affecting my work?' Marjorie asked.

'Oh, no,' said Nan, taken aback. 'No, your work is fine.'

'Then if you don't mind,' said Marjorie politely, 'I would prefer not to discuss the matter.' She opened her notebook. 'I do appreciate your concern.'

'Of course,' said Nan. 'Of course.' Matt was right about Marjorie being shy. Shy or frightened. Or one tough cookie, thought Nan. She was at once amazed by Marjorie's resistance and saddened by the overwhelming loneliness bred by such tenacity.

The Grand Jury met the following Friday, the seventh week of the quarter, February 22, at the Alameda County Courthouse, Oakland, from 7.00–10.00 pm.

As Nan and her attorney Amy climbed the stone steps to the white, 1930s edifice, Nan was suddenly visited with optimism. The last time she walked into this building, thirteen years before, she was a middle-aged radical, eager to claim divorce from the bourgeois Dr Charles Woodward. (No alimony, she had said, just let me out of the confinement and boredom of this marriage. Mental cruelty, ruled the judge. Nan knew that each had been cruel to the other. Each was guilty. Just let me out, she had said. And they did.) Now she was back with the same lawyer and her own name, Dr Nan Weaver.

'Just remember,' Amy was bearing down on her for the third time. 'Don't answer anything tricky until you've come out in the corridor and checked it with me.'

Nan noticed that Amy was wearing her tweedy attorney suit that evening. Years before, at the beginning of her career, Amy had believed being a feminist lawyer required blue jeans. In those days she was still flaunting her youth in the Brooklyn projects, still playing rough kid. Since then, Amy had accepted the tactical advantage of observing dress code.

'Right,' said Nan, smoothing a hand along her skirt. She was suddenly overcome with fear. Fear about being in this institution, fear about being a suspect. She winced, remembering the fear on Murchie's face as he lay dying.

Nan focussed on her friend again. 'I'll imagine you're my translator, and I can't understand a word of what they're saying.'

'Don't feel nervous,' Amy put her arm over Nan's shoulder. 'The DA is really an ass. He can't cause you any *serious* trouble.'

'I don't know about that,' said Nan, checking her watch, 'Angus Murchie was an ass and he caused quite a lot of trouble.'

As they turned the corner of the courtroom, they saw Matt sitting on a bench, sipping a cup of vending machine coffee.

'Matt,' Nan called, 'what are you doing here? You're not due on stage until nine o'clock.'

'Oh, you know me,' he said, nodding greeting to Amy, 'phobic about tardiness. Besides, I thought you might like a little comradeship.'

'Matt,' Nan kissed him on the cheek, 'you *are* a prize friend.'

'Better watch that,' he winked and wiped off her kiss. 'People might get the wrong idea.'

'Miss Weaver?' chirped a small, elderly man, who did not look unlike a scrub jay that Nan found hopping on her balcony last week.

'Yes,' she said, 'I am Dr Nan Weaver.'

'Oh, beg your pardon, Doctor,' he lisped as he checked his clipboard. 'Well, Doctor, the jury is ready for you now.' The elderly court clerk emanated an aura of wintergreen. Nan realised later, during the hour of questioning, that he didn't have a lisp, but was sucking a lifesaver, one of a series he was to consume with discretion.

Nan found nothing very grand about this jury of housewives and business managers. Italian knits and plaid sports jackets. Most of the jury looked as uncomfortable as she felt, all there out of some vague sense of civic duty or some vaguer sense of ennui. But were they frightened? Could they smell her own fear?

Nan was surprised by the ordinariness of the small, stuffy courtroom. Against one wall were filing cabinets and a table piled with telephone books. Dusty venetian blinds shut out the moon and the

skyline of downtown Oakland. Where was the dignity she antici-
pated? The power? This felt more like a library binding room than a
court. The one thing which captured her attention was the display
board, drawn with an outline of a man's body and marked with an
'X' over the stomach. The body was much skinnier than Murchie's.
How many layers of flab did Marjorie have to thrust through, Nan
wondered. From where did her strength come? How small was the
gut? Nan shook herself back to attention.

'How long did you know Angus Murchie?' the Assistant DA
asked. He was fair, lanky and rather pretty, much as Nan
remembered his second cousin, Laura Murchie, now the widow of
Angus.

The questions seemed easy enough, so she didn't bother to check
with Amy.

'Seven years.'

'I respected much of Professor Murchie's academic work.'

'We were not close friends.'

'Yes, we disagreed on certain political issues, as did many of our
colleagues.'

'I spent New Year's Eve with my family in Hayward.'

'No, I haven't any idea who would want to harm Professor
Murchie.'

After the testimony, Nan and Amy waited for Matt and his lawyer in
a small bar which smelled as if they brewed beer on the spot. The
rest of the witnesses would be called the next week, explained Amy,
and then, if the DA were smart, he'd bury the case.

'That was just a show,' she said, 'a token to the family. And if he
doesn't catch some bait soon, he'll have to drop the whole thing.
The Grand Jury isn't meant to investigate homicide.'

'You mean that's it?' asked Nan, feeling strangely let down, too
tense from her testimony to be relieved. 'We don't have to return
for another torture test?'

'Not unless something extraordinary happens,' said Amy.

Is that all there is, Nan wondered. Yes. Peggy Lee was singing 'Is
That All There Is?' inside her head. Well, maybe. Maybe Amy was
right. And maybe she, herself, had been right about keeping
Marjorie's secret. She could keep it for another week. And then it
would be all over. Wouldn't it?

'He'll have to drop the whole thing,' Amy repeated with a confidence which sounded only slightly forced.

110

Shirley's birthday seemed a month early; everything was happening at a different speed this year. All day Friday Nan looked forward to the party in the big yellow house. Commotion would be welcome after the brittle politeness of Wheeler Hall. She would feel easier in Hayward, safer.

Nan arrived to find Shirley cooking alone in the kitchen. Joe was singing in the shower; Nan tried very hard not to hear the lyrics. The boys hadn't shown up yet, and Lisa had run down to the Safeway for more beer and Coke. Shirley told her sister to sit down while she basted the chicken.

'What's this, cooking on your own birthday,' demanded Nan. 'I though that everyone was *bringing* the meal.'

'They are, they are,' reassured Shirley. She straightened her apron over the rose muu muu. 'Now relax, Nan. I'm just doing the roast and a few veggies.'

'Shirley!' exclaimed Nan.

'Well, the girls are bringing desserts and Lisa made a salad,' acknowledged Shirley.

'And Joe and the boys?' demanded Nan.

'Now, Nan, they've been working all day, the same as you.'

Nan was irritated by this gentle admonishment. Most irritated with herself. What had she prepared? Nothing. The two bottles of champagne she brought weren't even a very grand expense for a single person on her salary.

She walked over to the sink and rolled up her sleeves. The least she could do was wash and chop the broccoli.

Family, thought Nan, what on earth drew her to these people? Matt's family sounded equally nerve-racking. But they were bright, professional people who had interesting conversations between the guilt-tripping. Many families exploded in violent fights. Nan would have preferred that, would have appreciated some excitement. So what was her bond with these people who bored and enraged her and touched her by turns? She didn't know. If another civil war started, they would be on opposite sides. Yet, she knew Shirley and Joe would give her sanctuary and that she would do the same for them. Well, at least for Shirley.

'Now, Nannie,' Shirley was saying as she tied an apron around her sister. 'I want this to be a *peaceful* evening. I don't want people stirring up things.'

Nan noticed the way Shirley said 'people', as if she were referring to outside agitators.

111

'OK,' said Nan. 'It's your birthday, sweetie. I promise I'll behave. Cross my heart.'

Shirley wrapped her ample arms around Nan and gave her the sort of embrace Mom used to dispense when she said, 'You're both my girls, different enough, but you'll always be each other's sisters.'

Suddenly the commotion began – and didn't stop for four hours. First, the arrival of Tom and Bob and Lynda and Debbie. Debbie was 'showing', as Shirley called it, a good three inches. The next generation. They all walked into the kitchen with a chorus of 'Happy Birthday to You'.

'Enough,' laughed Shirley. 'Enough silliness. Pour yourselves some beer and go relax in the living room. Daddy will be out of the shower in a minute.'

'In less than a minute, my little butterball,' said Joe, pinching his wife on the ass, then hugging her.

Nan felt the same uncomfortable urge she had had twenty-five years before, to pry his arms apart and rescue her sister. In the intervening time, she had come to admit that Shirley was happy, that Joe was a decent man, that they lived in a different world with different choices. But she did wish Joe wouldn't act as if he owned Shirley.

Perhaps reading her mind, or at least chastened by the expression on her face, he said convivially, 'And how is the prettiest professor west of the Rockies?'

'Fine, Joe, fine,' said Nan. I will behave, she said to herself. I will behave.

'So how does it feel to be a Grand Jury witness?' he went on.

'Happy that the interview is over,' said Nan, hoping to detour the conversation.

'We were worried about you,' said Shirley, her eyes watchful. 'It's so scary, thinking there's a murderer on the loose.'

'Ah, Nan can take care of herself,' said Bob, 'She's a smart broad.'

'Who are you?' asked Lisa as she walked in, 'Humphrey Bogart, Jr? Watch your sexist language, brother.'

Shirley looked at Nan. Nan shrugged, then smiled quickly to Lisa. Lisa put up two fingers in the old peace sign.

'Pax familias and all that jazz,' said Lisa.

'Amen,' said Nan, touched by this unanimous complicity to celebrate Shirley's birthday peacefully.

Each of them made an effort to observe the evening the way

Shirley wanted it. Friendly and low key. Conversation was restricted to family memories – Christmases, birthdays, vacations.

One thing they did not discuss tonight was Lisa's illness. Lupus, thought Nan, staring at her niece across the dinner table. It could be Lupus. Or just anaemia. Or tension. They did not talk about it. But privately this evening, Lisa had whispered to Nan that she would be back in school spring quarter. And, later, in the kitchen, Shirley had confided to her sister that Lisa's vacation from college next quarter would do her the world of good.

Those lines from *To The Lighthouse* crossed Nan's mind again, 'And Rose would grow up and Rose would suffer so. . . Choose me a shawl, for that would please Rose who was bound to suffer so.'

After dinner, Nan looked around the oak table at Lynda, Tom, Debbie, Bob, Lisa, Joe and Shirley, wondering again what bound her to them. It was more than years. Tonight she had again noticed with pleasure how much Lisa resembled her. The high cheekbones, the deep hazel eyes. Also the gestures – the tense strength in her jaw, the wide-awake way she listened to people. And Shirley – with every visit Shirley reminded Nan more of Mom. Nan could not keep her eyes off Debbie's stomach. She had even bent down to feel the kicking and hiccoughing of the forthcoming generation. Would the high cheekbones and the hazel eyes survive? How much of Nan would be passed on?

Lynda brought in the cake. Lisa and Tom carried the presents. Shirley could barely sit still while the others served. Her skin was slightly pink from the champagne, and her eyes were moist.

'Ah, Mom,' teased Tom, 'you're not going to cry.'

'Oh, no,' Shirley began, 'not at all. . .'

'You leave her cry if she wants,' said Joe.

'It's my birthday and I'll cry if I want to,' sang Lisa.

'Oh, enough of this,' laughed Shirley, 'enough!'

Nan watched, smiling. Inside her smile she wondered whether Shirley was a person, distinguishable from her family. An individual. Then she wondered if perhaps Shirley hadn't made a better choice than her own – about individuality, about loneliness.

On the way home, Nan confided to Isadora how different her own birthdays were. She had spent the last three August 24ths dining with Matt at Chez Panisse. 'Much as I love the escargots and the pâté,' she confessed, 'it's not the same as a Hayward party.'

How had Nan and Shirley grown so far apart? They were equally bright; brought up by the same mother's love. Nan knew her sister would do anything to save her life – give up a kidney, fight for her place in the fallout shelter – even though they irrevocably disagreed on the purpose of that life.

'Enough sentimentality,' Nan scolded and turned on the radio. Then she heard herself whispering, 'You know, Isadora, if I ever tell the real story of New Year's Eve, it will be in that living room in Hayward.'

Fifteen

Amy told Nan not to worry. She spoke with clear, lawyer's confidence. At least one other person from the English Department had been called back by the Grand Jury, she had learned. The DA probably had no further evidence, but he had to make this last show of thoroughness.

At first, Nan hoped that the other witness might be Matt. They could support each other, talk it over afterwards. Afterwards. How Nan longed for afterwards. But the other witness wasn't Matt. Nor was it Hammerly, nor Augustine. She wouldn't ask further. No sense advertising her appearance before the entire faculty. Testifying to the Grand Jury wasn't the kind of consulting that won you tenure points.

Amy assured her that it would be a brief appearance, that it would all be over Thursday evening. Nan was relieved because Lisa was arriving on Saturday. She wouldn't bother to tell Shirley about the Grand Jury, no use worrying her for nothing.

As Nan and Amy reached the third floor of the courthouse that evening, Nan spotted a familiar figure walking away from them.

'Mr Johnson,' she called, half in surprise, half in greeting. She was reassured to see someone she knew.

Mr Johnson turned slowly and raised his hand in response. 'Hello, there,' he began.

Then the attorney, a large black man, pulled down Mr Johnson's arm and ushered him along the corridor.

Inside the stuffy courtroom, Nan regarded the now familiar faces of the Alameda County Grand Jury. During the last week she had often wondered about them, wondered what kind of job the thin, older woman had, how many children the red-haired man had. She felt easier with them now, not completely comfortable, but more *familiar*, the way you get used to strangers on a long train ride.

When she looked around at the faces, she expected a reciprocal familiarity, but found, instead, a formal coldness. She tried to ignore this by imagining them as nervous students on the first day of class.

Some of the questions were the same as last week.

So were the answers.

'I spent New Year's Eve with my family in Hayward,' said Nan, thinking of civil war sanctuaries and borrowed kidneys.

Then the District Attorney's mouth hardened; his voice seemed to come from somewhere else, as if he were a ventriloquist's dummy.

'We have other evidence, Miss Weaver,' he said.

Nan could not imagine where he had got his 'other evidence'. So, instead, she wondered how she could get him to call her *Dr* Weaver.

Of course she had nothing to fear, she told herself. She had committed no crime. Well, perhaps she had withheld evidence. But they couldn't give her the death penalty for that.

'I said, Miss Weaver, that we have other evidence,' the DA repeated.

'Oh, do you?' answered Nan with more indifference than she thought she could muster from her fevered body.

'Someone has testified to seeing you at Wheeler Hall the night of the murder, Miss Weaver.'

Nan's eyes had that faraway look that Lisa's often got. She wasn't too far away, actually, just out in the corridor watching Mr Johnson walk jerkily away from her. So he *had* been at Wheeler Hall all night. He had seen her light under the door earlier that evening. Of course he would be asked to testify. He might even be a suspect. Everyone knew that Angus Murchie had once referred to the quiet, omnipresent Mr Johnson as 'the Big Black Shadow'. One of the professor's unfortunate alcoholic slips.

Nan imagined that Mr Johnson's good lawyer had advised him, 'This is no time to protect her. You've got a family of your own. And a white woman has extra defences. Don't you be a fool, Clarence Johnson. Don't you go putting yourself on the line for some white woman professor.' The black man against the feminist, thought Nan, a final irony Murchie might have enjoyed.

'We would like to know a little more about the whole evening, Miss Weaver,' said the DA. 'Did you see Professor Murchie?'

Nan requested a chance to leave the room and consult with her attorney. 'Consult' was a difficult word, since she had told Amy

116

nothing about New Year's Eve. The fewer people who knew, the better, she reminded herself once again.

When Amy heard the question and Johnson's evidence, she blew up. 'Listen, Nan, we'll have to ask for a recess.'

'No,' Nan said firmly, 'there's nothing to discuss. I just want to take the Fifth Amendment.'

'What do you mean, "nothing to discuss",' said Amy, looking around the corridor to make sure they were alone. She lowered her voice, 'Nan, buddy, *we have to talk this out.*'

The argument lasted fifteen minutes. It was Amy's argument as she demanded various pieces of the puzzle. Nan remained silent. Finally, the birdlike clerk emerged and cleared his throat in their direction.

Nan waved to him politely. 'Just a minute,' she said. Then she turned back to Amy with finality, 'I just need to know if I can take the Fifth Amendment with a Grand Jury.'

'No, you can't. But you can do anything else you like,' said Amy, more furious than Nan had ever seen her, 'including getting yourself another lawyer.'

The District Attorney expressed profound disappointment with Miss Weaver's unco-operative stance. If she spoke, he assured her, she would be given unconditional immunity.

As he droned on, Nan stared at the display board with the forensic skeleton of Angus Murchie, an 'X' over the stomach.

'The evidence you give cannot be used against you, Miss Weaver,' he said kindly, slowly, as if she were deaf or stupid. 'We're just trying to get at the truth.'

'I understand that,' she said stiffly. 'But I'm afraid that I have nothing to add.'

'Did you see anyone on campus that night?' he asked.

'I did not say I was on campus,' Nan answered.

'Were you on campus?' he persisted.

'I have already testified,' she said, 'that I spent New Year's Eve with my family.'

The DA tried several other questions until it became apparent to everyone that Nan had nothing to say, nothing to say at all.

When Nan finished her testimony and walked out into the hallway, it was with a very different spirit from the week before. Then she had had Matt and Amy to talk to. Tonight she would be alone. She felt terrified, as if the nightmare were becoming relentlessly more real by the hour. She tried to push aside her fears about her impending murder trial and conviction. She was surprised to see Amy leaning against the wall.

'Hello,' she waved soberly to her friend and counsel.

'Bye,' said Amy briskly. 'I just stuck around to see if you saved your neck.'

'I can explain,' Nan began.

'No, no, not now.' Amy cut her short. 'We have a lot of talking to do before we make another public appearance together. But right now, I've got to go home and work on an appeal for another less lucky client already in jail in Santa Marta.'

Walking to the bus stop, Nan thought about Amy's client at Santa Marta and for the first time imagined herself there. No, it wasn't possible that she would be implicated. No, of course not. She was just getting timid about protecting Marjorie. Her mind rocked between faith in the power of her innocence and doubt in the fairness of the legal system. She swallowed the panic rising in her gut and tried to re-enter the normal world.

The bus ride did her good. The aisle was crowded with people and their everyday troubles: a black woman with four kids and two big bags of groceries; a blind couple, who almost fell on top of each other when the harried driver jolted to a stop. As the bus dodged in and out of traffic from Oakland back to Berkeley, Nan remembered that the Grand Jury was, after all, just another investigation. It was Mr Johnson's word against her own. In the dark. He couldn't have made a definite identification. Without any evidence, they would have to conclude inconclusiveness.

The next morning Nan arrived at Wheeler Hall just in time to dash up to room 205 for the discussion of Joan Didion. Once again it was hard to concentrate, and she found herself staring at the peeling ceiling. She felt closed in by the old beige room, confined by the expectations of her students. Was it the heat of the novels – the humidity of Boca Grande and the aridity of *Play It As It Lays*? Was it Didion's ominous symbolism – rattlesnakes and terrorists?

Nan heard herself speaking. She paused for half a second to hear what she had just said. It made sense, all right. She was probably giving a passable lecture. They could not know her stomach was bleeding with panic.

Outside, the sky predicted one of those cool, intermittently rainy February days. The air was the colour of boiled rice. And they all sat waiting for the answer from her. Maybe it was Didion's fault. Her tenacious sense of morality promised some distinction between good and bad. One expected. . .

All these students, Nan thought, all of them expected something from her. Normally, she thrived on this. But today she thought how a few people took the class because, as she once heard a student whisper, she was 'a notorious feminist'. Some people took the course because 'Women Writers' sounded like a mick, or a 'Mickey Mouse Course' as they used to say in the sixties. Some students took it because they wanted her to be their friend, mother, confidante, model. And some students took it because they were interested in the topic. At least she suspected that some took it for that reason.

Lawrence Craigmont was one of the mick students. Nan knew she should have discouraged him that day he sat in her office cleaning his fingernails with his IBM card. Since the beginning of the course he had insisted on comparing each writer to a male author. He took up miles of space and left it empty, rambling for minutes in the classroom, unaware of the ten others waving their hands in frenzy. He came every week to office hours. Rarely did he have any important questions. Perhaps he came because someone had told him you have to be visible to get a good grade, or perhaps because he regarded them like hospital visiting hours and thought Nan would be glad of the company.

Craigmont raised his hand.

'Yes,' said Nan.

'Is the rattlesnake a phallic symbol?'

'What brings that to mind?' asked Nan.

'Well, you know, it's long and pointed and injected threat into Maria's life.'

'Perhaps the rest of the class would like to comment,' said Nan. 'What do you think of Lawrence's point?'

As with most of Lawrence's points, the class could only think to change the topic.

Today's session felt like one of the longest hours of her life. The only thing that carried her through was the promise of a walk among the eucalyptus in Tilden before she went home. She would leave the grading until tomorrow morning and head straight up to Wildcat Canyon after class.

Waiting outside Nan's door was Marjorie Adams.

'The Road to Constantinople', Nan mused to herself as she considered Marjorie's chartreuse turban and matching silk dress.

'May I speak to you for a moment?' asked Marjorie.

'Sure,' said Nan, 'Come right in.'

Nan sat down and pointed to a chair, indicating that Marjorie should also take a seat.

'I understand that you testified before the Grand Jury last night,' Marjorie said.

'Yes.' Nan was taken aback that the younger woman was, herself, bringing up the murder case. She searched Marjorie's face for worry. She did detect a trace of tension under the muted green eyeshadow. 'Thank god it was brief,' said Nan, wondering if Marjorie could tell she was hiding something. 'But it's over now. Why do you ask?'

'Oh, just to commiserate,' said Marjorie nervously. 'It's hard on everyone, this constant probing.'

'Yes.' Nan was still waiting for her student to take the lead.

'I don't want to keep you,' Marjorie began. 'If. . .'

She regarded Nan intently, as if trying to communicate through telepathy. What would she say if she weren't so afraid of silence? That she knew Nan knew? That she appreciated her protection? That she had killed in self-defence? It was self-defence, wasn't it, Nan wondered. It was Marjorie, wasn't it?

'Oh, don't worry,' Nan looked at her watch. 'My next appointment is flexible.'

Marjorie sat straight on her chair. 'I came to discuss something of which you're already aware,' said Marjorie.

Nan noticed that the younger woman looked – was it timid? – for the first time in their acquaintance. And Marjorie had deep lines under her eyes.

'I want to tell you what I plan to do,' Marjorie continued more confidently.

Nan nodded and extended a package of chewing gum. 'I wish I had something stronger to offer than Trident gum.'

Marjorie smiled wanly, graciously waving aside the hospitality. 'I've been quite upset since Professor Murchie's death,' she said. 'We had become, well, friends, during the last quarter, as you may know.'

Nan was edgy. Jumpy. Just what was Marjorie doing, she wondered, auditioning for the demure debutante in a Walter Pidgeon movie? How could she stop the film and shake the girl into real life? Then she remembered she wanted to know as little as possible. Just last night at the Grand Jury, she had learned the value of limited information. If the DA had pulled out her fingernails, she could not have revealed all the circumstances of Murchie's murder.

'So my therapist,' Marjorie was continuing, 'suggested that I take a break, get a change of scene.'

Nan nodded sympathetically. Perhaps Marjorie hadn't seen her that night. But where did she think Nan had found the scarf?

'I wanted to explain this,' said Marjorie, 'because you have been so helpful on the thesis. And I wanted to ask if I might mail sections of the thesis for your consideration.'

'Of course,' Nan replied calmly. Of course, she thought, this was the wise thing to do. However, Nan was angry at Marjorie Adams. She resented her leaving. She felt like she was holding someone else's baby.

'Where will you be going?' Nan asked politely.

'Back to the family place outside Baltimore. Just for a couple of months, just until my head is clear.'

Does one clear the head by saving the neck, or vice versa, wondered Nan.

'I guess this sounds like running away. I've never been very competent with the practical parts of life, packing a suitcase, getting my car fixed.' Marjorie rambled as if she had lost the end of her sentence.

Nan waited nervously. She had never heard Marjorie get this unstrung, this personal.

'That was always taken care of,' Marjorie continued. 'Everything was taken care of at home. I know I've got to become more independent. But right now I just need. . .'

This is it, thought Nan. She waited. Then watched, amazed, as Marjorie composed herself.

'I hope to be back in May,' said Marjorie.

'Well now,' said Nan, pausing, waiting for some larger voice to take over, to say the right thing. When they both grew conscious of the silence, Nan said, 'I've found you to be one of my best students. I've come to respect you.'

Nan noticed a blush on Marjorie's right cheek. Her eyes were cast down. Was she going to cry? Nan could see just how young and naive Marjorie was under her chic feathers. And for the first time Nan felt more than compassion. She felt a real fondness.

'Please tell me if there's anything I can do.'

'Thank you. You've been a great help already. On my thesis.' Marjorie stood up to leave. 'Thank you again.'

'Good luck,' said Nan.

'Goodbye,' Marjorie shut the door behind her.

Nan rested her head on the desk. Clearly, Marjorie had done the best thing. Marjorie was a survivor. Best to get out of the picture. Nan tasted the panic again. It felt terrifying to be abandoned by the creature you were protecting. Yes, Marjorie was doing the right thing. But was Nan? Was she being self-destructive? Was she being stupid? No, she was innocent. Now, Nan felt possessed by fatigue. Groggily, she remembered that time in childhood when Shirley broke a vase at Sears. The clerk had insisted it was Nan. They were going to call her mother if she didn't confess. But Nan wouldn't tattle, and her clear brown eyes convinced them to let both girls go. Crazy thing to remember now. Not until a loud thumping broke into her fuzzy head did she realize she had been asleep. She looked out the window to a sky turned a dirtier grey. The Campanile said 4.30. She would have only an hour before sunset.

A loud thumping, a knocking on the door. Wearily, she answered, 'Yes, come in.'

Lawrence Craigmont ambled through the doorway.

'Good afternoon,' she said formally. These were not her office hours. She wasn't required to have a bedside manner.

'I just wanted to talk with you about the paper,' Lawrence said. 'Wouldn't it be better if I compared. . .'

'We discussed this for an hour yesterday,' said Nan.

'Yeah, I know,' Lawrence persisted. 'But I've been doing more thinking.'

'Why don't you just keep right on thinking,' said Nan, squashing the sarcasm that was creeping out the corners of her voice.

Lawrence looked confused.

'Please come back during office hours,' she said more patiently. 'I have another appointment and I'm already late.'

'Oh, OK,' Lawrence said amiably. 'I guess I could use some more time to put my thoughts in order.'

Nan felt a twinge of remorse as she thought about that question on the student evaluation forms: 'How available was the instructor for consultation?' But hell, if it were a choice between popularity and sanity, she would choose a solitary walk every time.

Prime time for a walk, thought Nan, one of those last afternoons in winter when the greyish-brown colour hugs the ground and the branches of the trees. Within the next week or ten days, the land would spill over in green. Nan liked the late winter, a time of simmering. For all the trauma of these last two months, she knew

122

the trouble would pass. But would she ever know if Marjorie had killed Murchie in self-defence? Regardless, was murder a justifiable response to rape? Nan ached from the urgency of these questions. But she had no doubts about her right to protect Marjorie. And despite Matt's warnings, she let herself feel that a spring without Angus Murchie would be a great relief.

The sun would last forty-five minutes. She had just enough time to climb to her spot by the radio tower and sit for a while. On the way up, she could see Contra Costa County on the left and over to San Francisco on the right. Sometimes the Bay Area seemed the most perfect part of the world – warm, beautiful, vibrant. Maybe this was a touch of spring fever, but Nan felt more optimistic than she had in months. Yes, she would get tenure. Marjorie would remain safe. And Lisa? Fantastic as it sounded, Nan felt that somehow in saving Marjorie, she was paying dues for Lisa. She would take care of Marjorie if god – sometimes she had to believe – would take care of Lisa. And from the look of this crimson and coral night, spring was coming sooner than any of them expected.

Sixteen

The slightest night sound always startled Nan. Her apartment was so small that she could hear everything. And everything sounded like a burglar fiddling with the lock or a rapist unhinging the windows. So, before she went to bed, especially these days when she was sleeping alone, she would take three or four Sleepese tablets. They could carry her through an eight-point earthquake. Thus it was with surprise and great drowsiness that she surfaced to consciousness on Friday morning in response to the persistent ringing of her doorbell.

Oh yes, Lisa was coming, Nan remembered foggily. No, that was tonight. And this was only – Nan peered at the clock – only seven am. Who could it be at this hour? She fumbled around for her robe, embarrassed by the big ketchup stain that she had been intending to wash out for days.

The bell rang once again.

'Coming,' she called, feeling around for her slippers. Suddenly she had a thought. They came in the morning. Recently many rapes around campus had been committed just after dawn.

She tiptoed to the door and looked through the safety hole. Outside was a husky policeman and, behind him, two other officers. One was a woman. The other was tall Officer Ross.

'What the hell,' she began to say and then swallowed it.

'Who is it,' she called. They could damn well announce themselves. Imagine waking a decent citizen at dawn, coming to her house without warning. Who did they think she was? Some kind of criminal?

'Berkeley Police, ma'am,' said the husky man.

Nan recalled the visit from Officers Ross and Rodriguez. 'Just the truth, ma'am.' These people probably did believe in facts and fairness, even in objectivity. Nan was not aware of how long she had spent in the dusty recesses of her mind until she heard the officer's voice again. Somewhat louder this time.

124

'Please open the door, ma'am. Berkeley Police for Miss Weaver.'

'I am Nan Weaver,' she said, opening the door while keeping one hand over the ketchup stain.

If They Come in the Morning, Nan now remembered, was the title of Angela Davis' prison book.

'Professor Weaver,' the man continued, 'I'm Officer Newman and I have a warrant for your arrest.'

'Arrest on what charge?' Nan said, with all the dignity she could manage. Could they detect the paralysis in her tongue?

'Homicide, ma'am,' Officer Newman replied.

Nan was wide awake now. Cool and practical. She recalled the night of Murchie's death. Again the automatic pilot took over.

'Well, I would like to call my lawyer.' Her voice sounded calm. However, Nan worried that Amy wouldn't speak to her after the Grand Jury scene. Of course she would. This was, this was an *arrest*.

'And I should like to get dressed properly,' she said. Even in her amazement, Nan had not removed her hand from the ketchup stain.

The husky policeman conferred with the woman on his right. Meanwhile, Nan was staring at silent Officer Ross. At Judas. Why had he picked her? Why of all the people they had interviewed? There was something unpleasantly familiar in Ross's face. Had he taken one of her classes? Perhaps one of those large lectures? Had he earned a D or an F and hated her forever after?

'Of course you may dress,' said the husky man who was beginning to sound more like a nurse than a cop. 'Officer Bendix here,' – the policewoman stepped forward – 'Officer Bendix will accompany you while you dress and make one phone call.'

The ride out to Santa Marta Jail was especially pretty early in the morning. Nan was being taken straight to the big county facility, they explained, because the Berkeley city jail was full. Nan had been to Santa Marta once before, ten years before, after a People's Park protest. She had been arrested with dozens of others for trying to stop the university bulldozers from making a parking lot out of a communal garden. (The demonstrators had been shoved into a paddywagon, their eyes smarting from tear gas. They had been transported in a windowless, airless van for miles and miles. Were they being taken into the Nevada desert? When the doors opened, Nan had been relieved to see the hills of Southern Alameda County.) Santa Marta, Nan now knew, was in Pleasanton, only a few miles from Hayward.

This morning she felt less like a criminal than she had as a political protester ten years before. Today she was a precious package, escorted in a car by two earnest couriers. Did they think she did it? Did Officer Newman, who was driving the car, and sweet young Officer Bendix sitting here in the back seat, honestly think she was guilty of murder? If so, they kept it to themselves. Perhaps they even sympathized. Nan remained silent. She had watched enough Perry Mason shows to know that she mustn't divulge anything except name, rank and social security number. At one point Newman asked if she minded him smoking. And since she didn't think she had any more to lose, she acknowledged that she did mind. The highway signs read Dublin, Tasajara Road, Eden Valley Road. Beyond them, Nan could see the fertile vineyards growing into an early spring.

Santa Marta looked more like a decaying resort than a jail. The weathered white buildings with green shutters reminded her of Spring Lake, New Jersey. And those irises in the parking lot! Nan was astonished by the profusion of pale purple irises. The first note of surrealism. As the day passed, she found it harder and harder to believe that she was really being stripped, searched, questioned, imprisoned. In the past she might have imagined many reasons for going to jail (as a participant-observer for Amnesty International, perhaps, or to teach creative writing, or to protest a traffic ticket). When she was a kid she had always regarded prison as a dramatic movie set, fancying herself as a Rita Hayworth type, a beleaguered widow fighting her way through an unjust sentence. That's it, Nan thought as they fingerprinted her, maybe the whole thing, the arrest, the imprisonment, was one of those cinematic Sleepese nightmares. Irises in the parking lot.

The day plodded on with a series of interminable questions. Interviews by the police, by the prison authorities, by the psychiatrist. Intense interviews executed in quick provocations and barbs and bordered by long periods in vacant waiting rooms which smelled of pee and disinfectant. Naugahyde couches and arborite tables rattled around in large, green rooms. She tasted fear, and when she swallowed the fear, she tasted terror. Arrested. She had thought this could never happen. Now the next step would be a hearing. And then? And then, Nan tried to convince herself, she would be acquitted. She sweated profusely in her prison T-shirt and green work pants. Mouldy green, so much green, a sadistic imitation of nature.

The buildings were hot and stuffy as if overheated with despair. Nan remembered reading in the *Chronicle* last month, or was it last year – time on the outside already marked a different order – that Santa Marta was overcrowded, yet somehow they had been able to preserve acres of waiting rooms and endless corridors which echoed with the reluctant footsteps of her new regulation shoes. All day Nan walked and waited and watched. The·matrons paced together in pairs, fingering their keys and whispering (why were they whispering?) like nuns saying the rosary.

Before Nan was assigned to a cell, among 'the females', the matron informed her about 'the feeding times'. She pictured baboons at the San Francisco Zoo.

Nan's cellmate greeted her with a doleful scorn from the bottom bunk. This woman was twenty at most. Silent, she clearly resented the intrusion. Nan looked away, trying to concentrate on the tiny space, but there wasn't much to see – two beds, a toilet in the floor – just a cold concrete cell. She wanted to apologise for imposing.

'I'm Nan Weaver,' she said, extending her hand.

'The professor,' said the small woman on the bottom bunk who kept her hands to herself.

'Yes,' stumbled Nan, 'how did you know?' (Maybe she *was* here to teach creative writing. Maybe this was her first student.)

'News gets around,' said the woman, winding a strand of long brown hair over her index finger. 'Lots of time to talk when there's time to talk. But that ain't now.' She picked up a Spiderman comic book. 'You'll excuse me, Professor,' she laughed, 'but I've got to catch up on my homework.'

Nan nodded and climbed to the top bunk. This could be more unpleasant than she had imagined. She stretched out and closed her eyes.

'Not to be rude, Professor,' came the small voice from below. 'My name's Judy Milligan.' She laughed again – in sarcasm or embarrassment, Nan couldn't tell.

Nan reassured herself that she would not be here long. She would have a quick hearing, establish that they had no evidence and that would be the end of that.

Tomorrow Amy would come back and settle everything. Yes. She would be out of this place in a week. Meanwhile, the experience would do her good. Rita Hayworth movies were no way to understand the prison system.

Bang, slam, bang. A sudden thunder above. Nan opened her eyes

127

to the strange sound and stared at the shoes of a guard on the catwalk above her bunk.

Nan was right about Amy. Of course Amy would pull through and take the case. But she was wrong about the arraignment. Nan was not released. Although it was unusual for a respectable university professor to be denied bail, Murchie's cousin-in-law was doing everything to turn the screw.

She would have a preliminary hearing in three weeks. Then a trial. She wished she could confide in Amy, but she knew Amy would not allow her to continue protecting Marjorie. Amy would not understand. Most sensible people would not understand. Nan, herself, did not completely understand. She was a sophisticated political person who knew that innocence was no defence in a sexist, racist legal system. The courtroom was not run with the same mercy as the Sears vase department. She knew she would get acquitted as much as she knew anything in her whole life, but Nan's confidence had nothing to do with clever pleas or California statutes. It came from an old place she used to call faith. It didn't make sense to defend Marjorie, yet Nan knew she was right.

One afternoon, Amy came to the visiting room bearing fresh news.

'Apparently Johnson, the custodian, is the only witness they have,' Amy told her.

'What do you mean *witness*?' Nan whispered hoarsely.

Amy ran a hand through her short black hair. 'Calm down, I talked to Johnson, a nice guy. But he says you were the only person there on New Year's Eve besides Murchie.'

'And besides him,' said Nan automatically.

'Yes,' nodded Amy, 'but he's not a very likely suspect.'

'What are you getting at?' Nan asked nervously, staring at the putrid green ceiling that was peeling worse than her classroom in Wheeler Hall.

'The coroner's report was clarified yesterday,' Amy was explaining, or was she accusing? Obviously, she knew Nan was holding back something.

Nan concentrated on the face of her lawyer, her friend, to prevent her own face from revealing anything.

'Apparently, Murchie was found with his pants down,' said Amy. 'The coroner says he was in the midst of "sexual activity".'

Nan nodded, again with a completely passive expression. All the

128

wretched smells of blood, semen, sweat and fear came raging back over her. Sometimes, in the intervening weeks, she wondered just what she had seen. What she had heard. How much of it she had just imagined. But now, with the coroner's report, her worst memories were confirmed.

'Nan,' Amy spoke anxiously, 'you've simply got to tell me all you know about this.'

'Nothing,' said Nan, watching a pair of women hunched together at a table across the room. Were they lovers? Lawyer and client? Mother and daughter?

'Nan.' Amy's voice was angry now. Her eyes were terrified.

Nan stared back at her friend. She wondered whether Amy would ever understand. She sighed, 'There's nothing to say, really. I didn't kill Angus Murchie and I don't know who did.'

The noises at Santa Marta made incessant assault. The slamming of iron doors, the whining radio music, the chattering voices, the billy clubs closing down with thudding finality. Nan remembered these noises as she tried to sleep, long after lights out. She couldn't buy Sleepese in the prison canteen, so she spent her nights in fantasies, a semblance of dreaming. She would imagine Marjorie Adams recuperating in rural Maryland, riding her mother's horses through the hills. Sitting in front of a huge fireplace sipping cognac and reading Iris Murdoch. (Iris. Huge pale purple irises.) Marjorie would sleep late in the morning, awakened by a servant carrying fresh coffee in a Limoges cup. Marjorie Adams was as safe in her distance as Nan was in her innocence.

One night, as Nan lay still, careful not to disturb Judy Milligan whose miraculous snores gave her great hope for human survival, Nan had more fearful fantasies. What if it came to conviction? She was no martyr. At that point, she would tell about Marjorie Adams. But what if Marjorie would not come forward? Nan had very carefully removed all of Marjorie's traces with the scarf. And she had returned the scarf. Shuddering under the thin prison blanket, she asked herself again, what if it came to conviction?

As much as Nan tried not to think about that, her mind turned to logical consequences. She would be sent up to Frontera, the women's prison in Southern California. That was where they had sent Wendy Yoshimura last year. Wendy Yoshimura, arrested with Patty Hearst, but not nearly so likely to have a Presidential pardon. Nan imagined talking with Wendy about politics and about a few mutual friends, but most of all about the brown hills of Alameda County for which they would both spend years in longing.

This was ridiculous, Nan reminded herself. She was getting carried away. She had to keep up her spirits. It was her only protection.

So she turned over and thought of Lisa. Of Lisa's letters. She had received one every day since the arraignment. Silly cards with joking messages. Long epistles enclosed about how Lisa wished she could visit Nan. About how she was beginning to feel better. Please god, she was recovering. More tests this week.

After ten days of iron doors slamming and ten sleepless nights, Nan heard that the English Department had formally disposed of her classes for the following quarter. 'Women Writers' would be taught by a very competent lecturer (Couldn't you just see it on her *vita*, 'substitute during murder trial'.) And the 'Mod Lit' class would be covered by a series of lectures from various faculty. Meanwhile, she had received several letters from former students who were setting up a 'Defence Committee' of women from all over campus. If the arrest weren't enough to lose her tenure, this defence committee could do it.

Matt brought all the details on his second visit. He had arrived with a bouquet of flowers for his lost duchess, but had to surrender them at the gate. Dear, sweet Matt. Loyal Matt. Loyalty, now there was a virtue no one discussed any more. Sure, people talked about 'sharing' and 'supportiveness', but loyalty ran deeper. Her people had come through – Matt, Shirley and Amy visited as often as possible. Their feelings about her didn't seem to change, except to intensify. In her most anxious moments, Nan worried that they would suspect her, but she was grateful to find they treated the arrest like some kind of disease from which she had to be rescued.

'So how's it going today?' Matt was trying to sound casual. However, he was nagging at his beard, so she knew how nervous he was.

'Just fine,' Nan told him. 'My cellmate actually spoke to me last night. Guess she figured that silence wasn't providing any more room in our little box.'

'What did she say?'

'Hooking,' said Nan, shaking her head.

'Sorry?' he said.

'Hooking,' Nan repeated, still shaking her head. 'Twenty years old and she's forced to prostitute herself to take care of two kids.' Nan was silent. When she noticed this, she added, 'And Judy didn't ask why I was in; she knew.'

'Honour,' said Matt.

'What?' asked Nan.

'Honour,' Matt pulled off his glasses and looked directly at Nan. 'I've been talking with Amy,' he said, his voice tightening with fear. 'And we think you know something, Nan. We think you're protecting someone.'

Nan turned back quickly to see if the matron was within hearing distance.

'Nan,' he stared at her so hard she thought her glasses might crack. 'Nan, dear, honour is a very old-fashioned defence.'

'Oh, Matt,' she tried to laugh. 'Sometimes I'm amazed at your penchant for melodrama.'

'Try the Victorian novel,' said Matt, his eyes on the matron who was, in fact, moving closer. 'Try *Tale of Two Cities*, for instance.'

'Oh, Matt,' sighed Nan, exasperated because she had so little time with him and she desperately needed some outside conversation to distract her from the obsessions with mealtime and recreational breaks and the dimensions of her tiny cell. These visits kept her from going crazy. She needed to hear that the world was as she left it so she could concentrate on returning.

'I'm not sacrificing *anything* for *anyone*,' said Nan. 'There simply is no evidence.' Even as she said this, she felt her pulse accelerate.

Nan wrote to Lisa that Santa Marta was just an enforced vacation. Santa Marta. It sounded like a little village on the coast of Spain. Or perhaps an old colonial port in Northern Morocco. She would have a lot of time to think here.

Nan knew she should take advantage of this time. She was always too busy at home. She could devise papers she wanted to write; reorganize her lectures for next year; dream about the trip to India with Lisa; meet Third World women. She was always complaining that most of her friends were white. Thanks to the racist courts, she now had plenty of time to talk with blacks and Chicanas. But Nan did none of this. For long hours of every day her mind seemed paralyzed, as though her head had been thrown into solitary confinement, without any ideas. Perhaps it was one of the consequences of being treated like a baboon. She could not think what to think about. If they had planned a torture, they could not have been more effective. She felt the weight of those early depressions in Hayward. She wished she was dead all day, save for those moments when she thought she was dead. She could not think what to think about.

But at night the pattern changed and her thoughts continued to keep her from sleeping. Nan ran through the incidents of New Year's Eve a dozen times, and she could find no evidence to convict Marjorie. If there was no evidence to convict Marjorie, surely there was no evidence to convict Nan? Matt was wrong. This wasn't about honour. She was sacrificing nothing. And during the few hours Nan did doze, her dreams connected Marjorie with herself; herself with Lisa; Marjorie with Lisa.

Seventeen

When the matron came the next day, Nan couldn't imagine who was visiting her. Amy was not due for three hours; Matt and Shirley had promised tomorrow morning.

Nervously Nan walked into the visitors' room. She looked around and saw Lisa, or rather, the back of Lisa's curly head. (The hair. Blonde hair in the dark night. Lisa's fair hair would have turned gold in the evening light.) What was happening to her? Hallucinating, rambling. Lisa was not Marjorie. Marjorie was in Maryland and Lisa was here. But what was she doing here?

Lisa seemed to be surveying sadness in the waiting room. The podgy, white-haired woman who visited her daughter every day; the two black men who visited one of the prisoners in the cell next to Nan's. She was glad Lisa hadn't been watching the door, hadn't seen her aunt ushered into the room by this cold sergeant. Nan tried to materialize her old self from the greyness around her.

Lisa turned and waved.

'Lisa, my sweet,' said Nan, for all the world like an Edwardian matron serving tea. 'How lovely to see you.'

'Oh, Nan,' Lisa worried, with no pretence of good cheer. 'How are you? I've been dying to come, but Mom wouldn't let me out of the house. Are you all right? Are you OK?'

'Yes,' smiled Nan. How could she smile now? How could she not smile? What else could she do with her nervous face? 'I'm just fine, love. But what about you? And does you mother know you're here?'

'No,' winked Lisa. 'I escaped! Oh, dear,' she gasped. 'Hope that wasn't in bad taste.'

'No, no,' smiled Nan. 'Prison rooms are wallpapered with lousy jokes.'

They both looked around at the patient, numb faces of the visitors.

'Seeing you here is like watching spring arrive,' said Nan. 'So tell me how you're feeling.'

'Well, I do have news,' Lisa spoke conspiratorially. 'I think that's why Mom looked the other way when I drove off this morning.'

'Yes?' said Nan.

'The test result came. Dr Bonelli says he doubts it's Lupus. Not one hundred percent sure, he said. He wants to take another set of tests in three months. But until then, I have a sort of parole.' Lisa paled. She put her hand over her mouth and looked down at the table. 'Oh, Nan, that's terrible; it just slipped out.'

'It's OK, honey,' Nan was laughing, 'it's OK.'

'Boy,' said Lisa, smiling and shaking her head. 'I must be more nervous than I thought.'

'But what does this doctor's report mean?' asked Nan. 'What is it you have, or had? What about this butterfly rash?'

'Don't know. It could be emotional, but we don't know. And that's what you said, Nan, remember, what you said all along.'

Nan nodded.

'Emotional,' Lisa repeated. 'It makes me feel a little crazy, psychosomatic or hypochondriacal or something.'

'Oh, no, honey,' reassured Nan. 'Pray that it *was* that. Those illnesses are real, just in a different way. And I'm so relieved that you're feeling better.'

'Well, this week I've been eating well, sleeping OK.'

'Lisa, honey, that's terrific. How are your mom and dad reacting?'

'Overjoyed. Mom thinks it's a certified miracle. She's going to say a novena in thanks this afternoon. Dad thinks that it's the result of staying away from Berkeley. As for me, I'm just glad to be off the drugs for a while.'

Nan noticed how sharp her niece looked – as if she had emerged from a pool. Her voice was strong and clear, with just an edge of exasperation when she talked about home. So different from the guilty hesitation which used to characterize every family reference.

'Enough about me,' Lisa went on. 'How are *you*? What is this place like? I mean,' her voice quavered, 'are you scared in here?'

'There's a certain comfort to the routine.' Nan pulled a small face.

Lisa stared back.

'It is difficult,' said Nan finally. 'It gets more frightening every day.'

'Who's visited you?'

134

'Matt, your mom, Amy. This has taught me a lot about love. And then I had those wonderful letters from you.'

'No one else?'

'No.'

'What about, what's-her-name, Marjorie Adams?' Lisa asked.

'Marjorie Adams?' faltered Nan. 'You mean my student Marjorie?' Nan was as frightened as she was confused by Lisa's question. 'Why do you ask about her?'

'Oh. I don't know,' said Lisa. 'Just that she seemed to be your favourite, I guess. Hasn't she been by to see you?'

'Well, no,' said Nan. 'I think she went home to her family for a while. Anyway, tell me more about your dad and the boys.'

'They're fine. Real worried, though. Everyone thinks it's outrageous they would arrest you. Dad has been alternating between wanting to rescue you with a crowbar and wanting to hit the cops over the head for stupidly wasting his tax dollars.'

'I tried to calm down your mother yesterday.'

'Yes,' nodded Lisa. 'She's very worried. And so's Aunt Betty.'

'You mean Grandma Weaver's sister Betty in Cleveland?' Nan was astonished.

'Yes.' Lisa smiled. 'We had a call from her this morning. It's the biggest thing to hit the family since Uncle Henry fell off the oil rig. And last night, Dad's brother Louie in Pittsburgh called.'

'It wasn't in the newspapers out there?' asked Nan.

'No, family telegraph, that's all,' sighed Lisa.

'Cleveland *and* Pittsburgh, eh?' asked Nan. 'Hmmmm, just two more places I won't get tenure.'

'Oh, Nan, how you keep from going crazy in this place, I just don't know. You really are amazing,' Lisa fumbled in embarrassment. 'Unique.'

'Unique, that's true,' volleyed Nan. 'I was the only one they arrested.'

Nan glanced at three visitors, waiting, silent. A podgy woman was biting her fingernails. Late morning sun poured through the small windows now, streaking a ray of dust across the grim room.

Nan turned back to Lisa and noticed tears rimming her eyes. She didn't know what to say. She had enough trouble keeping back her own tears.

Finally, Lisa spoke. 'Listen,' she whispered angrily, 'I'm going to do everything I can to get you out of here.'

'Of course,' said Nan, who understood this need to do something when there was nothing you could do. Nothing. 'I know that, Lisa, honey. I know you will.'

Eighteen

They brought Nan to the courthouse half an hour early. Her hearing was scheduled for ten. By 9.40 she was sitting in the ante-room watching the public gallery fill up. The widow, Laura Murchie, was among the first to arrive, supported by Professor Augustine. They both wore a kind of grudging pride, like parents of the bride at a shotgun wedding, present to see Justice done. They sat behind the Assistant District Attorney, Laura Murchie's second cousin. He turned to greet them and then faced back to his notes.

On the far wall, Nan saw a homely needlepoint of an American eagle. The judge's bench was elevated slightly above the witness chair which was elevated above the lawyer's tables. Amy was busy writing, her head nodding to a yellow legal pad. Nan wondered why she had left her homework until so late. But she tried to concentrate on how professional her lawyer looked in a handsome beige suit. The defendant, herself, was wearing a severe navy skirt and blazer with a Peter Pan collared blouse, the lay nun effect.

Nan caught her breath as Shirley and Lisa entered the courtroom. Too bad they had never met Amy. (Why had she tried so hard to keep Berkeley apart from Hayward?) Perhaps she could introduce them in court. Were civilian exchanges allowed?

Amy's husband Warren was handing her a pile of papers over the rail. His red hair shone iridescent under the fluorescent lights. Amy reached back over the rail and squeezed his hand warmly. This rail, Nan's mind wandered, like the communion rail in St Mary's, separated the rest of the sanctuary from the altar. The sacrificial altar. Old Latin rose from Nan's belly like a spell of gas. 'Agnus Dei, qui tollis peccata mundi, miserere nobis.'

Matt was next to arrive. Good old Matt. Also dressed in his most respectables. A grey tweed suit. He had even replaced his omni-present Birkenstock sandals with squeaking black loafers. Tuesday morning, Nan reflected, he must have cancelled his class. He sat

137

down stiffly behind Shirley and Lisa. His anxiety was diffused in a moment once Lisa turned around and introduced her mother. Nan saw Matt searching Shirley's face for traces of sisterhood. Shirley blushed and waved her hand in go-on-now modesty. They all laughed nervously, or rather smiled, and shook silently.

A small old man – not unlike the bird fellow who fussed around Nan during the Grand Jury – was ushering others through the door. Nan saw Millie walk in and sit beside Matt. This was like choosing sides of the bleachers in a football match. Now she saw Hammerly, who hesitated at the door and then chose the seat next to Augustine, behind the DA.

'Quickly,' the old man whispered. 'The judge will be with us presently.'

The judge – Nan wondered what kind of a person he would be. Not the worst, Amy had told her yesterday. Judge Harold Gordon was a liberal Republican. More liberal on race than on sex. Nevertheless, in Alameda County, he was what passed for liberal.

Nan watched, frozen, as two of her students arrived and sat beside Millie. Amy had gone to campus yesterday to quell the 'Defence Committee', who had been planning a group protest. It had taken an hour to convince them that they shouldn't sit at the back of the court and heckle. She explained that this would only alienate the judge. They agreed to postpone the protest until the trial. The trial, Amy had reassured them, would never happen. So now Nan held her breath as two – only two of them, thank god – took their seats beside Millie.

Nan felt a nudge on her arm. The matron was nodding now, 'Time to go in,' said Sergeant Fernandez, gently betraying the first trace of kindness that morning.

Entering the courtroom, Nan glanced around carefully. Two flags – the Stars and Stripes and the Golden Bear of California – stood on either side of the bench. On the dusty ledge near the window were three busts, two she could make out, John Locke and Oliver Wendell Holmes. The third she didn't recognize, only that it was a man.

'You'll be sitting with your attorney,' said the matron quietly.

'Yes,' said Nan, adding, 'Thank you.' After all, the poor woman was just doing her job. Were prison guards unionized? Did Sergeant Fernandez have children to support? What a terrible way to earn your living. Nan was relieved that the matron did not hold her arm. She didn't want to look like a prisoner. After all, her innocence would prove itself.

Nan was walking with as much confidence as she could conjure, reminding herself of the first time she gave a guest lecture in Wheeler Auditorium. How frightened she had been then, facing five hundred eager students. That day, and again this morning, she repeated over and over to herself the brave acts of her life: divorcing Charles, going back to college, working in Tanzania. Small heroics, but they did lend her some dignity and calm. As she moved toward the defence table, Nan repeated the words over and over, dignity and calm. Dignity and calm. As though on one foot she wore dignity and on the other calm.

Judge Harold Gordon entered, looking very much like Nelson Rockefeller. Never liked Rockefeller, thought Nan, never trusted his smile. Judge Gordon was unsmiling as he explained the court procedures. He spoke in such ponderous legal jargon that Nan wondered if he might put everyone to sleep.

The first witness called to the stand was the coroner, a squat young man who read his report as if he were reciting from the drawer in the morgue.

'Sixty-year-old man. Dead of a sharp wound in the stomach. Apparently in the middle of sexual activity. Body found fully clothed, except that the pants were pulled down around the thighs. Lower stomach and genitals exposed. . .'

The San Francisco Chronicle, true to its squalid mandate, Nan remembered, had published all the information, so this morning there were no surprised gasps of horror from the public. Nan thought she could feel the mortification of Mrs Angus Murchie. Without turning, Nan could sense the widow's stiff, almost brittle posture; she could hear the nervous, shallow breathing. In fact, Laura Murchie's presence was so palpable that Nan almost felt guilty.

The Chronicle had given the crime banner headlines on the front page whenever a new shred of evidence surfaced. Sometimes they simply repeated the old shreds. What was next, Nan wondered, would some hack volunteer to ghost-write her autobiography? Why was *The Chronicle* obsessed with this crime when San Francisco provided two or three murders and ten assaults on an average day? Perhaps this case did have a dramatic ring, 'Murder in the English Department'. The most galling aspect was the particular reporter, Beth Beale.

Beth was one of Nan's former students. (How many students

were out there. Seven years times three-quarters equalled twenty-one times a hundred students equalled two thousand one hundred students. Nan pictured herself as an excessively fertile frog who had spawned hundreds of unpredictable tadpoles.) Actually, Beth Beale was a sweet woman who had done well in school. (Unlike Officer Ross. By now Nan was almost convinced that Ross was that Vietnam veteran who insisted on smoking in class and interrupting the discussion with questions about why they weren't reading more *American* writers.) Beth had even confided in Nan that she was on her side. Apparently being on Nan's side meant long featured articles about discrimination against women academics, about the difficulty of getting tenure, about Nan's unselfish devotion to the Sexual Harassment Campaign. Poor Beth had been quite hurt when Amy asked her to 'tone down' her coverage of the hearing.

The next witness was Officer Ross, looking even taller than usual in his civilian clothes, a navy gaberdine suit which bagged around his thin frame. He testified to their thorough investigation of the English faculty, prior to the arrest of Professor Weaver.

As Ross was speaking, Nan heard a rustle from the back of the courtroom. Nan turned to see Clarence Johnson walk in and sit shyly in the last row. He looked tired and worried and Nan felt sad that he had got caught up in all this. Johnson was followed by his massive lawyer, who looked even more imposing today in a green sharkskin suit.

Judge Gordon rapped his gavel, and Nan turned back toward the bench, her eyes sweeping past, but not acknowledging, Beth Beale.

'Order,' the judge called. 'Let us keep our attention on the witness. Officer Ross, please proceed.'

The morning passed with one man after another pointing his evidence at Nan. Hammerly testified to the tension between her and Murchie, to political differences and temperamental difficulties. Augustine admitted that she would be the most successful of their junior faculty if she could be just a bit more 'low key'. Even in her professional work – like that panel on feminist criticism she had chaired last year at the Modern Language Association (Nan remembered how jealous Murchie was that she was asked to chair a panel) – she had insisted on being 'so political'.

As Laura Murchie climbed to the stand, she looked very willowy and blonde. (Blonde, Nan's mind raced wildly. Who had bothered to question Mrs Murchie's presence at the health spa? Blonde hair in the dark night.) The elegant widow spoke in short bursts of grief about her husband's devotion to students. She said she knew very little about Nan Weaver except that her dear husband had returned home several times, quite irritable about 'some disagreement'.

The prosecution witnesses returned to their seats on the right side of the courtroom with evident relief, as if their testimonies might wrest some evil spirit from their midst. Nan couldn't shake the image of football bleachers from her mind. What were the opposite teams? Those who believed in the honour of Angus Murchie and those who knew better? Or, perhaps, those who supported Nan Weaver and those who conspired to frame her?

Few people in the English Department really mourned the passing of Angus Murchie. And she knew few more would mourn the passing of Nan Weaver. Murchie was just a faggot lit at the bottom of her stake. Here they were ridding themselves of the Wheeler Hall Witch, even if they had to overlook evidence of a rape to do it.

Mr Johnson's testimony was the most pathetic. He said he knew nothing about the murder.

'I saw nothing,' he said quietly. 'Heard nothing. I've got nothing much to say. Yes, I did notice Professor Weaver's light in the building that night. . .'

Nan sneaked a look at Laura Murchie, whose eyes were closed in tense concentration.

Johnson explained that about 3.00 a.m. he finally went to turn off the light in Murchie's office. Getting no answer when he knocked, he unlocked the door and found Murchie's body on the floor. He had noticed only one other light during the course of New Year's Eve, from the office of Professor Weaver.

Mr Johnson did not look at Nan during his testimony, and avoided her eyes as he walked back to his seat.

After lunch, Amy called the defence witnesses. Other lawyers had advised against this, had told her to accept the normal procedure of letting the prosecutor present his case and saving her big guns until the trial. However, she said she didn't know her big guns yet. Perhaps they would emerge in testimony. Anyway, the evidence was so weighted against Nan that a few character witnesses couldn't hurt.

Matt was the first on the stand. How scholarly he looked in his tweed jacket, one hand on the Bible, the other nervously pulling at his beard. A quiet man of evident integrity. His testimony was brief and confident. Amy asked a few character questions to balance out the dark words of Augustine and Laura Murchie.

'Popular among students. . .'

'Great respect from journal editors. . .'

'A truly *loyal* colleague. . .'

Nan felt like she was at an awards ceremony rather than a murder hearing. She wondered whether Matt believed in her innocence. He probably wouldn't care if she had killed Murchie, acknowledging that she could still be 'innocent' in a larger, existential sense. Matt's morality was more intricate than Shirley's.

Shirley sat in the witness chair, red with indignation. Shirley Growsky, mother of three, President of the Altar Society, sister of a murder suspect. Hayward wasn't a tiny town, but news travelled. Nan knew that during the last month Shirley's mantle had slipped significantly. Nowadays she was identified more as Nan Weaver's sister than as Joe Growsky's wife. However, if Shirley was embarrassed or ashamed or frightened, she never revealed it. And now, as Shirley answered the DA, Nan watched her usual shyness turn to outrage at those who would accuse her sister.

'She arrived at our party shortly after one a.m.,' said Shirley, tersely.

'She told us she was working late,' Shirley answered.

'No, this didn't seem strange,' Shirley's voice was hot with anger. 'No, not even on New Year's Eve. Our Nan works harder than most people.'

When Nan was finally called to the stand, she felt dizzy, as if the room had tilted. Like her first day in prison, this testifying seemed so unreal. Inexplicable. As she rose from her chair, she silently repeated to herself, 'Dignity and calm. Dignity and calm.'

Nan sensed a hand on her shoulder. She turned to see Amy bending over her. 'You OK, kid?' her friend asked.

Nan realized that she had been standing still, not moving toward the bench at all for a minute, perhaps five minutes.

'Yes, sure,' she said, reaching for a glass and gulping down the dusty, warm water that had been standing on their table all day.

Nan swore on the old King James Bible that she would tell the whole truth (and she wondered briefly, in her scrupulous Catholic schoolgirl conscience, whether oaths on Protestant bibles counted).

Amy's questions drew out her devotion to scholarship, her co-operation as a colleague, her passion as a teacher.

The DA's questions about her relations with Angus Murchie were just what she expected.

'You had disagreements on which courses should be assigned for the English major?'

'At times,' said Nan.

'You disagreed as to the place of politics in campus life?'

'At times,' said Nan.

'You usually voted on opposite sides of issues?'

'Usually,' Nan said, regretting Amy's decision to put her on the stand. But from here she could look directly at Laura Murchie. Her chic pageboy haircut was too short for the figure she had seen running across campus that night. Had it been cut recently? Nan could not remember what she had looked like before.

'Do you know of anyone else in the department who had such a violent response to Angus Murchie?'

Nan heard several Ohhhs and Ahhhhs from the public gallery. She assumed they were a response to the prosecutor's leading questions.

She looked at the DA, past the DA, to the back of the court. The door had opened, admitting Joan Crawford–Grace Kelly–Marjorie Adams. She was wearing a stunning black suit, laced with long white pearls, and her gold hair was braided tightly on top of her head. She was accompanied by a tall, greying man whom Nan took to be Walter Pidgeon.

Nan felt faint again, strangely distant from the proceedings. She could see the prosecutor saying something to her, but she could not hear the words.

'Ms Weaver,' someone called.

Were they drowning? Was she drowning?

'Ms Weaver,' the judge called, as if from the edge of the shore. 'Ms Weaver, may we have your attention?'

She looked at the judge, feeling like a naughty child who didn't know what she had done.

'Ms Weaver, would you please address yourself to the prosecutor's question.' Then Judge Gordon, becoming a patient, protective parent, looked out toward the bleachers and said, 'Those of you who entered late, will you please seat yourselves with as little fuss as possible.'

How did Marjorie learn about this hearing in the wilds of Maryland, Nan wondered. And, her heart stopped for a terrified moment, on which side of the court would she sit?

Nan heard herself asking the DA, 'I'm sorry, sir, but I have forgotten the question. Could you please repeat it.'

She watched Marjorie sit behind Lisa and Shirley.

'Where were you on the night of December 31?'

'I was in my office, until about midnight,' Nan began. She was hearing two voices, as if she were speaking into a microphone. She heard her own voice and she heard Marjorie Adams hearing her voice. 'Then I drove to Hayward to attend a party with my family.'

Nan looked out at the gallery, at Marjorie Adams, sitting next to Shirley and Lisa. Marjorie so elegant in her New York fashions; Shirley like a Christmas tree in her best green jersey dress. Then Nan watched something she did not quite understand. Lisa was leaning over and offering her hand to Marjorie. Marjorie was shaking it and smiling thinly.

'Do you know of anyone else in the department who had a violent response to Angus Murchie?' asked the prosecutor.

Nan watched as Marjorie Adams passed forward a note to Amy. Her lawyer opened the folded sheet of blue vellum paper, read the note and, turning back to the strange woman, shook her head.

'Please.' Nan could see Marjorie's red lips around the word, 'Please.'

Amy was still shaking her head.

'Order,' said the judge, finally noticing the situation. 'Order, please. And, once again, Ms Weaver, will you answer the question.'

'I know of no one who had a violent response to Angus Murchie,' mumbled Nan. Was the microphone working? Did Marjorie know what Nan was trying to do?

The judge yawned and looked at his watch. 'Counsel,' he said, 'how much longer will you need for your questions? It is almost 4.30, perhaps a good time to adjourn for today.'

'If your honour pleases,' the prosecutor was saying, 'just three more questions.'

'And I should like to say something, your honour,' called Marjorie Adams.

Amy looked at Marjorie and then at her client. Nan was shaking her head frantically. Amy's eyebrows rose, as if she had found the last piece of the puzzle. People in the gallery were whispering.

'Order,' banged the judge. 'Order. Or I shall have to clear the court. Members of the public must be quiet or leave.'

'But, by your own admission,' the DA was continuing, 'as well as by previous testimony, we have discerned that you were the only one. . .'

Nan knew she would never have a chance to answer him.

'I'll answer that,' said Marjorie Adams, standing.

'Guard,' called Judge Gordon, who seemed more disturbed by this intrusion than by any of the day's bloody evidence, 'will you escort this young lady from the courtroom.'

Walter Pidgeon shook his head, stood and took Marjorie's arm protectively.

'I killed Angus Murchie,' said Marjorie Adams.

The guard stopped in the aisle.

'I killed Angus Murchie,' Marjorie was speaking directly to Nan, 'while he was trying to rape me.'

Nineteen

STUDENT CLAIMS RAPE/CONFESSES MURDER
MURDER IN THE ENGLISH DEPARTMENT TAKES NEW TWIST
PROFESSOR'S HEARING ENDS IN CHAOS

No doubt about it, Beth Beale's career at *The Chronicle* was taking off with this story. The out-of-town papers sent reporters after Marjorie made her confession. But Beth Beale kept scooping everyone because she had had an inside track from the start.

Nan was grateful for the clippings concerning the afternoon Marjorie confessed. She spent hours reading the newspaper coverage to pass her last three days in Santa Marta until the District Attorney developed a brief against Marjorie. Besides, Nan had been in such shock that she couldn't remember anything for herself, like Shirley's tears and Lisa's huge smile and the bloodless pale of Marjorie's face. She didn't remember Laura Murchie's scream, her shouting, 'You little. . .' *The Chronicle* left some details, but not many, to the reader's imagination.

The paper scoured the new defendant's history, helping Nan begin to solve the mystery of Marjorie Adams. This daughter of rich, conservative parents had attended only private schools until she finally struck a blow for radicalism and came to Berkeley. A straight-A student. She had little interest in socializing or in politics. But she wasn't completely a loner. Beth Beale discovered that Marjorie had worked with retarded children in Berkeley for three years.

Alma Pedersen, Director of Community Connection at the North County Children's Home, said Adams was one of her best volunteers. 'Prompt, reliable,' said Pedersen. 'A little on the cool side to the staff, but very involved with the children.'

146

Apparently Marjorie was also responsible to her god. A regular attender at St Mark's Episcopal Church, according to Beth's third investigative article. A member of the choir. No one had much to say about her. 'Modest, understated,' offered the minister. 'A superb contralto,' said the choir director.

Beth Beale did not neglect Angus Murchie in her investigations. She ran a long story about his reputation on campus. The Sexual Harassment Campaign had taken on a life of its own in Murchie's gory wake. Twenty-two woman had now made despositions to the Chancellor's Committee about Murchie's advances.

The story that Nan regretted most was the one which painted her as some kind of saint. Marjorie, in her rush of communication after the long months of silence, had told Beth Beale about Nan finding her scarf, about Nan covering for her. In turn, Beth asked Nan if she had done this sisterly act. Amy warned Nan not to respond. Concealing evidence was a serious offence, a felony. So, when Nan answered, 'No comment,' to these allegations of sorority, her modesty was immediately canonized by the Campus Feminist Caucus.

The day before Nan's release, Amy arrived at visiting hours ranting about Beth Beale's article.

'Who do you think you are?' demanded Amy. 'Joan of Arc?'

'No,' Nan was looking down at the wooden table where a dozen names and initials had been scratched into immortality. 'I'm sorry,' Nan said finally. She knew the relationship with Amy would need a lot of repair work.

'Lying to your lawyer is lunatic enough, but I thought we were friends, Nan, I thought. . .'

'Would you have let me go through with it?' asked Nan.

'You bet your boots I wouldn't. How self-destructive, putting your neck on the line when there was no need. Just how did you expect me to conduct a defence?'

'I was innocent,' said Nan. 'They had no evidence to convict me.'

'Oi, yoi, yoi, yoi, yoi. I'm stunned that you even hired a lawyer.'

'I know I was stupid,' said Nan, wondering, herself, if she had been naive or if her instinct had come from a different plane of wisdom. 'But I thought that if I was convicted then I could explain about Marjorie. I really didn't think I'd get convicted. Nothing very noble about that.'

'You're right,' agreed Amy. 'Nothing very noble, just very, very dumb.'

147

Nan shook her head and sighed.

'Besides,' said Army, 'how could you risk your life for that upper-class princess? You didn't even like her.'

'I didn't dislike her. I mean I respected her. Besides, that's not the point. She was another woman.' Nan paused. 'She needed help. You should understand that.'

As Amy left the waiting room, Nan wondered once again whether she had lost Amy's friendship.

Nan wasn't surprised that Amy sent someone else to pick her up from Santa Marta the next morning. She had expected to be greeted by a cordon of reporters. But luckily – how could she use such a word? – Marjorie's arraignment had been scheduled for the same day as her own release, so most of the press was down at the courthouse. Two photographers insisted on snapping Nan's picture as she walked through the prison gate.

Matt came in Isadora. It was a sweet thought, knowing how much she missed the car. But Nan wished that he had just driven his Triumph. Now she had an almost irrepressible urge to chat with Isadora. And she had never told anyone, not even Matt, about these tête-à-têtes with her automobile.

'So now that we've rescued Rapunzel from the tower, where would she like to go?' asked Matt cheerfully. 'I've taken the day off to be at your disposal.'

Rapunzel, thought Nan. Blonde hair in the dark night. Withholding evidence, thought Nan. She still couldn't tell Matt all that had happened on New Year's Eve. Amy had managed to get the DA not to press charges for withholding information. But she would have to remain silent. 'Felony,' she heard Amy's voice echo inside her head. 'Felony.' So even now, Nan concealed the concealed evidence. Sometimes she thought she might burst with this story. She felt like one of those dope freaks trying to smuggle cocaine by swallowing a balloon. Sometimes, she remembered darkly, the balloons fill up with air, expand, explode inside the body. Any second now, Nan might explode.

'How sweet of you,' said Nan to Matt, thinking that all she really wanted was to be at home, alone, in her apartment. 'Why don't we go somewhere with fresh air, somewhere warm and sunny and with a view of the ocean.'

So the two friends drove to Point Reyes and went hiking on Dillon Beach. Clouds flew across the cold blue sky on a high wind. Hills along the coast were heavy with green from March rains. Nan wanted to cry at this beauty after the long weeks in grim Santa Marta. She had looked forward to such freedom, to this chance for talking. She wanted to tell Matt about Santa Marta, about the guards and the inmates. But she felt stuffed up, clogged. Terrible company. Restless even on the wild Pacific Coast.

Matt understood, of course Matt understood, so he dropped her back at the flat in the late afternoon. She called Shirley briefly, then unplugged the phone, swallowed four blessed Sleepese and didn't wake until morning.

The desk was stacked with mail which had arrived during the last month. Bills. Telephone bills (she plugged in the cord, intending to call Shirley as soon as she had had a cup of coffee), electricity bills, insurance bills. Would the state pay for these extra interest charges? Could she sue for false arrest? Before she finished the questions, the phone rang. It was Shirley.

'So good to hear your voice,' said Shirley.

'Same here,' said Nan. But she was leary that an inch more sentiment might make her cry, so she added, 'You know you did see me five times at Santa Marta.'

'Nan Weaver,' said Shirley. 'We all have a right to be relieved at your release.'

'Yes,' Nan answered.

'And,' Shirley hesitated, 'Joe has planned a party tomorrow night, a kind of celebration, a coming-out party.'

'Oh, Shirl, do we have to. . .'

'It's just a little thing,' said Shirley. 'Family, and a few friends. Let him do it, Nan. Let us do something for you.'

'OK,' agreed Nan. She had searched so long for a way to love the family. Perhaps this was the best, the simplest way, by letting them love her. As Nan listened to Shirley, she remembered her on the witness stand, full of sisterly protectiveness.

'See you tomorrow night,' said Shirley.

'Right.' said Nan. 'Give my love to Lisa . . . and Joe.'

Coming out, thought Nan. Perhaps it was time for that. If they had stood by her at the murder trial, maybe she could tell them about . . . who knew what would come out next?

The telephone rang again. A reporter.

And again. Another reporter.

Before it could ring a third time, Nan unplugged it.

Prior to the coming-out party, Nan was faced with an even more peculiar social chore, a dinner engagement with Rose Adams, Marjorie's mother. Mrs Adams had let it be known to Nan that she was eager to talk, once discretion made it possible. Of course that meant once Nan was released from jail. Nan was prepared to dislike Mrs Adams. However, both Amy and Matt had told her she was a rather sympathetic character. A garrulous eccentric Eastern matron. The kind of sophisticated woman who always made Nan feel extra short and near-sighted.

Tonight, as Nan stood paralyzed in front of her closet, she wondered how she had agreed to this dinner. What more could she owe this rich family; they could take care of themselves. From what Beth Beale had reported about the Adams' merchandizing estate, they had enough money to hire a battery of fancy psychiatrists and fast-talking lawyers. What could Nan offer? What could she say to Mrs Adams? ('I'm sorry this had to happen' or 'Your daughter's thesis is coming along brilliantly' or 'My, what an awkward way to make your acquaintance.')

Isadora offered no advice on how to survive the social obligation as they began the drive to San Francisco. They were going to The Golden Hare Restaurant Français – Mrs Adams's suggestion. One of those terribly discreet places on Nob Hill. Discreet. Mrs Adams was so discreet she had even managed to keep her photograph out of the newspaper. The one, very touching thing that Nan had learned about Rose was her close friendship with Marjorie. Because Harold Adams was so preoccupied with his work, Rose looked to her daughter for company.

'Damn,' said Nan, as she missed the turn-off to the Bay Bridge. She found herself on Highway 580, headed in the direction of Oakland. Highway 580 would lead to Southern Alameda County, Hayward, and, if she went far enough, Santa Marta.

'OK, OK, Isadora, so I've obsessed enough about Mrs Adams. Let's change the topic. Tell me what I should do about the department.'

Professor Nelson had conveyed his good wishes through Matt yesterday afternoon. And when Nan returned home, she found Nelson's letter advising her to take off the Spring Quarter with full pay. This would allow her time to recover and to do some of her excellent critical writing. The tenure decision would be postponed until the following fall, of course, because technically she had not yet served a full seven years. This leave of absence seemed to everyone's advantage, didn't it?

Nan had agreed. Tenure. Somehow the tenure decision had lost so much weight for her. Tenure. She still wanted this job. Of course she did.

Soon Nan was lost on Nob Hill. Nob Hill. The damnedest thing about Nob Hill was finding a parking space which cost less than $5.00 a minute.

It was in this harried and rather belligerent mood that Nan entered the dim vestibule of The Golden Hare Restaurant Français. Adjusting her eyes to the half-light, she stopped still. Sitting at a small table in the corner, her head in a book, was Marjorie Adams.

Not possible, realized Nan as she gingerly resumed walking. She couldn't have received bail yet. Not until after the arraignment. Not possible, Nan repeated to herself. Then she noticed that this woman was slightly softer around the edges than Marjorie. In this dark light, she could pass for Marjorie's twin. The pair of them might pose for one of those mother-daughter Palmolive commercials. Nan's reverie was interrupted by the double herself.

'Why hello there,' she called. 'There' sounded more like 'theyah'. Her voice carried across the restaurant softly but clearly. Nan nodded, smiled politely and concentrated on not tripping as she approached the small table.

'Welcome,' said Rose Adams, extending her hand. 'Welcome, and thank you for coming. Why thank you for everything, for trying to save our daughter, for being such a fine professor, a real inspiration, I'm given to understand.'

'Not at all,' said Nan, finally untangling her hand from Mrs Adams' firm grasp and sitting down.

Rose Adams talked incessantly – like Shirley – as if words might shut out her anxiety. She paused only when sipping her pink cocktail through a tiny striped straw.

'How can I express my gratitude for all you've done, for all you've tried to do for my little Margie?'

It felt like an eternity before the waitress brought Nan her Bushmill, straight up. Nan wondered if Amy had been right, if she had been foolish risking her neck for these rich people.

'Marvellous,' said Rose.

Nan was calling her Rose by now.

'You drink just like my husband,' said Rose. 'No fooling around with these sodapop ladies' beverages. Whiskey straight up. That does suit your strong character, from what Margie tells me.'

151

The idea of Marjorie and Mum chatting about Nan in the seclusion of their formal garden was slightly unnerving.

'I'd like to know more about you, Nan,' Rose continued warmly. 'All about you. You must be a remarkable person to do this for my daughter. But of course Margie told me just how remarkable you are. You worked in East Africa, where was it?'

'Tanzania,' Nan answered. But how did Marjorie know about that? From the posters on her wall, perhaps, or the framed Visitor's Pass to State House in Dar es Salaam? She had never noticed Marjorie noticing anything in her office except perhaps dust on the bookcase and a fallen hem on her skirt.

'Isn't that fascinating,' said Rose. 'Why on earth would you go all the way over to Tanzania? As a Professor of English, I mean. I understand, of course, that the region holds certain archaeological fascinations. I was an anthropology major at Bryn Mawr, myself. None of these grand tours of Europe for Rosie, no; I spent three summers in Olduvai Gorge. . .'

Before Nan knew it, they had each finished three drinks and were waiting for their entrees in the plush dining room. She was confiding in Rose about New Year's Eve and Rapunzel's escape.

'So you saw all of it,' Rose signed and leaned back into the brown leather booth. 'That's just the way Margie described it.'

Rose seemed tired. Nan noticed for the first time that she and Rose were about the same age. She quite liked this Eastern lady. She admired the spirit and honesty which had weathered the best finishing schools.

'Poor Margie,' said Rose. 'She was always such a moral, guileless child. I know this is my fault. She never had to take care of herself. Never had to clean her room or pack her bags. I wanted to do so much for her. But I never prepared her for anything like. . .'

'No,' said Nan, reaching for Rose's hand. 'You can hardly take responsibility for this. Angus Murchie was a selfish, harmful man. Angus Murchie is the one to blame.'

'How comforting it would be to believe in right and wrong and retribution,' said Rose, who was more composed now. 'To believe that guilt was punished and innocence, in all its different forms, was protected.'

'I don't know about all that,' said Nan. 'But I know that what happened isn't your fault, isn't Marjorie's fault.'

'Of course,' said Rose. 'Margie spoke of your compassion. . .'

Yes, a rather sympathetic character, thought Nan on the way back over the bridge. Totally devoted to her daughter. No thought of family reputation, like the bastard father.

Tonight wore that kind of clear blackness brought by winds of early spring. Nan could see the Campanile from the bridge and, way beyond, up to the top of the hills.

What an innerspring, thought Nan. No wonder Marjorie is so reserved. As a child, she must have had to hold back tides and tides of Rose's ebullience. What was the father like? A real villain, incredible, to be withholding support for his own daughter's defence.

That was the hardest part to digest. Apparently Harold Adams, a very religious man, did not understand how Marjorie could get herself into such a compromising position. Rose Adams was still trying to talk with him, making pleading phone calls every night. She was going back to Maryland next week to stop him before he legally disowned Marjorie.

Families, what would she have to endure tomorrow with Joe and Shirley? Who would they invite? It was a sweet idea, but after a month in prison, thirty days of wall-to-wall people, all she wanted was to be left alone.

Alone to think, especially about Marjorie's trial. What could be done now? Margie, thought Nan. 'My Little Margie' with Gail Storm. No, not Margie, no diminutives for Marjorie Adams.

The next evening Nan found a number of cars parked in front of the jellybean yellow house. That horrible bright shade. She had hoped that the spring rains might have paled the colour, but no such luck.

Nan's attention was caught by a broad wave from the kitchen window. Shirley smiling and waving and saying something Nan couldn't decipher. Everything was the same, except the two broken-down Ford sedans in the driveway had grown a little more rusty. The door opened before Nan reached it. Lisa ran out, hugged Nan and took her by the arm into the crowd of well-wishers.

'For she's a jolly good fellow. For she's. . .'

A lot of people. Off key. Very loud. At first Nan was too overcome by the volume of noise and goodwill to notice faces.

'Hello, Nan.'

'Welcome, Nan.'

'Bravo, Nan.'

Nan focused in on the faces of Lisa, Joe, Shirley, Bob, Debbie (was she going to have the baby any moment?), Lynda, Tom. Amy was leaning against the well. Nan nodded sheepishly. Warren smiled. And Matt, Matt waved from the back of the chorus next to, my god, next to Rose Adams. How bizarre, thought Nan. Perhaps the balloon *had* exploded. Well, what the hell, she took a glass of champagne and drank it down in one long, thirsty swallow.

The drinks flowed freely, and soon everyone seemed to be great friends. Joe and Matt swapped stories about the best fishing spots in Northern California. This was a side of Matt she hadn't known.

'Oh, yes,' Matt turned to her, blushing, 'Knut and I have gone fishing the last three weekends in a row.'

'Congratulations,' said Nan.

Matt smiled and nodded.

'Well,' said Joe. 'Maybe me and you and your friend there can all go sometime, maybe to that place up by Donner Pass you mentioned.'

'Yes, well,' said Matt, 'perhaps.'

Rose Adams was leaning across the burlwood table accepting a piece of homemade cheese crumb cake from Shirley.

The Yosemite picture calendar was turned to a photo of snow melting down to Tuolomne Meadows. What were these two ladies discussing, Nan wondered. They both looked comfortable enough, much more comfortable than she was. By now, Nan had guessed that she owed the presence of their Eastern visitor to Amy. Earlier that day, she had been persuaded by Rose Adams to take her daughter's case.

Amy and Lisa seemed absorbed in each other. Nan overheard Amy trying to recruit another good woman to the bar.

'Rape law,' Lisa was saying, 'now that's something I could get interested in.'

Shirley's house felt cosy tonight, not at all confining. Of course, what could be as confining as an eight-foot by six-foot cell? No, it was more than that. This cosiness had something to do with her people being there – Matt, Amy, Warren, and even Rose Adams. Tonight she was more than Aunt Nan or Sister Nan. The family had to speak in a neutral dialect. And so Nan could imagine an open door between her two sanctuaries.

Noticing that Amy and Joe were engaged in a lively battle over the Equal Rights Amendment, with Matt moderating, Nan pulled Lisa into the kitchen. The bright overhead light caught a shine on the faucet and the aluminium counter edge. They sat across from each other at the familiar linoleum dinette table.

'There's so much to catch up on,' Lisa was saying.

'Yes, like Marjorie Adams, for instance,' said Nan, carefully watching Lisa's face.

'Mmmmarjorie Adams,' asked Lisa, opening her eyes wide.

'Yes,' said Nan. 'How did Marjorie learn about my hearing in far off Maryland?'

'Why ask me?'

'Oh, I don't know, just intuition.'

'Well, maybe she read about it in the papers,' said Lisa.

'Lisa, honey, we know the case didn't go national until after Marjorie's confession.'

Lisa shrugged.

'Maybe you wrote to Marjorie?' suggested Nan.

Lisa was tracing the linoleum swirls with her thumb.

'Lisa,' Nan spoke slowly, 'how on earth did you know about Marjorie?'

'Nan, you used to talk about her all the time.'

'Did I?'

'Sure, you were always going on about her clothes and how smart she was. I guess I was even a little jealous.'

'Oh, Lisa.'

'And then all of a sudden you stopped talking about her. Right after the murder.'

'Sherlock Holmes,' said Nan.

'Nope. Agatha Christie,' said Lisa. 'I read ten of her novels when I was home. The only escape from daytime television.'

Nan was shaking her head, abashed by that mixture of pride and awe that Shirley and Joe always had for their daughter.

'So I got Marjorie's home address from school. At first I was afraid she was too much of a snob to register in the student file. But there she was. So I sent her some *Chronicle* clippings and then phoned her three days later.'

'Why didn't you tell me, or Amy?' Nan asked.

'Marjorie told me not to. She was afraid you wouldn't let her into court.'

'Oh, Lisa, honey, how do I thank you?'

'But *I* have to thank you,' said Lisa. 'You really did save me, Nan. Your hearing got me out of myself, out of my troubles.'

Nan was shaking her head in confusion.

'This got my mind off the illness,' said Lisa. 'It made me think of someone besides myself; it got Mom and Dad to lay off for a while.'

Nan couldn't respond. She shook her head again to keep back the tears, but they came again anyway. Now it didn't seem to matter.

'And who knows?' said Lisa. 'This might be the beginning of my career. Amy's offered me a clerkship in her office during my first year of law school.'

Twenty

'We have a right to protect ourselves,' the young woman was shouting. Sunlight gleamed in her fair curls and in the silver threads of her cowgirl blouse, giving Lisa a gentle fluorescence on this early summer day.

'In fact, society requires us to protect ourselves,' Lisa's voice reached down Sproul Steps and across the plaza with the strength of a seasoned propagandist.

'Rape was not taken seriously as a crime against women until the last decade. Until then, it was an offence against property, against the male owner.'

Nan listened, off to the side of Sproul Steps, under one of the late-budding sycamores, as her niece gave this final speech in the rally for Marjorie Adams' defence. Self-defence. She had explained that she never intended to kill Murchie. He attacked her. She fought back. In self-defence. The preliminary hearing would begin tomorrow, and still they had so much more money to collect for the Defence Fund, so much more attention they needed from the press.

Perhaps two dozen people were listening to Lisa. Most of the summer school students passed through the plaza with a lazy June gait. But what 'The Marjorie Adams Defence Committee' lacked in members, it had in spirit. Their red and black banners proclaimed, RAPE IS A CRIME AGAINST WOMEN. WOMEN STUDENTS UNITE. FIRST SEXUAL HARASSMENT, THEN RAPE.

'We have heard the same story again and again,' Lisa was chopping the warm afternoon air with her right hand. 'Inez Garcia; Yvonne Wanrow; Joanne Little.' Nan felt proud. Who would have imagined that all those rhetoric classes might come to this? A little nervousness, a few stammers, but great determination. Amy was wise to invest in Lisa's legal future.

And this was the same Lisa Growsky, hospitalized for two weeks in winter? The kid who couldn't weather the stresses of Berkeley?

The spring had filled Nan with more hope than she had known for years. Some people recover from disease. Some people escape Hayward. And maybe, just maybe, some people are acquitted of murder.

They were applauding Lisa. Nan looked up. Applauding something Lisa had said. Such guts, thought Nan. Here was Lisa addressing people from Sproul Steps like Mario Savio and Tom Hayden did in the sixties. Of course *now* you could be a Lisa Growsky. Today, plenty of women spoke from Sproul Steps.

Not Nan. She felt a twinge of guilt at her absence, mixed with envy at Lisa's exhilaration. But Matt was right. She must keep a low profile on campus now. As an ex-professor she would be little use to anyone. And it was best to leave this work to the students.

Interesting, no astonishing, the way Lisa and Marjorie had taken to each other after their meeting at Nan's hearing. Lisa had immediately joined Marjorie's Defence Committee. Perhaps it was natural because Lisa had long ago inherited a feminism from Nan, and public speaking was her forte. More importantly, Lisa had come to *like* Marjorie Adams. They were *friends*. Shirley and Joe had no time to object. They were still breathless from Lisa's apparent recovery, Nan's hearing, all the press coverage. And now Lisa visited Marjorie at Santa Marta more often than Nan did.

'As we pass these cans among you,' Lisa was saying.

Over forty people had now gathered around the steps.

'Just think, about what it would be like if you were arrested for the crime of defending your own body.'

Nan checked her watch. Almost one o'clock. She had better get back to work. She felt tired as she walked through Sather Gate. In the nine weeks since Marjorie's dramatic surrender, all of them had been caught in an avalanche of activity. Two months in Santa Marta, Nan shook her head. The DA was determined to make an example of Marjorie, before or after her lawful hearing. Originally, they formed the Defence Committee as a means of earning legal expenses. (Marjorie's father was unrelenting about the money. Beth Beale had reported that he blamed Marjorie for the rape as well as the murder. Rose Adams was back East with him now, trying to break through his born-again Christianity, but she would return for the hearing tomorrow.) The Defence Committee was also a good method of consciousness-raising. But Nan hadn't expected it to turn into a travelling road show.

As Nan opened one of the heavy wooden doors into Wheeler

Hall, a woman student whom she didn't know smiled at her. This had happened a lot lately. In the past month, Nan had appeared on four local television programmes. The publicity about the case wasn't always the right kind of publicity. Many reporters still wanted to interview Nan on what Matt called 'The *Tale of Two Cities*' angle, or How-the-Feminist-Professor-Covered-for-Her-Woman-Student. Eventually, Nan learned how to turn around the questions to the prevalence of sexual harassment and to the frequency of 'civilized rape' that goes unconvicted and often unreported. With this amount of coverage, Marjorie might as well be running against Dianne Feinstein for Mayor of San Francisco.

Nan stopped at Matt's office. But he was out, probably at the Pogo Cafe where he had been spending a lot of time during Summer Quarter. Dear friend Matt, the cautionary chorus in this long drama. Not only did he keep her off Sproul Steps, but he warned her to drop the Defence Committee. What more could Nan do for Marjorie? he demanded. What could Nan accomplish that a dozen other people couldn't? She had no delusions of omnipotence, but the Defence Committee needed workers, phone callers and stamp lickers. Ultimately, it was Matt who gave in, donating money and spending an evening typing labels. Who knows, thought Nan, with a camp like this, maybe Marjorie could beat Dianne Feinstein.

Nan had just closed the door to her office when she heard an impatient rap and a familiar voice, 'Professor Weaver. Professor Weaver.'

'Yes,' said Nan, summoning her friendliest tones. She was attempting to make as few enemies as possible this summer. 'What can I do for you, Lawrence?'

'I've been looking for you all quarter,' he said anxiously.

'I was, er, out of town for a while,' said Nan evenly. 'And since then, I've been working away from the office.'

'I know,' he smiled at her. 'I just wanted to say how brave I think you are.'

'Oh, well,' said Nan, embarrassed and ashamed that she had underestimated him.

'And to tell you,' he continued, 'that I enjoyed your course, even if I did get a B-. I think you're the best professor I've ever had, even if you're not, uh, um, the most objective.'

She nodded wearily, but, she hoped, graciously.

'I should let you get back to work,' said Craigmont, mistaking her fatigue for impatience. 'I just came by to, well, to pay my respects.'

Quickly, he pumped her hand and shut the door.

'Objective,' thought Nan. There was that word again. Objective. Dispassionate. Objective. Nan sat at her desk remembering how Nelson, the chairperson, had greeted her return to campus.

'Now, Professor Weaver,' he had said, 'we're delighted to have you back with us. And if I may offer some advice, do try to keep your politics off campus. Do try to stay as objective as possible.'

Nan had answered simply, 'I understand your concern.' She was tempted to ask if he would advise a black professor not to discuss poverty in regard to the Harlem Renaissance.

Nan looked out the window at the Campanile now, considering all the words she had not said.

Was she a coward? No. Just a survivor. Let Nelson think she was cooperating. Let him remember her publications, her celebrated lectures. They could argue academic decorum after tenure. Perhaps. Nan sometimes worried that she had lost the distinction between double entendres and lies, between being a survivor and being a hypocrite.

She tossed her pencil on the desk. She could not concentrate on this damn journal article. Nan closed her folder, locked up the office and hurried across campus to pick up Isadora.

She would be driving out to Santa Marta alone today; Lisa had an examination. Now, as often happened when she passed the Doe Library, Nan thought about her spring of six months before, through the dark campus, chasing the gold thread of Marjorie Adams. What would Nan have said if she caught up with Marjorie that night? 'I'm glad you did it.' No. 'Don't worry, I'll take care of you.' No. Somehow, she still didn't know what to say to Marjorie.

Nan went to visiting hours at Santa Marta out of a sense of duty. But, as time passed, she did begin to feel more and more affection for Marjorie. Rose had helped with that, explaining how Marjorie had always been a wholly honourable girl, whose reserve came from cautious inexperience. Logic and hard work had always been her defences against a world that might overwhelm her. Abstractly, Nan knew that Marjorie was grateful for her visits. But Nan wished for more emotional connection. She had never seen Marjorie Adams laugh, smile, maybe, but not really laugh. She could not even conceive of Marjorie crying. Surely, these last six months must have changed her, must have broken through some of that inner reserve.

When Sergeant Fernandez escorted Marjorie into the waiting

160

room, it was the Sergeant who smiled at the visitor. Nan still cherished the matron's kindness during her hearing. She hoped Sergeant Fernandez was also kind to Marjorie. Did she see through her sophisticated veneer to Marjorie's fear?

Even here in the austere prison clothes, without make-up, it was difficult to perceive the real Marjorie Adams. She still looked like a movie star. Young Ingrid Bergman in 'For Whom The Bell Tolls', her hair in a modest bun, her face scrubbed and shining.

Marjorie smiled at Nan as they both settled stiffly on their chairs.

Maybe Nan was touching her, but Nan, in turn, could not feel Marjorie Adams.

'I've done ten more pages on the thesis. They're with the guard. She'll give them to you as you leave.'

'Perhaps we should forget sending students to the library, and direct them all to Santa Marta.'

'The hours are not quite as flexible.'

The two women managed quick smiles.

'Besides,' Marjorie added matter-of-factly, 'I have to do something with all this time. I can't just sit around thinking about myself.'

Nan wondered how Lisa had reached through this cool practicality. She didn't understand the friendship between the two young women. Perhaps age made a difference. Yes, more than she liked to admit.

'You do amaze me,' said Nan. 'The hearing starts tomorrow and you're reading Iris Murdoch. I'm sure she'd be flattered, but . . .'

'What else can I do?' asked Marjorie. 'I've already confessed, so I don't have to spend time practising an alibi. It's all in Amy's hands. She's a very competent attorney.'

Competent attorney, thought Nan. Yes, she is a very competent attorney and you are a very confident defendant.

'But,' Nan blurted, 'you're too objective about it. Aren't you . . . I mean, aren't you . . .'

'Scared?' finished Marjorie finally. Her voice was husky now – with anger or sadness Nan could not tell.

'Well, yes,' said Nan. 'Maybe it would do you good just to admit you're afraid, to say how you feel.'

'But I'm *not* scared,' answered Marjorie. 'When Angus jumped on me, I was scared,' she said bitterly. 'When he pulled up my dress, I was scared. Since then, since I picked up the letter opener and defended myself, I have not been *scared*.' Marjorie put her head in her hands and wept softly.

'I'm sorry,' said Nan. 'I didn't mean to make it any worse.'

'No,' said Marjorie, 'it's good to talk about it. The panic and the desperation. At first, I couldn't believe it was happening. Then everything became very clear. I had to stop him. I had to. My screams were useless. And my fists. I didn't think the letter opener would hurt him badly. I didn't know my strength. And then he was, oh my god,' she sobbed, 'and then he was lying there limp and bleeding. All I could think of was to get away. Every day since then I've wondered why I didn't call an ambulance. But it didn't occur to me. I was frozen. No room for anything. Except panic. Except escape.'

As Nan watched Marjorie's tears, she felt drenched by the memory of her own fear and loneliness at Sanata Marta. 'I just wish there was something I could do.'

'Something you could do,' repeated Marjorie, wiping her eyes in astonishment. 'But look at all you have done, with your silence, with your own hearing, with the Defence Committee, the fund raising, the visits out here to see me, the criticisms of my thesis. . .'

'Your thesis!' Nan laughed nervously.

'That's been very important,' said Marjorie. 'It's given me hope that there's life after all this, that there's some kind of continuity.'

Nan was smiling at Marjorie, with a kind of admiring pride.

'Oh, that reminds me,' said Marjorie. 'Remember Judy Milligan?'

'My old cellmate,' Nan said. 'Sure, I remember her.'

'Well, she's back in again. And she sends best regards.'

On the last day of June, the Yosemite picture calendar was turned to sunflowers at Bridal Veil Falls. Everyone laughed at the baby trying to shake a pink rattle in her crib. Life in Hayward moved at a more predictable pace (pregnancy, motherhood, infancy) than in Berkeley. The baby was a month old, and Marjorie Adams was out on bail.

'My first grandchild,' Shirley was explaining to Marjorie. 'Her mother drops her off for several hours every day.' Marjorie laughed and tickled Katherine Growsky under her double chin.

Nan was amazed at Marjorie's even spirits since the hearing. Of course getting bail helped. And now she had a two-month respite, because the trial was scheduled for September. Maybe her good mood was explained by all those support letters from Europe and Latin America and Maryland. Or maybe it was simply that

Marjorie, like Nan, held a firm belief in innocence.

'The baby is lovely,' said Marjorie. 'She has your eyes, Mrs Growsky. Lisa's eyes.'

'You should see the rest of the family,' said Shirley proudly.

No, this is not a dream, Nan reminded herself. But it was harder to accept Marjorie Adams being here than Rose's visit two months before. It had been Lisa's idea to invite Marjorie. Nan understood that there was something about Marjorie's confidence, about her assumptions, that she would never possess. Marjorie had always accepted her right to be in the world, ever since she was a child. It was still a distinction of class. Marjorie could walk through any door. Nan always knocked.

'How about the Fourth of July?' Shirley leaned across the burlwood table to Marjorie. 'Can you join us?'

'Why thank you,' said Marjorie, who looked genuinely interested. 'My bail allows me to go as far as Hayward.'

'Terrific,' said Lisa, showing only the slightest deference to Marjorie. Perhaps Lisa would have the friendship that Nan could never have. Her defences were younger, more flexible. 'And I'll take you down to the rodeo the day after.'

'We'll do fireworks in the backyard,' Shirley said. 'And then a barbeque. Just hamburgers and hotdogs, I'm afraid. . .'

'And Taco chips,' added Lisa.

'When it's dark,' said Shirley, 'we can see the skyworks from over by the Navy Base.'

Nan sat back on the old armchair and considered the scene before her. Here was Marjorie Adams in her turquoise jump suit, leaning back on Shirley's faded red brocade couch. Here was Marjorie Adams, whose father owned half of Baltimore, having a perfectly comfortable conversation with good old Shirley. They had taken to each other for several reasons, not the least of which was Marjorie's fondness for Shirley's cheese crumb cake.

Snobbery, thought Nan. Observing Marjorie now and remembering Rose's visit, Nan reckoned that she, herself, was the biggest snob about Hayward. Too bad Rose couldn't join them, but she was back in Baltimore again, still lobbying Mr Adams for the defence fund.

'And you'll be here for the Fourth, won't you, Nan?' asked Shirley.

'Sure will,' said Nan. 'The Speak Out doesn't begin until the tenth.'

163

'Do you have to, Nan? I liked the Himalayan scheme much better,' said Shirley. 'You're still going through with this feminist extravaganza?' Shirley glanced apologetically at Marjorie.

'Ah, Mom,' said Lisa, as she cut herself another large slice of cake. 'It's not an "extravaganza". It's a three-day conference about sexual harassment. People are coming from all over the country. It's a crucial forum for women who have been silent. . .the issues are crucial. . .'

'It's going to get your aunt in a lot of trouble,' said Shirley.

'What more trouble can I get into?' laughed Nan, a little too forcefully. 'I realized it's too late for a low profile on campus now.'

Marjorie and Shirley exchanged worried glances. Abruptly Shirley got up and walked into the kitchen to reheat the kettle. 'You could lose your job,' she called from the other room. 'She's right,' said Marjorie. 'Don't you think you've done enough – at least for a while – at least until you have the security of tenure?'

'But if we don't have the Speak Out this summer, it'll be no good to you,' said Lisa. 'Besides, your case is important to exposing the problem. And Nan's presence is important to exposing your case.'

Shirley carried the teapot back into the living room. She stood still, glaring at her sister. 'This could be bad for you, Nannie.'

Lisa answered, 'You don't know what you're talking about, Mom.'

'Don't interrupt me, young lady,' said Shirley.

Nan winced.

'When will you accept that you've done enough, Nan, honey?' Shirley asked soberly.

Nan had thought about this. It was the same question Matt asked again and again. She held up her cup for her sister to fill. Then she took a deep breath, as her friend Francie had instructed her ('Breathe, Nan,' Francie would say. 'Everything is easier when you breathe.'). Finally, Nan answered.

'Why must you see me either as a martyr or a fool? What am I risking? What is one person's job compared to the safety of women to attend night classes, to visit male professors during office hours unmolested? to. . .'

'You're on a soapbox, Nan,' Shirley said.

'No, let me finish. Now, I don't know, any more, where they measure up lives. But if you balance that "propagandizing" as you call it with teaching English, it's easy to figure out which is more important.'

164

'All right,' Shirley said, exasperated.

'I'm sorry,' said Nan, 'about my high horse tone. . .'

Shirley smiled her familiar, affectionate smile, 'You always did know your own mind, Nannie.'

'Speaking of which,' Nan said, 'I should get back to Berkeley, back to work. Including your new thesis chapter, Marjorie.'

'Now there's a great topic for a journal article,' Marjorie pulled an exaggerated poker face, '"Innovative Functions of the Thesis Adviser".'

'Hmmm,' smiled Nan. Perhaps there was still hope for Marjorie's sense of humour. Perhaps some day. Clearly it was doing her good hanging around Lisa. 'When the bad jokes start flying,' said Nan, 'I know it's time to leave.'

'Ahhh, Nan,' said Lisa, 'I wanted to take you both on a walk down Crow Canyon. Remember our New Year's walk? I was telling Marjorie about it last week. Remember?'

How could she ever forget that New Year's walk, Nan wondered. The hangover, the hope that Murchie's death had been a nightmare, the prayers that Lisa would recover.

'No,' said Nan. 'I haven't forgotten.'

'All right,' teased Lisa. 'Rest your old bones. And I'll drive Marjorie back to Berkeley later.'

'OK,' agreed Nan.

It was more than OK. She had a lot to think about, a lot to discuss with Isadora, who was the other woman who had not failed her in all of this.

Twenty-One

Three months later, instead of going back to school, they were driving into the sunrise, just Nan and Isadora. The back seat was so loaded with suitcases and camping gear that Nan could only see out the side mirror. Dangerous. She would stop somewhere – maybe Reno – and rearrange the pile, put more of it on the front seat next to her. The early start was worth it. She would be through the Sacramento Valley before the heat of the day, which could be blistering in late September. Eerie, driving in the pre-dawn light, like trailing through ghost territory. She switched on the radio for company.

'Feminists are hailing it as a victory for women,' said the hearty disc jockey voice. 'Last week, at a landmark case in Oakland, Marjorie Adams was acquitted of the murder of a professor at Cal's English Department.'

Nan turned up the volume. 'Judge Marie Wong ruled that rape is an act of such physical violence that it warrants substantial use of force in self-defence. This morning, we have pre-taped interviews with the defendant, Marjorie Adams, and with Lisa Growsky, a member of her Defence Committee. We failed to reach Nan Weaver, the woman originally charged with the murder. Apparently she left town after Adams' acquittal. Professor Weaver is unavailable. . .'

'Professor Weaver is unavailable,' mused Nan. Is this the notice they would put in Wheeler Hall to mark her six-month 'leave of absence'? She sighed with relief. Six months free from courtrooms and classrooms and office hours and tenure rumours. Six months to visit friends around the country and to finish her long article about sexual harassment. Nan was enjoying this article more than she had enjoyed the writing of anything in a long time. Television programmes and radio interviews were all very well. But some of these broadcasters never used verbs. And Nan came from a generation who believed in literacy. This was not the kind of article which would win her tenure; she could hardly care any more.

'Professor Weaver is unavailable.' Nan doubted that Professor Weaver would ever be available again at Berkeley.

'Wake up Jake. . .' Ian and Sylvia singing an old favourite. Good station, thought Nan, as she watched the tulle fog rising from the flat farmland on either side of Interstate 80.

Matt had warned her not to take the leave.

'You're crazy, Nan, to go now,' he told her two nights before at the Pogo Cafe. 'The department's sympathy is with you. You could get tenure, just by being inconspicuous for a few months.'

'Do I really want to work in a department where half of my colleagues fear or despise me?'

'The English Department is part of the real world,' said Matt, looking over his shoulder and trying to catch Knut's attention. 'You're just complaining about the state of misogyny in the real world.'

Matt knew Nan was determined; he didn't push the argument. Besides, most of his attention was absorbed by domestic bliss. Knut had moved in with him during the last month.

Back to Ian and Sylvia. Nan tried to sing along with the familiar words, but the argument kept running through her head. She didn't need Matt to play Devil's Advocate. She could argue both sides herself.

'I don't want to give up teaching,' she said.

'There are other places to teach,' she answered herself.

'But I turned forty-eight two months ago. I'm almost half-a-century old and I'm still not settled.'

'Maybe that's OK. Maybe knowing what you *don't* want is just as good as knowing what you *do* want.'

'But security is hard to come by nowadays.'

'I can get other teaching jobs. Maybe they won't have as much prestige as Berkeley. Chances are they won't have as much sexism.'

'Don't fool yourself. There are pigs under every rock.'

The morning was growing lighter, into the quiet pale preceding full dawn. Nan watched Highway 80 stretch straight ahead through miles and miles of pasture. She savoured the names of the towns through which she would be driving – Roseville, Nevada City, Sparks, Winnemucca. The Golden West.

167

Sunrise. Joe and Shirley always got up at dawn. Joe showering for his early shift at the shipyard and Shirley frying his eggs. Nan had been right about the fallout shelter. Joe and Shirley would always take her in, no matter what. 'I don't know anything about this murder, Nan,' he had said, 'but I know that if you did it, you must have had good reasons. And let me tell you that a thing like that really takes balls.'

Nan suspected Joe had been a little disappointed when he learned she hadn't murdered Murchie. But he handled it generously, with the coming-out party.

'I woke up this morning. . .' Nan tuned back to the radio, 'and you were on my mind.' A familiar Sylvia Fricker song. Yes, Nan would stay with this station until static descended.

Neither Joe nor Shirley was keen about Lisa's involvement in the Marjorie Adams Defence Committee. However, they were so over-whelmed by Lisa's apparent recovery, they kept quiet. Recovery, please let it last, thought Nan. Shirley thought Lisa should concentrate more on school, but timid around her daughter's new temper, left the arguing to Nan.

'Marjorie's a terrific friend,' Lisa had told her. 'She studies all the time.'

'But don't you think the case will be distracting for you?' asked Nan.

'You know better than to ask that,' said Lisa.

Lisa seemed different now – stronger and more independent, even from Nan. All of them were different for having survived these nine months. They were closer. In a funny way, Marjorie had brought them together.

And maybe Shirley found it easier to let go of Lisa now that there was a baby nearby. Delighted with the extending family, she sat with yards of soft wool on her lap as she watched over Debbie's child and knitted. Since the first baby had proved such a success, Lynda was now pregnant. This grandmotherhood was not what Nan had wanted for her sister. But Amy reminded her that she didn't have the screen rights on Shirley's life.

Sun was beginning to show over the golden hills. Nan loved autumn best, these days of Indian Summer, these last long nights before the end of Daylight Saving; the spring green baked away by the hot summer sun, the clean smell of dry dust. Where else could you live where every year the hills turned to gold?

She would come back to California, if not to Berkeley. After a rest. For a while, Nan would just drive east, into other sunrises. Maybe she would discover she really was 'the shortest professor west of the Rockies'. Maybe she would relax.

'So, Isadora,' said Nan, 'where should we stop for coffee? And how about waffles? Blueberry waffles smothered in butter?'